GW00391159

The Firstborn

Quenby Olson

World Tree Publishing

The Firstborn is a work of fiction. Names characters, places and incidents are products of the author's imagination or are used fictitiously. Any resemblance to actual events or locals or persons, living or dead, is entirely coincidental.

ISBN-10: 0-9981012-4-9
ISBN-13: 978-0-9981012-4-8
Published in the United States of America by World Tree Publishing.

First Edition: May 2017

1 2 3 4 5 6 7 8 9 POD B1720

Cover design by Ash Navarre

To my father.

I miss you. But don’t worry, I’m happy and I’m still here doing what I love.

Chapter One

There were too many letters. An inordinate amount of them, spilling out of crevices and sliding out of their well-organized stacks. Most were invitations, a fact that irritated Finnian to no end. Invitations to balls, to routs, to garden parties and afternoon teas, where he would be expected to deal with the attentions of no small number of simpering females. And all of them with their eyelashes fluttering while a mere turn and snap of their fans spoke a language he would never care to decipher.

This morning's stack of cards sat on his desk, the light shining through the window and sending a solitary beam across the topmost letter. A glance at the direction told him more than he needed to know. The lettering was too fine and flowery—a woman's hand—and a noticeable aroma emanated from the paper, as if glazed with rose water before being sent round to his townhouse.

He understood their interest in him, and his position in polite society. He was a man. A gentleman. A titled gentleman with a rather large fortune. And, most bothersome of all, a titled gentleman, possessed of a large fortune, who—according to that polite society which insisted on tossing flowery cards and invitations at him as if they were tossing bread crumbs to a duck in a pond—had decided to remain stubbornly ensconced in his current life as a bachelor.

He gave the corner of his newspaper a shake and reached out for his cup of tea. From another part of the house, he heard a knock on the front door, followed by the measured step of Gleeson showing no haste in his effort to answer it. Finnian waited, his eyes gazing at a vague point beyond the edge of the newspaper as the butler's steps made their way towards his study. Another knock, this one on his own door, and a grey, tonsured head bowed itself into the room.

"Lord Haughton? It's Mr. Winston. Shall I...?"

He nodded in reply. Gleeson disappeared, the steps receded, and Finnian folded his newspaper into a stiff rectangle that landed with an audible smack on top of the pile of invitations.

"Finn?"

He glanced up at the door as another man, this one dressed in a coat and trousers of a dull, forgettable colour, entered the sunlit room.

"Winston." Finnian sat up in his own chair and indicated the one opposite him with a wave of his hand. "I didn't expect to see you again so soon."

Winston strolled forward, his hands clasped around both hat and gloves, neither of which had managed to be relinquished to the butler upon his arrival. He let out a sigh as he lowered himself into his seat, scratched his chin, and ran a bare hand over his neatly-trimmed brown hair.

"Have you breakfasted?" Finnian asked, his eyes taking in the obvious wear on the man's suit and the scuffs on his boots.

"Yes, early." Those two words revealed an accent that held no connection to any town or borough within fifty miles of London. Finnian had never inquired after Winston's origins, and Winston had never made any move to volunteer the information.

"So." Finnian cleared his throat. "Since you're not here to dine with me, I take it you've..."

"I've found her."

He looked up from his cup. The dregs of his tea slid down his throat, leaving a bitter aftertaste that threatened to linger on his tongue for some time. "And the child?"

Winston nodded, his chin dipping down to touch the simple folds of his neckcloth. "A bouncing, blustering specimen of childhood. Quite a healthy thing, he looks to be."

A breath slid out of his lungs as he allowed his own head to tip back. He found himself staring up at a ceiling painted with all manner of cherubs and pudgy, angelic creatures, their grotesque smiles having beamed down on his own head, and his father's before him, since his mother had commissioned the ghastly artwork some three decades before.

"The woman." Finnian shut his eyes. He would have to paint over that damned ceiling one of these days, perhaps once this latest mess was cleared away. "What was her name? Susan?"

"Sophia," Winston provided. "Sophia Brixton."

"Sophia..." An image of a young woman appeared in his mind: short and curved, with dark hair and fair skin beneath rouged cheeks and rouged nipples and anything else that it was fashion to have rouged. It was a type, he realized. His brother's type, and never had David dared to deviate from the original template. "What have you learned about her?"

"Currently lives in Stantreath," Winston said, as he sat up in the chair and reached inside his coat for a small pad of paper. A brush of his thumb across his tongue and he began to flick through the pages. "Up in Northumberland, right near to the coast. She's got herself a tidy little cottage that she shares with one sister." He licked his thumb again and turned another page. "Parents are gone. Father was a tradesman, ran a rag and bottle shop of some sort. The younger sister, that would be one Lucy Penrose, has no fortune of her own. Mrs. Brixton possesses an annuity of a mere fifty pounds per annum."

"Wait." Finnian held up one hand as one of the details finally wriggled its way to the forefront of his thoughts. "Mrs. Brixton? She is married?"

"A widow, as far as the gossip travels. But I was unable to discover any proof of a previous marriage or of the prior existence of a Mr. Brixton."

Finnian raised one eyebrow. "You believe she's lying?"

Winston tilted his head to one side. "You know I'm not one for guesses and conjecture. But I would not rule out a false marriage in order to pass off the child as legitimate."

"Of course." Finnian grumbled under his breath and pushed himself out of his chair. He shook his head, ran his fingers through his own dark hair, and moved to stand in front of the window. "Go on," he prompted. "I want to know everything."

"Well..." Another lick of the thumb, another turn of the page. "There's Stantreath...cottage... Ah, yes, here we are. There's no maid in the household, but there is a hired girl who helps out several times a week. Ah...Mrs. Brixton attends services regularly, dresses modestly, above average height, red hair—"

"What was that?" Finnian spun on his heel as he turned away from the window. "That last bit? What did you say?"

"Erm...red hair?"

"No." Finnian shook his head. "That cannot be right. My brother abhors red hair, especially when it comes to the fairer sex."

Winston raised one shoulder as he tipped his head to one side. "Perhaps the boy has had a change of heart."

"Or perhaps he succumbed to a moment of uncharacteristic desperation."

Winston's eyebrows pushed upwards into his forehead. "Or perhaps this Mrs. Brixton possesses some other charm, something beyond a mere head of hair."

Finnian sniffed. "You know as well as I, my brother is incapable of looking beyond anything but the most superficial of charms."

"Which means...?"

"Which means that he was probably so inebriated at the time that he wouldn't have known whether he was making love to a real, warm-blooded woman or a freshly plumped cushion."

Finnian abandoned the window and began to pace around the study. He had not bothered to make many changes since taking over the room from his father's reign as Marquess. The furniture was the same, all of it leftover from the previous century, and all of it showing signs of wear and the many batterings of brooms from the previous four decades. The colour of the room was too dark, too rich to adhere to the current fashion of light and brightness that had begun to invade every London household. And then there were those damned cherubs...

"I take it my brother is ignorant of the fact that he has a son? This woman, this Sophia...she's made no further move to contact him since the birth of the child?"

A letter. A simple missive had begun it all. One tidy sheet of paper, its lines written in a messy scrawl and signed by someone bearing the appellation, "Your Love." And within those blots and flourishes, the news that his brother David was soon to find himself welcomed into the state of fatherhood. Finnian had discovered the correspondence among his father's papers in the days following the old man's death, among a tremendous collection of letters, debts, and other evidence of his younger brother's poor decisions.

Winston gave his little notebook a final glance before he closed it and returned it to its home inside his coat. "As far as I can tell, she's done nothing but keep mostly to herself and spend her days in the rearing of the child."

"An uncommon woman."

"Finn?"

Finnian winced at the use of his nickname, but he didn't bother to reproach the man. He'd known him too long for that. "Uncommon that such a woman as the one you've described would ever find herself in the company of my little brother."

"The birth of a child can do a great deal towards reforming a person's character." Winston shrugged. "Or so I've heard."

"Or so you've heard," Finnian echoed, and continued his progress around the outer part of the room.

The notebook now out of sight, Winston again leaned back in his seat. The muted shade of his hair, of his clothes, indeed of his entire person blended in with the worn leather of the armchair. "And now that you know," he began, his fingers lacing and unlacing themselves across his chest while his hat bounced on his knee. "And David does not know, what do you plan to do with this information? A little, light blackmail? Bribery of some sort?"

Finnian waved his hand, clearing the air of Winston's suggestions. "No, no. In fact, that's precisely what I wish to avoid. All I need is some forgotten conquest of my brother's to storm into my parlour, a baby dangling from her hip as she demands some absurd amount of money in exchange for her silence about the bastard."

"But is silence even something that needs to be bought in this day and age?" Winston tapped his fingers against his sternum as Finnian paused in his pacing. "Who doesn't have a bastard? It could almost be counted as a symbol of status among some. And as I've seen, the woman seems to be doing everything within her power to pass off the child as legitimate."

But despite Winston's assurances, Finnian could not ignore the threat that this woman posed to his family, to his nascent status as the ninth Marquess of Haughton, and how blithely determined his brother seemed to be to see the lot of them swept into scandal and bankruptcy. "If there is a child, which we know there is, and she decides to go to the press... Or if there are letters, private correspondence between the two of them? And do you remember Regina? The actress who nearly absconded across the channel with half of my mother's jewels in her keeping? Jewels that my brother gave to her after having spent a mere three hours in her company?"

Winston's fingers continued to tap out their quiet melody on his chest. "From what I've seen, this one doesn't seem likely to make trouble for anyone."

"For the moment," Finnian said. "But what about when the child grows larger, when he becomes a handful? And what of new clothes, and food? You tell me this woman and her sister and this child are all to survive on a scant fifty pounds a year? No, you mark my words. As soon as that child is large enough to ride a horse, she'll be down here clutching a list of demands."

Winston blew out a loud breath that sounded as a hiss from between his teeth. "So how do you propose to avoid such an intrusion?"

Finnian moved towards his desk, the neat stacks of invitations, of previous days' newspapers, of filed and folded documents pertaining to the care of his family's estates proving only a minor impediment as he shifted a few things aside and produced a sheet of vellum. "A simple thing, really. I merely offer her the money she would certainly come to claim at a time when it would be more inconvenient for me. A fixed sum, enough to ensure the child will receive the proper care and guidance he deserves as my brother's offspring."

"And in return?"

"In return..." Finnian brandished the document. "She does not interfere. She does not leave her tiny cottage. She does not set foot in London. Nor does she attempt to contact myself, my brother, or any other member of our family, except within the terms laid out for her."

Winston let out a long, low whistle. "And do you think she'll agree to that?"

"I've found that most people will agree to anything, if the proper incentive is offered." Finnian glanced down at the document in his hand. There was a mercenary twinge in his bones that did not agree with him, but the fact of the matter remained: he could not allow this woman to gallivant about the country with his brother's illegitimate offspring in tow, no matter her attempts to keep up appearances to the contrary. Their father, the previous marquess, was barely cold in his grave, and now such a scandal threatened to destroy the family's name.

Finnian looked down at the desk, his gaze flicking towards the rear panel that hid a secret compartment. It was a small nook where he hid all the other documents and notes connected with his brother David's dissolute ways. There were numerous gambling debts that needed to be paid, reports of a duel that Finnian bribed no less than three people to keep out of the papers, public displays of drunkenness, along with various items connected with the family's history—apart from their departed mother's jewels—that had to be recovered anytime David saw fit to use them as currency when his own pockets were empty.

It wasn't until the week after their father's death that Finnian discovered how much the late marquess had done to keep his younger son out of both financial and social difficulties. Thousands of pounds spent to either rectify or erase David's various mistakes. And now with the appearance of this child, it seemed that those mistakes were nowhere near to finding an end.

A soft creaking noise preceded Winston sliding forward in his seat. "How do you plan on informing this young woman of your most generous intentions?"

Finnian sighed. There were too many things that called for his attention, too many matters left to languish during the final weeks of his father's illness. He shouldn't leave London, however... "I'll go, as soon as I can arrange it."

"All the way to Northumberland? That's not exactly a day's jaunt, you know. Send Briggs, or one of your other solicitors to take care of the matter for you."

"I'm well aware of the journey's length," Finnian admitted. "And I don't trust an intermediary in such a matter." He glanced at Winston and bowed his head. "No offense intended towards present company."

Winston returned the gesture. "None taken."

There was the sound of another knock on the front door, then the familiar shuffle of the butler's steps through the foyer to answer the call. More visitors, Finnian realized. More demands on his time, on his family's slowly dwindling fortune—no thanks to his brother and the young man's extravagance. They were still supposed to be in a state of mourning for their departed father, but something would have to be done about David's spending. Their father had been stringent with a meager allowance, but when the debts piled up, there was little to do but pay them off in order to prevent the appearance of any collectors on their doorstep.

"I will let you know when I depart," Finnian said, his eyes glancing over the document once more. He had drawn it up with his solicitor only the day before. It would be a nuisance, he thought, settling a pension on this woman and her child, but he was not a monster. He would make sure that any blood offspring—whether legitimate or not—should not lack for care or education. And as for the rearing of the boy...

Well, Finnian had another reason for wishing to make the journey to Northumberland in person. If this woman was to be in charge of his nephew's health and wellbeing—at least until the boy went off to school—then he wanted to see for himself what manner of influence she would have on the child. Would she instill him with bad habits? Was she a negligent creature, the type to drink away any of the money that he planned to settle on herself and the baby?

"And when you return?"

Finnian looked up at Winston's voice. "Yes, when I return as well. I'm sure you'll want to know how I fared. And I don't plan to be gone for any longer than the entire matter should require. Once I've arrived, I can't see it taking up more than a few hours of my time. I simply have to gain her word that she will keep quiet about the boy's true parentage should the question ever arise. And for as much as I'm willing to offer, I have no fear of being rejected."

Chapter Two

"Well, aren't you a cheerful thing this morning?"

Sophia swept a lock of red hair back from her cheek before bending down over the small, wooden cradle. George stood on the balls of his feet, both hands reaching up towards her while his plump fingers made grasping motions in the air. As soon as she clasped him beneath his arms, the infant let out a terrific squeal of delight, his blue eyes shining as Sophia swung him over the edge of the cradle and into a full circle through the air before finally settling him on her hip.

"Did you sleep well?" she asked, the sound of her voice only increasing the boy's grin, a grin that sported two white teeth from his bottom gums. As Sophia changed the boy's diaper and put him in clean clothes for the day, she spoke to him of what she'd dreamed about while she slept, of the sun that shone in through the bedroom windows, and of the white roses that had begun to bloom along the hedge. George babbled in reply to her queries, his hands clapping excitedly when she again picked him up and carried him downstairs for his breakfast.

"Would you like some apples?" Sophia asked as she opened a crock of applesauce and poured it into a dish. The boy chattered from his corner of the kitchen, where there was an assortment of wooden blocks and a toy horse—complete with a wooden carriage—that rolled along the floor on clackety wheels, a remnant from Sophia's own childhood.

"We should get a new bit of string for that carriage," she went on, her hands deftly slicing off the end of a loaf of dark bread that she passed down to the child. He began to gum the tough bread eagerly, while a sheen of drool collected on his chin and ran down to soak his collar. George kicked out his pudgy legs as Sophia lifted him from the floor and set him in his high chair at the end of the table. She sat beside him on a tall stool, feeding him bites of applesauce as he lost interest in the bread and began to tear it to crumbs.

"Perhaps we should go for a walk this afternoon," Sophia suggested, taking the now empty bowl to the wash basin. "If the sunshine holds, we could even have a bit of a picnic. How would you like that?"

She continued to chatter to the babe as she fixed her own breakfast and cleaned up the kitchen. She ate standing up, slipping bites of buttered bread and bacon between sweeping the floor and wiping down the table. The windows would soon need a good wash, she reminded herself as she glanced out into the garden behind the cottage. And the garden needed a good weeding, and the hedge needed a trim, and...

"Or perhaps we'll save the picnic for tomorrow, hmm?" She pinched one of George's cheeks as she passed by his chair, but the boy was too occupied with banging one of his blocks against the tabletop to notice the brief touch. "Besides, Lissy should be coming today to help wash the curtains, and I'm sure she'll want to take you out to search for caterpillars, that is, only if you're a very good boy this morning."

The chores, she hoped, would be enough to take her mind off of other things. Of course, she held the same hope every morning, that the work of running the household, of taking care of little Georgie would succeed in distracting her from her thoughts. But each day, without fail, her smile faltered as she settled into her work, her arms tiring too quickly as she mixed the dough for the fresh loaf of bread she planned to bake later that afternoon.

When she spoke to George, she never allowed those thoughts to show in her words or expression. He didn't need to know that his mother had abandoned him, without a single card or letter to let them know of her current whereabouts. But that had always been Lucy's way, to run away without looking back, to leave everything and everyone behind her the moment something, or someone, happened to catch her attention.

Sophia wrung out the cloth she had used to wipe down the table and draped it over the edge of the basin. It wasn't even mid-morning and already there was an ache in her back, the knot of tension that lingered between her shoulder blades. The last three months had been the most difficult. Until George was six months old, Lucy had been content to stay with her at the cottage and take care of the boy. But as soon as George had begun to crawl and show some signs of infant independence, Lucy had grown restless. She had complained of the toils of motherhood, of how it was aging her beyond her nineteen years. And then, one morning, Sophia had woken to find Lucy, along with all of her worldly possessions, gone.

That had been a Tuesday. The mail coach always came through Stantreath on Tuesdays, and seeing as how Lucy and her battered trunk had up and disappeared on a Tuesday, near to the very hour when one could find the coach outside the inn...

And then she had discovered the note on Lucy's dressing table. It had not been a particularly long missive. No apology, of course. But then, that wasn't Lucy's style. "You'll do much better than I, I'm sure" it had said, signed off with a heart and a looping "L" with which Lucy had taken to signing the majority of her correspondence.

"Come along, darling." Sophia lifted George out of his high chair and dropped a light kiss on the top of his blond head. "Let's go make the beds, shall we?"

It was five minutes past ten in the morning when Lissy arrived at the kitchen door, a crisp white apron already tied around her waist and a large basket slung over her right arm. "Sorry I'm late, Mrs. Brixton." The young woman shook her head as she apologized. "But Mamma would have me bring these biscuits along for little Georgie. They're a bit stiff, so she thought they might be good for his teething."

"Oh, wonderful!" Sophia took the proffered basket and peeked beneath the cloth that protected the still-warm biscuits. "George is down for his morning nap, but I'm sure he'll love to nibble on one or two of these with his milk once he's awake."

While Sophia set aside the basket and reached up to replace a hair pin that had slipped from the braid at the back of her head, she surveyed young Lissy. The miller's daughter was a beautiful creature, made even more beautiful by a fine plumpness that gave shape to her burgeoning figure and a roundness to her complexion, with cheeks and skin as smooth as fresh cream. Sophia grimaced beneath her own freckles, freckles that had dogged her since she was a child and that had failed to disappear completely with the descent of womanhood.

Lissy, Sophia thought, would make a fine wife and mother one day, though the girl seemed to be completely oblivious to her own attractions. Sophia, on the other hand, knew the extent of her own marital limitations. She had little to recommend her towards a prospective husband. Aside from the physical (for who would wish a red haired and freckled young woman on any man?), her sister's behavior had further removed any chance that Sophia had of ever finding a husband. No matter that they had arrived in Stantreath under the pretense of a young widow and her sister attempting to create a new life for themselves.

She knew of the rumors that circulated about them—about herself, in particular. That she had never been married at all, that the child had been born to her out of wedlock, and that they'd absconded from their previous home a dozen counties away in order to escape the stain of scandal. And so she remained in her cottage, teaching herself to budget her fifty pounds a year while enduring the haughty looks and outright meanness of the townspeople who chose to look down upon her for having a murky past tainted further by several months' worth of gossip.

If they'd had more money, Sophia often wondered... More family, a *better* family, perhaps they would have been in a place to send Lucy away for the duration of her confinement, away from the prying eyes and judging looks of the neighbours. And then, after a few months had passed and the gossip died away, she could have returned with the new baby and claimed it as a cousin or even a foundling left to their care. But Sophia had neither the funds nor the connections for such a scheme, and the recent demise of both their parents had made it clear how few connections they truly had.

And so Lucy, only eighteen years old when she'd discovered she was with child, had been forced to bear the censure of nearly the entire town in which they'd been raised. That was, until after the child was born and Sophia had embarked on the scheme to pass herself off as a widow and pack up their meagre belongings for a new life in Northumberland.

"There's a small hole here, ma'am. Right along the seam."

Sophia and Lissy had spent the remainder of the morning taking down the curtains and drapes and examining them for any sort of damage before setting them aside for washing. Sophia picked at the knot in her thread and began on the small hole that Lissy had pointed out to her, her fingers moving with more speed as soon as she heard George begin to fuss from her bedroom upstairs.

"I'll go and get him," Lissy offered, and bounded towards the staircase before Sophia could say a word. A minute later, the young woman returned with an already-smiling George tucked against her hip, his hands batting at a small ribbon she'd removed from her hair for use as a plaything.

"Mama assures me that he'll be walking before he's aged another month," Lissy said, her smile growing as she flicked the green ribbon out of George's reach before allowing it to slip down between his fingers again.

"I wouldn't be surprised." Sophia matched the young girl's grin with one of her own as she watched the baby and his near-comical efforts to grasp the thin piece of fabric. "Lucy walked early—around nine months, if I'm not mistaken."

"What about you?" Lissy gave the ribbon another flick, only to have George suddenly lunge out and catch it, his knuckles turning white as he held on with all of his strength.

"Oh, no." Sophia laughed. "I was a late bloomer, or so my mother took care to remind me on several occasions. I was late to walk, late to sleep through the night, late to speak my first word, and tragically late to grow a full head of hair. In fact, I was nearly three years old before any of this finally made an appearance." She paused in her sewing long enough to give the end of her braid a gentle tug. "Lucy used to joke that my hair had spent so much time inside my head that it had turned sour, and so came out such a ghastly colour."

Lissy laughed out loud, then coloured with embarrassment.

"Don't fret." Sophia waved away the girl's awkward countenance. "You're not the one who has to live with it." She smiled again, and Lissy seemed to relax.

"What colour do you think Georgie's hair will be?" Lissy asked after several minutes had passed. "It's quite fair already," she said, and ran her fingers over the short, nearly white hairs that decorated the infant's scalp.

"I'm not sure." Sophia set down her mending and looked at George's head.

Lissy continued to run her hand through the wispy hair on the baby's head, each pass of her fingers producing another coo of appreciation from little George himself. "Perhaps his father is fair, or was as a child. Maybe..." She stopped herself, her eyes growing wide at her own mistake. "I'm sorry," she said, her voice low while her gaze sought out the patterns in the parlour rug.

"Please, do not worry yourself." A twist of her fingers, a snip of the scissors, and the hole in the curtains was stitched out of existence. "It's simply not a matter one can avoid entirely. It will come up, and more than once, I'm sure. And it does not pain me. At least, not as much as you may think." She experienced a brief twinge at this dishonesty, but attempted a small smile to put the girl at ease.

But despite Sophia's words, Lissy continued to chew on her bottom lip. "Do you...?" she began, and faltered into silence.

"Yes?"

Lissy cleared her throat and tried again. "Do you miss him? Georgie's father, I mean."

Sophia sighed and set aside her sewing. She was struck by the same fatigue that had dogged her for the last few months, that same knot of tension tightening in the middle of her upper back. "Of course I do. He was my husband, was he not? Though sometimes I feel as if we did not have enough time together for me to truly miss him as I should."

"Miss Lucy told me about him," Lissy went on, and Sophia swore silently under her breath at her sister's inability to practice more caution when speaking with others. "She described him as a 'fine gentleman'."

Sophia resisted the urge to roll her eyes. "Well, perhaps we shall leave it at that, hmm?"

Lissy set George on her lap and continued to fuss about him, adjusting his collar and tugging at the knitted socks that kept his little toes warm. She was nervous, Sophia realized, and yet the urge to ask questions, to engage in a bit of gossip was greater than any embarrassment she felt about the subject at hand. It must be the product of having been born and raised in a small village, Sophia mused, that created a need to talk about others and pretend that their world was so much greater than what existed between the vicarage and Mr. Bingaman's sheep farm.

Sophia stood up in an effort to put a full stop to the previous conversation. She brushed the spare strands of thread from her apron and moved towards the kitchen. "I think it's about time for some tea, and then George can tuck into his biscuits and milk."

In the kitchen, she put on a cup of milk to warm and set out a handful of the now cool, stiff biscuits in front of George's chair at the table. The tea things were laid out, along with a few slices of bread and some fresh strawberries for themselves, and then she rolled up her sleeves and planted her fist into the bread dough that had been left to rise since the morning.

The sound of the coach outside of the cottage made no impact on her thoughts as she worked. The road beyond the front gate entertained enough travelers throughout the day to make the rattle of wheels and harness and the clomp of horses' hooves as familiar as the call of the gulls that circled inland from the coast. It wasn't until Lissy stumbled into the room, her cheeks flushed, her hands twisting the edge of her apron, that Sophia finally looked up from her work.

"There's someone at the door," Lissy said, her eyes glancing back over her shoulder, towards the parlour, as if there were an exotic animal ready to burst in through the doorway. "I didn't know. I mean, his carriage... There's a coat of arms, and he looks..."

Sophia wiped the worst of the flour from her forearms and preceded Lissy out of the kitchen. The front door stood open, the narrow frame filled by the silhouette of a man dressed in a dark coat and trousers. He still wore his hat on his head, the brim keeping his face in shadow. But she saw enough to make out the line of his profile, and the set of his jaw was enough to fill her with a sense of foreboding.

"You didn't show him in?" Sophia whispered to Lissy, who remained behind her.

"I don't know what came over me!" Lissy hissed in reply. "The way he looked at me, and all my nerves turn to jelly, and I wouldn't have even been able to remember my name if it was asked of me."

Sophia placed a hand on her arm. "It's all right," she said, and smiled. "Just see to George, please? His milk should be warm, and I've already set out some biscuits for him."

Lissy nodded, relief evident in her expression before she collected the baby from his place among his toys and took him into the other room.

As soon as she was gone, Sophia returned her attention to the stranger still standing in the doorway. "I'm so sorry," she began, aware of the streaks of flour on her arms and dress as she took in the precise cut of the man's fine clothing. "May I help you?"

He dipped his head, his eyes casting downward before they found her again. The blue of them was striking, a pale colour that reminded her of the water that beat against the shore not more than a few miles away. But it wasn't the colour that made the next words pause at the tip of her tongue, but rather the cold displeasure that emanated from them, as if he had come to scold her for some crime which she possessed no memory of having committed.

"Mrs. Brixton?"

He spoke the name with a distaste that matched the cool glint in his eyes. But she noticed how the rest of his face remained calm, his expression giving away nothing of his reason for being on her doorstep.

Her mind worked quickly. It was obvious that he was a gentleman, a gentleman of some distinction judging by his clothes and his manner. And he wished to speak with her as if she were actually Mrs. Brixton, which meant that he must not know her true history.

She blinked up at him and pushed her shoulders back against the twinge of tension that had lodged itself there. "I'm sorry, but I did not catch your name."

She saw the look of irritation the passed across his features before it was quickly tamped down. "My apologies." He dipped his head in the slightest of bows, so slight that she recognized the insult that lay behind it. "I am Lord Haughton."

"Lord Haughton." She inclined her own head but did not bow. "And you find yourself on my humble doorstep today because...?" She tried to keep her tone light, polite. But the line of his mouth, the faint curl at the corner as he surveyed not only her own person, but the parts of the cottage that were visible to him from where he stood were nearly enough for her to step back and slam the door in his aristocratic face.

"Mrs. Brixton," he said, his bright blue gaze pinning her in place. There was no question in his voice now, and something in his tone told

Sophia that he suspected she had taken to residing beneath this roof under a false name. "You know very well why I am here. Unless my brother managed to keep his identity a secret from you, a fact I highly doubt."

"Your brother?" Sophia shook her head. "Again, I am sorry, but..."

"Oh, this is ridiculous!" He stepped inside, without invitation, and began to remove his hat and gloves. Sophia stared at him, rendered into a state of shock by the man's boorish behavior.

"Don't play the coy miss with me!" Lord Haughton snapped, each word punctuated by the slap of a glove against his hat. "You and I both know that my brother is the father of your child!"

Sophia opened her mouth and closed it again. His brother. She closed her eyes and pressed her fingertips to her temples, willing away the headache that had already begun to form there. "Come in," she said finally, her voice sounding weary to her own ears. "Have a seat in the parlour, and then...we'll have a nice little chat."

Chapter Three

She was not at all what he expected.

Finnian had encountered a fair number of his brother's...women over the years, and so he had sketched what he assumed would be a fairly accurate portrait before he had even raised a hand to knock on the door. She would be silly, he had assumed. Silly but with a light of avarice in her eyes, eyes that he hoped would shine the brighter as soon as he explained what had brought him all the way up to this godforsaken place.

And godforsaken it surely was. All the way at the edge of the country—at the edge of the world, it seemed—in a tumbledown stone cottage, with the smell of the ocean carried in on a breeze that threatened to continue blowing until it had bent every stalk and tree to its will...

And the trip had been long, and there had been nothing but rain and mud and bad roads and worse inns between here and London. His body ached, and he wished for nothing more than to shut his eyes and find himself back in his own home, preferably facing the prospect of sleeping in his own bed for the night. But after he left here, he knew it would be another night in some vermin-infested inn, picking at food that he wouldn't dump into a trough for the pigs, and all before climbing back into his coach to travel over roads that were as comforting to his joints as being tossed about on the waves during a storm.

After he dealt with this woman, he reminded himself. This woman who had turned his thoughts upside down from the minute she'd met him at the door.

He watched her as she set down the tea tray, her hands careful but each movement driven by purpose. There were no wasted flutters, nothing of a performance in her ministrations. And then she passed a cup to him, smoothed her hands down the flour-covered apron she still wore, and took a seat in a high-backed wooden chair across from him.

"Your brother..." she began, and picked up her own cup before taking a tentative sip.

Finnian watched her. He had never seen the likes of her on his brother's arm. Her build was wrong, too broad across the shoulders and wider in the hips than David preferred. And the hair...

No, David detested red-heads. And here was this woman, her strawberry hair bound back from her face in a braid that was decorated with myriad wisps and curls that had worked their way free from the pins. And there was something else, a boldness that David would not have cared for, would in truth have most likely been repulsed by.

Because David wanted to be flattered. He wanted a woman who would gaze up at him with adoration in her eyes and tell him in the most irritatingly coquettish voice possible that he was her moon and her stars, more often than not while the creature pressed her ample bosom against his arm in an effort to better pick his wallet straight from his pocket. David would never have gone for a woman such as the one before him, and Finnian was strangely relieved to know that his younger brother had not suddenly altered his preferences. At least that was one thing on which he could still depend.

"Mrs. Brixton," he said, smiling at her over the rim of his own cup—a chipped thing, decorated with rows of poorly rendered periwinkles. "Perhaps we should start again, don't you think?"

"Start again?" Her fine eyebrows drew together. "How so?"

"I am afraid I have arrived here under some misapprehension."

The woman drew in a deep breath, her chest rising beneath the ghastly, high-collared frock she wore. And it was grey, a faded colour that clashed horribly with her own vibrant complexion. "I do not understand what you mean."

He said nothing. He would watch her fidget, watch her attempt to play whatever game she had most likely used upon his brother, and then he would tear apart her poorly constructed facade.

"Allow me to be blunt, Mrs. Brixton, as I do not believe we will get on well together with any amount of prevarication between us. Now, tell me the truth. Are you or are you not the mother of my brother's child?"

He expected her to squirm. Aside from a slight tightening in her jaw, he witnessed no other change in her composure. "I am not," she said, her voice irritatingly calm and clear.

"And would you know who is?"

She took another sip of tea, returned the cup to the tray, and pointedly ignored him as she aligned the handle of the of the cup with the spoon beside it. "Perhaps you should provide the answer to your own question," she said without looking up. "Seeing as how you already know so much about my family."

He set down his own cup and shifted forward in his chair. The thing creaked beneath him, likely its death throes as the spindly piece of furniture appeared ready to collapse into a pile of tinder should he dare to relax too fully against its frame. "Where is your sister?"

"Ah, so you know I have a sister. I thought as much."

"And she would be Miss Lucy Penrose, correct?"

Her pointed chin tilted at what he took to be a defiant angle. "She would, yes."

"And your sister? Miss Penrose? Is she currently at home? I believe I'd like to speak to her."

Sophia's mouth moved as her teeth sought out the corner of her bottom lip. "She is not at home," she admitted finally.

"She is out?"

Another hesitation, this one lasting one beat longer than the first. "Yes."

"Well." Finnian again reached for his cup and downed one long swallow. "Then I shall simply wait for her to return. If, that is, you do not mind my prowling around your parlour for the next hour or so."

Her lips thinned, and then he watched as she smoothed her hands down her apron a second time. She was nervous, he realized. Something was wrong. "I'm afraid you'll have a longer wait than that, my lord."

"How long of a wait, Mrs. Brixton?"

Her eyes met his. The light from the curtainless window fell across her face, illuminating the flecks of gold and green that twined together in her irises. "She's been gone these last three months. I don't know when she'll take it upon herself to return."

Finnian replaced his cup on the tray, careful not to slosh any of the remaining liquid before he stood up and walked towards the window. So the silly chit was gone. Yes, he'd bet every bank note in his pocket that she was the mother, and not this infernal redhead in front of him. But the child...

He had seen the boy for an instant, when the girl who answered the door had carried him back into the kitchen. A glimpse of chubby arms and legs beneath a blond head, and that was all. He sighed. "Where is she now, your sister?"

He heard the clatter of the tea things behind him, but he did not turn round. He would let her fidget away her discomfort without his eyes glaring down at her.

"I do not know," came the quiet reply.

"You've received no letter, no communication whatsoever?"

"There was a note," she began to explain, and then she fell into silence. He turned around then and saw her still seated in her chair, her hands in her lap, her thumbs picking at the flour that was embedded beneath her nails. When she noticed his gaze upon her, she sat straighter, her shoulders pushing back again as her chin lifted an inch. "Aside from that... No, I've heard nothing."

She stood then, without another glance in his direction and began to gather the tea things. "Now, if you'll excuse me, I've much to do. Should my sister return, whenever that may be, I'll be sure to inform her of your visit."

She was sending him on his way, he realized. And quite rudely, as she simply hefted the tray off the table and walked out of the parlour, leaving him to gawk after her.

It was an insult, and an unmistakable one, at that. He wanted to account it to nothing more than pure ignorance as to the matter of proper etiquette and manners, but she was no crude farmer's daughter, cut off from polite society. This woman, Sophia... There was a gentleness to her movements, along with a carriage that spoke of having been well-instructed in her youth. And she had simply glided out of the room, without a care as to what he should do with himself now that he was out of her sight.

No, he thought. This would not do.

Finnian followed her through the low-ceilinged doorway and into the small kitchen. She stood with her back to him, giving no sign that she would acknowledge his presence. But the other girl, the one who had answered the door was seated at the table, helping the infant to sip from a cup of milk while his short legs kicked out from the seat of a battered high-chair.

The girl looked up at him, her hands going still in the act of raising the cup to the infant's mouth, eyes widening at Finnian's appearance in the kitchen. The baby, however, seemed unconcerned about the visitor, and took this opportunity to make a grab for the poorly attended cup. A moment later, there was a squeal of delight from the boy as the cup, and all of its contents, spilled across the table and onto the floor.

Sophia spun around at the noise, her attention caught between the baby slapping his hands down into a milky puddle and the uninvited gentleman standing at the far end of the table.

"Here, Lissy." Sophia passed a dry cloth to the girl and together they began to wipe up the mess before it could spread any farther.

Finnian noticed her gaze flicking towards him as she worked, the muscles in her neck and jaw growing more tense as she scrubbed the squirming boy's face and attempted to sop some of the spilled milk from the front of his clothes.

"Would you be so good as to take him upstairs and change him?" Sophia asked. Lissy scooped the squealing boy into her arms and moved towards the door, careful to cut a wide path around Finnian as she sidled out of the room.

"I see you've decided to be tenacious," Sophia said without pausing in her work. She leaned across the table, wiping from corner to corner before returning to the wash basin to wring out her dripping cloth. "All right, then." She slapped the cloth over the edge of the basin and spun around, her arms crossed over her chest, her mouth set. "What brings you here? And no attempts to baffle me or to evade the truth, if you please. Just tell me...what do you want?"

Finnian shifted his weight from one foot to the other. Up to this point, nothing had transpired in the way he'd imagined it would. And as for Sophia, she was too blunt, and too intelligent. And that was what worried him most.

He gestured towards the recently vacated table. "Will you be seated?"

Her shoulders pressed back. "I'll stand, thank you."

He cleared his throat. She was not going to make this easy for him. A point for her, since he doubted she had any idea what had brought him all this way. "The child—"

"George," she said, interrupting him. "His name is George, after our father."

"Of course."

"No," she spoke again, while his next words still danced on the tip of his tongue. "Not 'of course'. Such a phrase denotes your being aware that our father's name was George, or knowing what type of man he was and why we would choose to honor him in such a way. But here you are, darkening my doorstep nine months after his birth. A fact which proves to me that either you didn't know about him before now, or you simply didn't care."

He inclined his head, yet dared not take his eyes off of her, not for a second. "My apologies. I assure you it was the former, and as soon as I discovered that my brother had a son—"

"And where is your brother? And why are you here in his stead?"

Finnian could feel his temper beginning to rise. Never before had he allowed himself to show anger in front of a woman, and yet she was the most infuriating creature he'd ever encountered. "He is in London. I assume."

"You assume?" To his surprise, her mouth broke into a smile and a soft laugh emanated from the back of her throat. "In other words, you have about as much sway over the life of your brother as I have over my sister."

"I'm not here to discuss my family," he said, his voice taking on a note of warning he hadn't even intended to be there.

"Oh, but I'm sure you're here with the sole purpose of discussing mine. Or am I wrong?" A flash in her eyes countered the steel in his voice. "The mere fact that you've arrived today with a prior knowledge of not only both our names, our location, George's existence, and no doubt a myriad other trivial items concerning our past and present life tells me that you've gone to great lengths to find out all you could before traveling here from..." She waved her right hand in a vague circle. "... wherever you call home. Which means, no doubt, that you wanted the upper hand in this discussion. Which also means that I will most likely not care for whatever it is you've come to tell me."

Finnian fumed in silence. If the baby's mother was even half as maddening as the woman standing before him, he wondered how David had survived with his manhood and his sanity intact. "I had come here with the intention of speaking to the mother of my brother's child," he ground out between clenched teeth.

"But she is not here," she said, delivering the confession with the precision of a wielded weapon. "And she is not like to be anytime soon. And since your appearance here is most likely connected with George, then you will have to make do with speaking to me."

"Very well." He sighed. His confidence drained away from him, and the surety he'd experienced upon arriving here that the matter of the child's welfare would be swiftly dealt with—and in his favor—had been skillfully chipped away by every word to come out of Sophia's mouth. "Shall we?" He inclined his head towards the chairs that flanked the table.

"Of course," she said, and slipped gracefully into the seat that he pulled out for her.

Chapter Four

Sophia's heart hammered inside her chest. She would not allow him to see how afraid she was, though the panic that had begun to rise within her at the mention of his identity had neared a pitch that caused her ears to ring and her hands to tremble.

She laid her hands, one on top of the other, on the scrubbed wooden table top, the better to prevent any traitorous shaking from giving away the current state of her nerves. That he had come to take away her George, she did not doubt. But then, George wasn't hers, not really. Though she had spent the last nine months caring for him, including the time her sister had been in residence, she knew that the child didn't belong to her. At least, not in a way that any court or legal document would acknowledge.

And she, stupid creature that she was, had allowed her anger and the shock of Lord Haughton's arrival to get the better of her and confessed that George was not her child. But she didn't doubt her visitor already knew as much. In fact, she wouldn't be shocked if the man also knew that her life here in Stantreath as the widow of the late Richard Brixton was nothing more than a bit of playacting to erase the footprints of scandal that had dogged them before their departure to Northumberland.

Her breath stalled in her lungs as she waited for him to begin. *I have come for the boy.* Those were the words that played over and over again inside her mind, and so she shut her eyes as she attempted to push them out of her head.

"I have a legal matter, of sorts, to discuss with you."

She swallowed, an action that sounded so loud to her own ears that she thought Lissy must have been able to hear it from the floor above.

"I had wished to broach the subject with George's mother, who I assume is your sister," Lord Haughton continued when she made no move to contribute to the conversation. "But as you've pointed out, she's not here, and since you appear to have taken over the care of young George since her departure..."

Taken over. Two simple words, and yet they were so painfully deceptive. For there had never been any exchange of caregiving from Lucy to herself. There had been a few weeks, at the beginning, when Lucy had relished being a new mother. But as the novelty had worn off, and as the difficult work of raising a child set in, Lucy had become more churlish, her complaints growing in variety and frequency.

Sophia recalled late nights and too-early mornings when Lucy would take the time to nurse George, but then immediately set him back into his cradle. There, he would kick and fuss, the cries growing louder, his face becoming redder, his eyes leaking tears until Sophia would come in and scoop him into her arms. During those trying months, she had learned to burp him and to change his diapers, and had discovered which songs he loved and which set his bottom lip quivering. It had taken her only days to learn that he loved to be carried facing forward, so that he could look around with ease. And when he laughed for the first time, it was because she had found the perfect spot beneath his arm that when tickled, brought out the most gleeful series of hiccuping giggles.

With a small shake of her head, Sophia forced herself to return to the present. Seated in front of her was a man who threatened to take that away from her, and she would be a fool if she allowed her mind to wander while she spoke to him.

"... five hundred pounds per annum." Lord Haughton finished speaking, and Sophia blinked up at him, cursing her nomadic thoughts for having let her miss the beginning of his speech.

"Five hundred pounds?" she echoed, and struggled to understand what he was saying.

Lord Haughton nodded. "That should be more than enough to cover any expenses accrued by yourself and a small child."

Something clicked into place inside her head. "You're offering to give me five hundred pounds a year? Every year?"

"The cost of his education will also have to be discussed," he continued now that he had her full attention. "And, of course, once he is finished with his schooling and finds himself an occupation, there will be an annuity settled on... Well, I had planned for it to go to the boy's mother, but I'm sure we'll be able to work out something that will satisfy all the various parties involved."

Sophia leaned back in her chair, until the high, wooden back pressed hard against her shoulder blades. She looked at this Lord Haughton, at his dark hair and his eyes, so much like ice it unnerved her to stare at them for too long. And so she let her gaze dip lower, to the strong line of his jaw, just touched by the faint shadow of a beard he must have neglected to shave before coming to see her. He looked tired, worn down by travel, and yet there was still a rigidity within him that seemed unwilling to bend under any conditions.

Her gaze flicked down to his hand, his left hand, fingers drumming out a steady rhythm on the tabletop. She wondered if he, too, was nervous, if he had to struggle to hide any and every sign of weakness from her.

But, no. This was a man who would not waver from his purpose. Unfortunately, she still could not discern exactly what that purpose entailed.

She moved her own hands towards her and clasped her fingers together. The contrast between the condition of their hands was almost laughable. Whereas his were smooth, his nails neatly trimmed and displaying the obvious signs of a regular manicure, the skin on hers was red and dry, her knuckles cracked and flaking, and her nails were bitten down into the very bed.

He had never worked, she realized. Not physical labor, at least. And here he was, offering her more money than her family had seen in decades, and for what? Her gaze returned to his eyes, those cold, blue shards of colour that watched her, waiting for her reply.

He wanted something. This wasn't merely a gift, given out of the goodness of his heart. This was a man who most likely lived by the way of business and transactions. This was a man who would not give unless he expected something in return.

"Five hundred pounds," she said again, even the words sounding like an extravagance on her lips. "That is..." *Inconceivable*. "... most generous."

And still, she watched him. One corner of his mouth lifted with a hint of a smile. He thought he had won.

"Most generous," she repeated, her knuckles tightening as she squeezed her hands together, the red, chapped skin growing paler before her eyes.

"The boy is my brother's child," Lord Haughton pointed out, while Sophia struggled to keep her breathing even. "No matter any ignominy accompanying the facts of his birth, he is still a member of our family, and I would not see him deprived of his due as such."

No matter any ignominy accompanying the facts of his birth...

Never before had she heard the word "bastard" stated in such florid terms. "Again, that is more than generous. However," she said, and noticed at once the muscle that jumped in his jaw. "I cannot help but wonder what is expected of me, or my sister, in return?"

She saw his nostrils flare as he drew in a sharp breath, but everything else about his expression seemed carefully drawn to show that she had not caught him off guard. "I don't know what you mean. I simply want what is best for the ch—for George," he amended.

"No," she said, and exhaled. "No more prevarication, if you please. I've had enough of that from too many people over the years, so I would prefer that in any matters pertaining to the care and wellbeing of my nephew, we both remain completely and utterly honest with one another."

"So you fully admit he is your nephew?" He did not crow over the fact—she would give him that much.

"Yes. Lucy is his mother."

Lord Haughton nodded. "But she is not here, nor has she been for some time."

She watched as what seemed like a battle waged itself behind his eyes. A minute passed, or perhaps longer, and Sophia heard the rippling laughter of George and Lissy float down to her ears from the rooms above.

"Very well." He shifted forward in his chair, until both of his elbows rested on the tabletop and the position of his hands matched her own. "I would prefer that you agree to several conditions before this matter goes forward to my solicitor. First, that the boy never takes his father's surname."

"I see." Sophia licked her lips, her mouth having gone uncommonly dry at the sudden change in the tone of the conversation. "Pray, continue."

He drew in another deep breath. "You are to make no claim, public or otherwise, on the boy's parentage. No one is to know the identity of his father, and should word arrive to me that you have done so, then any and all payments towards you will immediately cease."

Her gaze drifted down towards the table, her focus concentrated on a knot in the wood. She suspected that if she dared to look into the man's face while he continued to speak, she might be tempted to do him physical harm. "Anything else?"

"You are never to come to London, or to any of my family's estates throughout the country, unless first issued an invitation to do so. Failure to comply with these conditions will mean—"

"—an end to the promised annuity," she finished for him. "Yes, yes, I understand."

She continued to breathe, measured breaths that required her to count three seconds for each inhalation and three seconds for each exhalation, or else she thought she might be ill.

"So..." His voice sounded from the other side of the table. "Mrs.

Brixton, are there any comments or questions you may have for me before we move forward with this?"

One...two...three... "Only one thing," she said, her voice tight as she attempted to speak between clenched teeth. "My own condition, actually." Her eyes met his. *One...two...three...* "And that is that you must leave this house. Now."

He swallowed. She saw the rapid up-and-down motion of his Adam's apple before it again disappeared behind his neatly tied cravat. "Mrs. Brixton, I fear you misunderstand—"

"No," she said again, this time with more vehemence. "I understand perfectly well. You have come here from your elegant townhouse, or your estate, or from wherever you choose to rule over your perfectly ordered little world, and you have insulted not only myself and my sister, but also a mere child, one who had no control over the *ignominy* associated with his birth. And on top of all else, you have chosen to throw a bit of money at me in the hope that your brother's mistake will not become a scandal that should reflect badly on you. Now tell me, *my lord*, is there anything else I may have misunderstood?"

She heard the sound of her own heart pounding in her chest, the noise of it drowning out all else. It had been a mere guess as to the reasoning behind his actions, her assumptions based on what little body language he had given her along with his words. But she was not a stranger to those who had attempted to deceive her, and so she had known, from the first instant that Lord Haughton had set foot inside the cottage, that he had not arrived with any intention other than obtaining something that would be of benefit to him and his blasted family.

Sophia stood up, the legs of her chair scraping across the freshly swept floor. She said nothing more. In fact, she doubted if she had the courage to speak another word without descending into a litany of shouted name-calling. She simply wanted the man out of her sight, out of her thoughts, forever.

"Mrs. Brixton." Haughton stood and made a low bow, the gesture more insulting than if he'd done nothing at all.

She did not follow him out of the room. The heavy strike of his boots as he left the kitchen, followed by the slam of the front door was more than she needed in order to trust that he was gone, finally gone.

It wasn't until Lissy appeared at the kitchen door, her shoulders rounded forward in the meekest of postures that Sophia realized she had not moved from her place beside the table.

"Ma'am?" The poor girl took a single step into the room.

"George," Sophia said, her voice barely above a whisper. "How is he?"

"Nearly asleep in his cradle."

Sophia nodded, her thoughts someplace far away. "Good." She stirred herself, enough to shift her gaze towards Lissy and give the lovely girl a smile. "And thank you, for everything."

Lissy blushed prettily and took another step forward. "Is all well? That man..."

"He will not be bothering us again," Sophia said, her smile gaining strength. "Now, let's return to those curtains, shall we?"

Chapter Five

The next morning arrived on the wings of a cold wind that carried a mass of heavy, grey clouds along in its wake. There was no rain, however, and so Sophia wrapped a shawl tight around her shoulders, tucked George's sparse hair beneath a knitted wool bonnet, and set out towards Stantreath.

The town itself was situated roughly two miles from the front door of the cottage. The majority of the buildings fanned out from the walls of Stantreath castle, a decaying fort that had spent the last two centuries of its existence bending to the will of the wind and the waves that beat against it. The castle loomed larger with each step along the rutted and potholed road, its crumbling walls standing stark against the grey, shifting sky. Sophia put one hand to her bonnet as she looked up at it, her sharp eyes seeking out various shapes and shadows in the ruins, all of them transforming into characters in the story she told to George as he bounced cheerfully on her hip.

She had decided on the morning walk to expend some of the energy that had built up since her encounter with Lord Haughton the previous day. She had slept fitfully during the night, her pillow receiving countless thumps and poundings from her fists, as if the lumpiness of the filling was the sole cause of her insomnia. Everything about his visit had filled her with ire; his unexpected arrival on her doorstep, his knowledge and supposition of too much of her family's situation, his poorly veiled insults against George's illegitimacy, and then the self-aggrandizing posture he'd assumed when making his offer to her, as if she should have been thanking him on bended knee for his charity.

And where was his miscreant of a brother throughout all of this?

The man was George's father, and she or Lucy had yet to hear a word from him, the man behaving as someone incapable of carrying on normal human interactions. But then, perhaps he wasn't. If he was the sort to tumble about with young women of Lucy's class without any offer of protection or marriage, it followed that he most likely wouldn't be the sort to check in with his conquests after they'd adjusted their skirts and returned to their previous life. And any letters they had sent, any energy expended in discovering his whereabouts and informing him that he was a father had amounted to nothing.

But along came the illustrious lord, ready to clean up the mess made by his younger sibling. Sophia's thoughts suddenly came to a halt. How many times had Lord Haughton had to do this? How many other women had been seduced and then abandoned? For all she knew, little George could have a passel of half-siblings scattered across the country, possibly over parts of the continent, as well. She had no idea how *prolific* this David was, and the more she considered it, the more she realized she did not wish to know.

A slight turn in the road brought her into the main part of Stantreath. Its neat rows of low houses seemed to hunker down even closer to the ground this morning, as if threatened by the heaviness of the clouds that shifted above them. Tucking George against her shoulder as a strong blast of wind pushed out from between two stone houses, Sophia slipped into Kirkland's Tea Shoppe for a brief respite from the chill.

The Tea Shoppe sold more than simply tea, its dark shelves filled with coffee, spices, laces and ribbons, bolts of fabric, patterns, books (no novels, as Mrs. Kirkland frowned upon such nonsense), and various other knick-knacks that could easily distract a person from their original purpose in entering the establishment.

A bell jingled on the door, alerting the shop's proprietors to Sophia's entrance. Mrs. Kirkland was the first to appear, that woman gliding out from the back room in a fuss of starched lace and frills, her cap so heavy with ribbons that the woman's neck seemed ready to crumble beneath the weight of it.

There was a smile on Mrs. Kirkland's face as she entered the front room, but as soon as her eyes alighted on Sophia, her grin faded and her already thin lips became nearly nonexistent. "Can I help you?"

Sophia stepped away from one shelf in particular, displaying an array of watch-fobs that had caught George's attention. "Some sugar, I think." She didn't need any sugar, but she did need an excuse to loiter about the shop until she'd shaken the chill from her bones, and sugar was the first and only thing to come to her mind.

While Mrs. Kirkland reluctantly filled her order, Sophia switched George to her other hip and gave his mittened hands a squeeze to make sure they weren't bothered by the nip in the air. Without a word, Mrs. Kirkland dropped the paper-wrapped cone of sugar onto the counter and named a price that Sophia knew was higher than the one given to other customers.

Sophia sighed. There were several people throughout the town who insisted on treating her like a pariah, no matter that she had arrived in town months before claiming to be a proper widow charged with the care of her child and younger sister. She knew the gossip that had begun to circulate not long after their arrival, gossip that increased tenfold after Lucy had taken it upon herself to abscond from Stantreath without any word as to her whereabouts. The stories went that Sophia had never been married at all, or that she had been mistress to some titled gentleman who had tucked her away in the country once her husband had died and she'd found herself heavy with the man's child.

After taking the overpriced sugar and tucking it into the bag she had slung on her arm, she exited the shop, prepared to be struck in the face by another great push of air from the direction of the coast. But it was an uncommon stillness that met her as she stepped out onto the main street, the sound of the various types of traffic—both wheeled and pedestrian—sounding especially loud now that they weren't swept away by the wind to another corner of the county.

It wasn't until the roof of the vicarage came into sight that the first drop of rain landed on her forehead. She was about to turn back towards home when the rumble of carriage wheels came up beside her, the harness of the horses jangling as the driver ordered the great beasts to a halt.

Sophia glanced up at the carriage and smiled. A moment later, the window dropped down and an elderly bonneted head poked out of the small, rectangular space. "Silly girl!" the lady's reedy voice came from beneath the oversized piece of millinery. "What are you on about, taking a child out in such frightful weather?"

"Lady Rutledge," Sophia replied with a curtsy. "I was just on my way back to the cottage."

"Nonsense!" The feathers on the old lady's bonnet shivered in accompaniment of her feigned horror. "You'll bring that baby into this carriage at once, and then I'll see you back to Rutledge House for cakes and a bit of warming in front of the fire."

Sophia knew not to argue, and so allowed the carriage door to be opened to her. She even permitted Lady Rutledge to place a blanket over her legs before the carriage set off again.

"Now, give me that child, dear!" Lady Rutledge removed her gloves and held out both of her bare, spindly hands, her bejeweled fingers sparkling in even the dim light inside the carriage.

Sophia obliged and passed George to the other lady, who took him eagerly before bestowing a loud kiss on the boy's nose. "Such a treasure," Sophia heard her remark under her breath. "Such a heavy thing," she then said at a much louder volume. "I believe he's grown since... Oh, when did I see him last?"

"It was Tuesday." Sophia settled back in her seat, feeling a quiet pride at the boy's obvious good health and appetite.

Lady Rutledge counted it out on her fingers. "Too long, too long," she muttered. "And if it wasn't for my nearly running over the two of you in the road, I wouldn't be able to see you today either. You need to escape that dreadful hovel of yours. Keeping yourself locked away won't do any good, either for yourself or for this little terror." She pressed another kiss to the child's head.

"We are not locked away," Sophia protested.

"No, of course not. But neither are you *doing* anything."

"I'm taking care of George," Sophia pointed out. "I'm keeping a home, cooking, and cleaning."

"And what of *you*?" Lady Rutledge punctuated the question with silly face that made George squeal with delight. "Are you visiting? Do you attend any of the assemblies? Do you have any friends or close companions?"

"Lissy visits quite often." Sophia clenched and unclenched her hands in her lap. "And I am not a hermit, as you seem to be insinuating."

"Oh, I am not insinuating anything! I am saying quite plainly that you are languishing in that house, punishing yourself and this child for something you're not even guilty of doing."

Sophia looked out the window as the gates to Rutledge Hall came into view. "I don't have to punish myself. The majority of the town seems more than capable of doing that for me."

As they passed through the gates and started up the long drive that led to the main entrance of Lady Rutledge's home, Sophia let her gaze rest on the elderly woman as she doted on George. Her family had been acquainted with Lady Rutledge for years, Sophia's maternal grandmother having shared her debut season in London with the venerable lady when she herself was nothing more than a fresh-faced young woman on the lookout for a suitable husband. And if it hadn't been for Lady Rutledge's intervention, Sophia reminded herself, she and Lucy would never have been given the cottage for their use. It was because of Lady Rutledge they were allowed a second chance at a life untainted by scandal. At least, that had been their hope at the time.

"The people in this town are a great lot of fools," Lady Rutledge announced as the footman opened the door to the carriage and let down the step. "They take to shunning others over the silliest things. Do you remember the Latimer girl? The one they claimed created a scandal because she didn't have the proper amount of lace on her gown? Psh!"

Sophia took George back into her arms and waited for her companion to descend from the carriage. Lady Rutledge, for all her vitality and bluster, was not steady on her feet, and so it took the aid of the footman, along with Lady Rutledge's cane, to help her arrive at her own front door.

"And that vicar!" The older woman pushed into the house, nearly knocking her butler off his feet with the end of her cane. Sophia nodded to the equally-aged man, who returned her attention with a genuine grin for both herself and the baby. "What's his name? Finley?"

"Fenton," Sophia supplied, and followed Lady Rutledge into the drawing room after one of the maids appeared to divest her of her bonnet and shawl.

"Fool, more like." Lady Rutledge hobbled over to the sofa, a grand, plush thing upholstered all in dark green velvet. "I've never seen such a hypocrite, not in all my years. And such a slimy creature, too. Why, I cannot count the times he's stood in this very room, oiling his way around the furniture while he eyes my trinkets, probably hoping to stash them into his pockets the moment my back was turned. Pull the bell, will you?"

Sophia gave the bell pull a hard tug and then settled on the floor with George, the better to keep him within arm's reach and away from Lady Rutledge's fine trinkets.

"It's why I won't invite him or that wife of his to dine here. I can't trust that I'll still have all my silver intact by the end of the evening."

"Their son is not as oily, as you put it."

"No," Lady Rutledge agreed, though with some reluctance. "But I cannot say I care for the way he looks at you."

"At me?" Sophia glanced up sharply. "What do you mean?"

"Oh, you're young, so you don't know. But believe me when I say that young man has his eye on you from the minute you enter the church until the second you leave again. If not for his parents or the fact you're supposed to be grieving a dead husband, I'd say he would've already made his feelings known."

Sophia shook her head and unhooked George's fingers from the edge of a lace tablecloth that he seemed intent to drag down onto his head. "You're mistaken," she said, and attempted to distract the child with a small, tasseled cushion. "He's hardly spoken to me once since we've arrived here."

"Because his parents probably won't allow him near you," Lady Rutledge said with a point of her cane towards Sophia's head. "If I can see how goggle-eyed their boy is when he's within twenty paces of you, then so can everyone else. And I've no doubt they've already lectured against him chasing after one such as you."

"Such as I?"

"Poor," she began, ticking the first item off one of her gnarled fingers. "Lacking connections," she ticked another finger. "And much too opinionated for their liking." A tick for a third finger. "If there's something a pompous bag of air such as our dear Reverend Fenton detests more than anything else, it's someone who would dare to open their mouth and utter a word against him. And that's you from head to heel, m'dear."

Sophia's mouth opened and closed several times before she could utter a word in reply. "You make me sound quite dreadful, like the most belligerent of harridans."

Lady Rutledge shook her head. "No, you are incorrect. That particular coronet belongs to none other than myself, and I will lay waste to anyone who attempts to steal that title away from me."

She reached down as George crawled over to her, her wrist turning sharply from side to side as she shook her bracelet before the infant's grasping hands. "Of course, the fact that I possess a title along with this estate, which has become refuge for a rather large quantity of mice and bats, I'm afraid, permits a fair number of the town's inhabitants to forgive a greater share of my eccentricities."

She straightened up again, though the bracelet was now gone from her wrist, the shining pearls clutched between George's pudgy fingers. "Unfortunately, that same piddling title and this drafty pile of stone is not enough to lend my connection with you the same measure of forgiveness. Perhaps if I had another ten or twenty thousand guineas to my name, I could provide you with more than a drafty cottage and the occasional ham from the smokehouse."

Sophia extricated the bracelet from George with a deft sweep of her hand. She slipped the jewelry out of sight and managed to secure his attention with the tinkle of a small, silver bell before his lip could tremble over the loss of the beaded bauble. "An astounding thing, the power a bit of coin can wield over one's transgressions."

"Or how others perceive them," Lady Rutledge was quick to add.

The arrival of the maid was enough to turn their conversation towards lighter matters, and when the tea things were brought in, Lady Rutledge amused herself with the task of feeding George bites of cake from her own fingers.

"You'll spoil him for all other foods," Sophia warned, though there was a smile on her face.

"Let him be spoiled," the older lady cooed. "His lot is already a more difficult one than he deserves, and so I'll thank you not to begrudge him a few crumbs of lemon cake and cream before he's even made the transition to proper trousers."

Sophia tucked into her own plate of delicacies, one that was swiftly followed by a second when Lady Rutledge threatened to have the leftovers packed up and delivered to her doorstep if she refused to eat her fill.

"And now it is time for us to be leaving," Sophia said as she dabbed the last crumb from her mouth and bent down to retrieve a yawning George from his post at Lady Rutledge's skirts. His own hands and face were sticky, but she didn't mind the mess as he burrowed his face into her shoulder and settled more comfortably in her arms.

A glance at the windows told her that the harsh breeze and spitting rain had yet to relent, but when Lady Rutledge called to have her carriage again brought around, Sophia waved the offer away as she settled her shawl around her shoulders. "You've done more than enough for us this morning," she said, and wrapped one edge of the shawl more snugly around a dozing George. "I'll make better time on foot, and the jostling of the carriage is more likely to wake him from his nap. But you have my gratitude."

Lady Rutledge tapped the end of her cane on the floor, a sign of her agitated mind. "I don't deserve your gratitude, and that will be enough on that subject. Though I do wish you'd take my advice and move into my home permanently. I have enough room, and you'd have more than enough spiders and mice to keep you company, should my own presence ever become too much to bear."

Sophia stepped forward, dropped a light kiss on Lady Rutledge's cheek, and watched as the older woman touched the soft curls of George's hair that peeked out from beneath the edges of his bonnet. "You've done so much for us already," she told her. "You've given us our own home, and a chance for George to grow up away from the scandal associated with his birth."

"Your sister," Lady Rutledge began, her voice lower now that she was speaking so near to the infant's sleeping form. "She wasn't ready. To be a mother, to face the responsibility that comes with it." A click of her tongue and Sophia looked up to see the woman shaking her head. "You're made of stronger stuff, m'dear."

Sophia fought against the urge to sigh, to allow her shoulders to droop beneath the weight of all those countless responsibilities that had been added to her burden since Lucy had confessed to being with child.

The image of Lord Haughton arose in her mind, unbidden, and a frisson of tension course through her limbs. The day before, his offer had been nothing less than repellant to her, but now that she was once again free to dwell on the bleak prospects her future contained, she wondered which path would be the show of greater strength: To take his money, to acquiesce to his demands? Or to fight him, merely to assuage her own pride?

"I am curious," Sophia said, before stepping out the door. "Have you ever heard of a Lord Haughton, or encountered any members of his family?"

"Haughton?" Lady Rutledge pursed her lips, her eyes squinting to better peer back through the annals of time and memory. "Rings a bell. Of course, when you arrive at my station in my life, nearly everything sets off the ringing of some bell, somewhere, and yet I can never recall where I last saw my favorite pair of gloves. But Haughton, yes..." She gave her cane another strong tap on the floor. "Proud, disagreeable, and overly concerned with the importance of rank. Probably kept a dog-eared copy of *The Peerage* tucked beneath his bed pillow. Though I will admit his wife was an uncommonly beautiful creature, and about as welcoming as a day old fish dinner."

Sophia bit back a laugh while George squirmed and shifted against her chest. "So is this the former Lord Haughton, I assume?"

"Oh! Is there a new one?" Lady Rutledge raised one shoulder in a thoroughly unladylike gesture. "I hadn't heard. Of course, when you live at the edge of the world, it does take a bit of time for news to find its way here." She raised one eyebrow. "Why do you ask?"

"No reason." Sophia hoped the lie wouldn't show on her face. "Lissy thought she had heard a bit of gossip, and... Well, it looks as if the rain has nearly quit," she said hastily. "I really should be on my way."

The butler opened the door for her, and she ducked her head as she set a brisk pace down the length of the graveled drive. The rain had indeed stopped, though the breeze seemed more inclined than ever to buffet her from every direction. But the wind would dry the roads, she thought, and if the vexatious Lord Haughton was already on his way back to London, then she sent up a quick prayer that it would only serve to further hasten his journey away from her.

Chapter Six

Finnian had not yet left Stantreath. The roads, he'd been informed, were too wet to facilitate an immediate departure following his interview with that confounded Brixton woman. The streams and local canals were too high. Several of the bridges he would need to cross were rendered impassable by a rainstorm that had occurred several days ago some miles inland, the effects of which were only now visiting their destruction on the village and its outlying areas.

This, of course, was the explanation for why he had, in contrast, experienced little difficulty upon his journey to Stantreath. There had been some mud, and one of the horses had thrown a shoe, but apart from that, nothing more than a few minor inconveniences had marred his forward progress.

But now, the owner of the inn—a Mr. Treacher, who had become the most irritating of bootlickers the moment the crest on Finnian's coach, along with the contents of his wallet, had become known to the odious man—did nothing but protest against his plans for departure. Surely he should stay for at least another night, possibly two, until it was certain that all roads toward London were passable again!

And every person in the inn seemed to be in collusion with one another, the stable boys reporting that his coach needed repair, while the maids insisted that he needed to change rooms and wouldn't he more comfortable on another floor? And all while Mr. Treacher added more items to the bill: Another meal, a fresh set of linens for the new bed, two more scoops of coal for the fire.

He sat in a private sitting room at the back of the inn, a space that bore more resemblance to a spacious cupboard than an area intended for the comfort of a fully-grown person, and sipped at a tepid cup of tea. He could ring for someone to bring him a fresh cup, but no doubt the avaricious Mr. Treacher would add three more items to his bill (quality tea being such an expense, the landlord had informed him) and he would be expected to place a gratuity into the palm of whichever overly-obsequious maid took it upon herself to deliver the tray.

And so he took another swallow of cold tea, and he made a third attempt at reading the same newspaper he had been nursing for as long as his dismal beverage had rested near the arm of his chair.

The knock at the door that interrupted this rare instance of leisure was faint, but considering the scant size of the room, there was little chance of him pretending not to have heard it.

"Enter," he said, and didn't deign to look away from his newspaper as the red-faced Mr. Treacher puffed into the room.

"Beg pardon, your lordship." Mr. Treacher attempted a bow, but managed to upset a small table decorated with cheap, vulgar figurines. The landlord apologized profusely, while attempting to set everything to rights, and Finnian shook out his paper and rolled his eyes heavenward. Four ghastly figurines shattered to pieces. He'd be shocked if they didn't show up on his bill as the most precious examples of Ming China in all of Northumberland.

"Yes?" he prompted while Mr. Treacher continued to fuss over the now wobbling table.

One table, broken, was how he imagined it would be transcribed. Along with: *Chippendale, irreplaceable.*

"You've a visitor, your lordship," the landlord said, before he wedged a book beneath one of the crooked table legs and stepped back to survey his handiwork.

"Oh?" Finnian straightened in his chair. There was only one person he'd called on since his arrival in Stantreath, and he wondered if a night spent thinking over his offer had finally brought Mrs. Brixton around to his view of things.

"The Reverend Fenton, my lord. Sir. Your lordship." Mr. Treacher took up the corner of his soiled apron and used it to wipe the sweat from his upper lip. "Come to pay his respects, I'm sure. He asks for only a brief moment of your time."

"Of course." He folded the newspaper twice, needing some activity with which to engage his hands. He should have known that his presence in this godforsaken little town would not pass unnoticed. His carriage bore his crest, and in a village of this size, he might as well have simply ridden through the main street with a town caller announcing his arrival. "Send him in."

Mr. Treacher glanced at Finnian's cup. "Some more tea perhaps? Or some cold meats and a bit of cheese—"

"No trays, no food," Finnian interrupted. "I'm afraid your Reverend Fenton will not be staying long enough to enjoy whatever parade of victuals you may have for our perusal."

Mr. Treacher bowed. "Right you are, your lordship. Sir. I'll just..." Another bow, and the landlord backed out of the room, his hand searching blindly for the doorknob before he slipped out into the hall.

But his respite was short-lived. Less than a minute later, a tall figure, clad from head to toe in varying shades of black and dark grey, ducked into the room.

Finnian took him into immediate dislike. It was something about the man's eyes, he decided, how the gleam in them failed to match the expression on his long, angular face.

"Good morning, my lord." The Reverend Fenton dipped his head and shoulders in a slow bow, while his voice—deliberately stentorious, he suspected—reverberated to every corner of the tiny room. "How condescending of you to allow such a humble personage as myself to intrude upon your time of leisure. You know, it is quite often that I tell my parishioners to find a quiet moment during their busy days, merely a minute or two in which to sit and reflect upon the glories of this life, which is our Lord's gift to us. But often..."

Finnian reached into the pocket of his waistcoat while the speech continued. He retrieved his pocket watch, flicked it open with his thumb, and glanced at the time. *Good morning*, the Reverend Fenton had said on his arrival, but no doubt it would be well past midday by the time the man was finished reveling in the sound of his own voice.

"Ah, yes. Of course," Finnian said, as soon as he detected a lull in the Reverend Fenton's soliloquy. "And I assume you're here on some errand of divine beneficence? Prayer books for the poor, no doubt. Or an extra piece of coal for the widows?"

The Reverend bowed again, this time going so far as to set one foot in front of the other before his upper body creaked forward. "You pay me too great a compliment, my lord, to assume that all of my earthly endeavors are for the welfare of those less fortunate than you and I. Indeed, their plight weighs heavily on my thoughts, even now as I stand here before you. But I must confess that my appearance here pertains to more social matters, if you will."

"I see," Finnian said carefully. Now there would be an invitation, he realized. For tea, or perhaps even for a full dinner, complete with five courses and accompanied by the unctuous sermonizing of the Reverend Fenton and guests. "It's unfortunate then, that I'm to depart for London this very afternoon. But if you will give me your direction, I'm sure that my secretary can arrange for a donation to be made to..." He shrugged. "Whichever charity you would deem fit."

"Oh, that is most kind of you, my lord. Most kind!" This was followed by another bow, during which Finnian rose from his chair.

"If you'll excuse me," he said, and nodded towards the door.

The Reverend Fenton's brow furrowed in confusion, before he realized that he was being dismissed. "Of course, my lord. Don't let me keep you. But I did wish to ask you—it is, I'm sure, no concern of mine—however... What was it that brought you all the way to Stantreath in the first place, my lord?"

Finnian stopped near the door. His shoulders stiffened while his fingers tightened around the rough metal of the latch. "You're correct, Reverend. It is no concern of yours."

"My apologies!" the Reverend cried, and continued to hover in the background as Finnian stalked into the dimly lit corridor. "My sincerest apologies, my lord. It is just... Well, when word reached me that your most elegant equipage had been sighted at the home of the Brixton widow, I thought it my duty to come here and deliver a warning."

Finnian turned around quickly, causing the Reverend to nearly stumble into him. "A warning? Against what?"

"Well." The Reverend stepped back and began to rub his hands together. It was a gesture that Finnian associated with a feeling of glee, and he wondered how much this Man of God was delighting in the opportunity to tell tales about the various inhabitants of his parish. "It is a pair of sisters, my lord. Their parents died a few years ago, succumbed to a fever, I believe. I *suspect*, that it may have been due to some profligate way of living, considering the characters of their daughters."

"Indeed." Finnian eyed the man with renewed distaste, but he fought to keep his features as bland as possible. "And it is their characters, I suppose, that you felt compelled to warn me about?"

"The older sister," the Reverend said, leaning forward, his voice lowered to an exaggerated whisper. "She purports herself as a widow, but there is no mention of her deceased husband's family, or where he was supposed to have come from." He raised his eyebrows. "And the younger sister," he added, the dark lines of his brows rising higher still. "Has since run off!"

"Run off?" Finnian echoed. "And what leads you to believe the elder of the sisters is putting forward a false impression of widowhood?" He thought of auburn hair and a pair of fiery eyes that flashed at him in shades of gold and green.

The Reverend released a heavy sigh. "There is no mention of her deceased husband's family, and she is always quite vague when it comes to revealing where she and sister resided before coming here. It leads one to think, my lord, that the child did not find its way into this world under a banner of legitimacy. And to see her flaunt the creature, to fly in the face of propriety..." He shook his head. "I must confess that the Lord, in his wisdom, did not see fit to bless me with a daughter. But when I bear witness to this supposed *Mrs.* Brixton, parading through the town, for all the world as if the child in her arms were not—" He sniffed, his eyes closing against the mere image he'd conjured with his words. "There are indeed times when I am thankful I have no female issue to be spoiled or influenced by such a deleterious example of womanhood."

"Quite," Finnian said, and looked away from the man, suddenly bored by the entire conversation. His irritation, however, was barely kept in check. The Reverend had referred to the infant as a *creature,* relegating the child to a status measuring less than human. And all because some foolish girl had fallen for his brother's charms? "Good day to you," he said, and shouldered past the man without another glance.

And what had he said about Sophia Brixton? That she was *flaunting* the child? How? By not taking up residence in an uninhabited cave in order to spare the townspeople from creating more gossip about her and the infant's *deleterious* behavior?

Finnian returned to his bedroom on the third floor, his arm aching to slam the door behind him. He couldn't understand the true reason behind his irritation at the Reverend Fenton's words. Hadn't Mrs. Brixton accused him of insinuating some of the same things, of speaking poorly of the infant George's birth only the day before? But he pushed aside the reprimand towards his own behavior as he changed his coat, as he adjusted the folds in his neckcloth, as he reached for his hat and his gloves. And he continued to hold himself without blame in the matter as he walked downstairs, ignored the inquiries of Mr. Treacher as to his intentions, and set a course for the home of Mrs. Sophia Brixton.

Chapter Seven

Sophia held George on her hip, his fingers grasping at the frayed edge of her shawl. Above them, the rain clouds had begun to break apart, while the breeze tugged at the strings of his bonnet.

She had hoped he would sleep for the entirety of the walk from Lady Rutledge's manor back to their cottage, but the rumble of a passing coach had disturbed him from his slumber, and so she attempted to keep him happy and distracted by the various sights and sounds the outdoors had on display.

Ahead of her, she noticed the hulking form of the inn, and near its entrance, the familiar figure of the Reverend Fenton. He was clad in his usual black, and what she could see of his expression across the distance between them seemed particularly severe, even more than what she was often forced to endure when his glance happened to fall upon her during Sunday morning services. Making a quick turn, she skirted around the side of the large building. She held her breath until she was certain she had succeeded in slipping by without garnering the reverend's attention.

After the appearance of Lord Haughton on her doorstep the previous day, Sophia wasn't confident in her ability to face another overbearing man, especially one intent on imparting his opinion on how best to rear her sister's child. If she was to be honest, she was tired of being treated as little more than a blight on polite society. All she wanted, more than anything, was to be able to go about her daily life and raise her nephew in peace. Why the rest of the civilized world seemed unable to allow her such a small freedom, she could not begin to understand.

She stepped into a narrow, muddy lane that kept the main traffic of Stantreath behind her while still leading her towards home. A few seagulls, dipping overhead, caught George's attention, and he squealed in delight as they fluttered on the breeze before circling toward them again.

Sophia heard the step of someone walking behind her, but she didn't look back right away. It wasn't a private lane, and now that the weather had begun to clear, no doubt several other townspeople would be wanting to dry out after the morning rain. But when the steps quickened, she finally stopped and turned around.

"Mrs. Brixton!"

A young man, his cheeks flushed in his apparent attempt to dodge the various puddles and holes that clogged the lane, ran up to her side.

"Mister Fenton," she said, and dipped her chin in greeting. The man before her was a startling contrast to his father, both in looks and character. Where the Reverend Fenton was tall and angular, his eldest son carried his weight across broad shoulders and possessed a tendency towards plumpness in his jaw. His hair was fair, the ends of it curling out from beneath the brim of his hat. But the greatest difference of all was in his eyes. Josiah Fenton looked at her with kindness, while Sophia suspected that his father would be hard pressed to deliver an adequate definition of the word.

"Mrs. Brixton," he said again, while his gaze darted from her face, to the ground, and back again. "I do hope you and your family are in good health?"

Sophia blinked at him, until George reached up and gave her earlobe a tug. "Why, yes. Of course. And you? You are well, I suppose?"

"Quite, especially now." Again, his gaze met hers. Then, suddenly, he cleared his throat and looked back over his shoulder. "My father is at the inn. He wished to call on someone, and I thought I would take the opportunity to get a bit of fresh air. And then I saw you, and-and little George, and I thought..." He stopped, swallowed, and cleared his throat again. "Well, I thought perhaps I could accompany you. That is, unless you'd prefer to be alone."

At first, Sophia could think of no reason why he should not walk with her. But Lady Rutledge's comments, about the young Mr. Fenton's marked interest in her, rang through her head. For them to walk together, in the open, where anyone could see... Well, in a town of this size, it was tantamount to a proposal of marriage.

"I am only walking home," Sophia said, as the warmth of embarrassment flooded her cheeks. "And I would not wish to take you away from any of your other errands."

"It would be no trouble," he told her, as a hint of a smile appeared on his lips. "No trouble at all."

Sophia shifted George to her other hip and continued walking. Mr. Fenton fell into step beside her, his hands clasped behind his back. Several minutes passed in silence. But as the cottage came into view, Mr. Fenton coughed nervously and began to speak.

"I-I had hoped to discuss a matter of some delicacy with you, but it's difficult to find the courage—"

At that instant, a yawn from George developed into a bout of crying as he rubbed his eyes with his fists.

"Oh, I'm sorry." Sophia put the child's head to her shoulder and rubbed his back. A more fortuitous circumstance, she could not imagine. Whatever Josiah Fenton had been about to say, she was quite certain it was not something she wished to hear. He had always been kind to her, even when the other members of the Stantreath populace had done their best to exclude her and George. But never had she thought of the young man in terms of marriage, and she doubted she ever could. "He missed his nap, and I fear he'll be a right little terror until he's had a chance to rest."

"Of course." Mr. Fenton bowed and began to back away, his shoulders slumped forward as one dejected. "I'll not keep you."

"Good day, Mr. Fenton."

"G-Good day, Mrs. Brixton." His eyes met hers once more, before he ducked his head and his face slipped out of view.

Sophia hesitated in the lane, then turned and went up the path that led to the cottage. Mr. Fenton's behavior had unsettled her already beleaguered mind, and by the time she'd placed George in his cradle and returned downstairs to the kitchen, she wasn't surprised when the first twinges of another headache began to pound at her temples.

She needed to eat, she realized. A few bits of cake and some tea with Lady Rutledge were all she'd consumed since an early breakfast that morning, and so she tied her apron around her waist and set about preparing a small meal.

There was a bit of bread leftover from the previous evening, and some smoked ham that she had been saving for a rainy day. Well, it had rained that morning, and so she loaded the ham and all of her edibles onto a tray, along with some cheese and a crock of mustard she snatched from the cupboard as she sidled past.,p>

As she placed the tray on the table, there was a knock at the front door. She shut her eyes and sent a silent prayer heavenward. Perhaps, if she ignored this uninvited visitor, they would simply go away and leave her in peace.

There was a pause, then. Her hands twisted in the stained folds of her apron. Another minute, and she would know they'd moved on. She could simply pull out a chair, proceed with her uninterrupted repast—

The next series of knocks was louder than the first. Loud enough, she realized, to wake up poor George from his second attempt at a nap. The baby's cry sounded through the house. Sophia swept out of the kitchen, down the hall, ignoring the front door and whoever may have been standing on the other side of it, and fetched the squalling infant from his bed.

"Shh, shh," she soothed as she returned downstairs, her arms filled with a fussing, squirming child. George's face was soaked with an impressive mixture of fluids from eyes, nose, and mouth, and Sophia did her best to wipe off his cheeks and chin with the corner of her apron before she reached for the latch on the front door. If whoever had interrupted her nephew's nap was intelligent, she hoped they possessed the forethought to dispatch themselves from her doorstep before she could set eyes on them.

"Good afternoon, Mrs. Brixton."

Lord Haughton stood there, irritatingly stiff and starched. Sophia's own clothes, she knew, were blotted with all manner of stains and spills, along with a fresh patch of drool on her shoulder from where George dribbled on her.

"Of course," she muttered under her breath. "Good afternoon," she returned the greeting in a louder voice. She bounced George on her hip, while he continued to fuss and cry in her ear.

"Is something wrong with the child?" he asked, and a little more of Sophia's patience slipped away from her.

"Yes, there is something wrong with the child," she snapped. "Twice he has attempted to nap today, and twice he has been interrupted, most recently by a knocking sound that was quite loud enough to raise the dead."

He raised one dark eyebrow. "My apologies," he said, though she could not tell if he meant it. "I had no idea that it was so difficult for children to sleep during the day."

"Normally, it isn't. But when one of those children is teething..." She switched George to her other hip and stepped back from the door. "You may come in, if you wish."

It was all the welcome he would receive. She was not normally so impolite, but the fact that she could already guess at Lord Haughton's purpose in visiting her a second time siphoned away the last of her good manners and graces.

She did not look back to see if he followed her. There was the click of the door closing, and the heavy footfalls from his boots as he trailed her into the kitchen. She saw her tray, and its delicious contents, still sitting on the table where she'd left it.

"Here," she said, and turned around, holding George out to him.

"Not only did you interrupt his rest, but you interrupted my meal as well. So, if you would be so kind..."

He looked down at the baby as if she were about to thrust a two-headed serpent at him.

"He's not poisonous," she assured him. "Though he does bite, and I can't vouch for the survival of your neckcloth should he get his fingers into it."

A deep noise of discontent emanated from Lord Haughton's throat. A grunt or a groan, she couldn't be sure, but since he failed to put any further argument into actual words, she tucked the baby into his arms.

"You don't need to support his head," she said, and tugged at his sleeve. "He can sit up very well on his own, but I fear that if you were to set him down on the floor or in his chair, the entire populace of Stantreath along with most of Northumberland will be able to hear the result."

Sophia watched as he tried to shift the child in his arms, his movements awkward, as if he held something both ridiculously fragile and covered in filth. For some reason, the sight of it made her mouth quirk into a smile, and she had to bite down on the twitch of her lips before he happened to glance up and see her.

"Now, then," she said, once she was confident that he wasn't about to let George tumble to the floor. She turned back to her tray and fixed a sandwich for herself, heaping large amounts of ham and mustard onto the thick slices of dark bread. "Shall I fix something for you?" she offered, and picked a crumb of cheese off the tray and popped it into her mouth.

"I'm fine," he said, though it was apparent he was anything but. George kicked his legs in an attempt to leap out of Lord Haughton's arms, while his cried intensified until his face was blotched and slick with a fresh layer of tears.

"Poor thing." Sophia reached across the edge of the table and gave George's back a few gentle pats. This, unfortunately, was more than enough for poor George, who promptly spit up all over the lapels of

Lord Haughton's coat.

"Ahh..." was all he said before Sophia picked up a damp cloth from the edge of the basin and wiped up the mess from his shoulder and sleeve.

"You've been christened," Sophia said, and glanced up at him, her mouth beginning to twitch again. "And look! He's much happier now."

Indeed, George was all smiles again, and clapped his hands playfully as she cleaned the last drops of sour milk and half-digested cake from his chin.

She sat down at the table then, pulled the tray with her sandwich towards her, and without further ceremony, began to eat. Lord Haughton seemed discomfited by her ability to tuck into her meal while he stood beside the table, a babbling baby boy in his arms. But she ignored him, except to pass a crust of bread up to George, who happily gummed the tidbit.

"Have you reconsidered my offer?"

Sophia glanced up at him and back at the food in her hands. "No," she said, and took another bite.

Lord Haughton shifted restlessly, then turned to pace the length of the small room. The entire time, George continued to laugh and talk around a mouthful of soggy bread.

"Why should the answer I gave you yesterday change with the passage of a single night?" Sophia asked after she'd swallowed her own bite. "I will not be bought off. It's unseemly."

"And raising your sister's bastard is not?"

She breathed in sharply through her nose. "I should have you thrown out of this house for that," she said, without looking at him. Carefully, she wiped the crumbs from the corners of her mouth and smoothed down the folds of her apron. "But I'd rather take this opportunity to remind you that George is as much your brother's son as my sister's. So take care to recall that every insult you so carelessly toss over that child's head, he is your flesh and blood."

"I am sorry."

That was enough to tear her eyes from the food. He appeared slightly stunned by her words, and when he pulled out the chair opposite her and sat down, she thought there was even a slight air of contrition in his posture.

"I'll take better care to keep that in mind the next time I speak."

Sophia continued to stare at him, her lips parted. If he was sincere, then it was a change in him she never could have imagined occurring. "It's easy to allow ourselves to focus on the wrong thing," she said, and toyed with the edge of her half-eaten sandwich. "But regardless of how my nephew made his passage into the world, he deserves to be loved and taken care of without having to bear the shame of his parents' stupidity."

Lord Haughton set George on his knee, and when the child proved to be happy there, he brought out his pocket watch and dangled it in front of the infant's hands. "And you're the only one to undertake such a task? There are no orphanages, no—"

"Oh, an orphanage?" She pronounced the word with as much distaste as she could muster. "How silly I've been! Now that you've reminded me of their existence, I can simply wrap him up and drop him off like a bundle of laundry. And I'm sure he'll be cherished and given every amount of attention and opportunity that such institutions are known for providing."

"Don't be facetious," he chided her, as he bounced George on his knee.

"Then please refrain from being such a clod, stomping in here with your bags of money. Not every problem can be whisked away under the influence of a few battered coins."

He shifted forward in his seat, and Sophia thought he was about to stand up and pace again. But instead, he merely retrieved the entire pocket watch from his waistcoat and placed it in George's fingers. "I am offering the boy a chance," he said, his calmness a contrast to the irritation that continued to bubble up within her. "I wish for him to have a good education, a future that you alone may not be able to provide."

Sophia nodded. "In exchange for my silence."

He stared at her, his mouth working around something she wouldn't give him a chance to say.

"Because that's what this is, correct? A few pounds settled on him now, your promise that he'll be duly cared for in terms of his education and his future prospects, and then you leave here puffed up with the knowledge that you will never have to hear from me, never have to be reminded of your brother's indiscretion except for once a year when the annuity pays out."

As soon as she stopped speaking, she wondered if she had gone too far. But Lord Haughton's arrival into her quiet, secluded existence had thrown a considerable measure of uncertainty into every facet of her life. Because what would happen if she continued to refuse his offer? Would he simply take George away from her? And what of his brother, the baby's father? If, in a year, or ten years, he decided to take a passing interest in his son's life, what power did she have to deny him? And this was all without even considering what would happen if Lucy ever decided to return.

"If this is some attempt at bargaining for more money…" he began to say.

"No," she said, and dropped her hands into her lap. Her sandwich was forgotten, her appetite having abruptly fled as she imagined a life in which she would not have her nephew to care for. "We are all not as mercenary as you make us out to be. I don't want anything from you, not now, not ever. In fact, if you wish for me to sign a contract to that effect, promising that we need never again cross paths with one another, I think you would find me more than willing to put my signature to such a document."

He sat, not looking at her, but toying with the chain of his watch, tugging at it in order to make the thing bob and spin in front of the baby's enchanted eyes. "And that is your final say on the matter?"

She nodded, then realized she would have to speak for him to know her answer. "Yes," she said, her voice tight.

"Very well." He stood up and passed George back to her. The baby kicked his legs and shouted happily at the exchange before he began to gnaw on the edge of the watch. "You need sign nothing. I'll take you at your word. If you wish to be left alone, and swear to make no claims on us, George's family, then I will wish you a good day and leave it at that."

Sophia blinked up at him. This sudden shift in his behavior…it couldn't be real, could it? And yet, when she looked at his face, she saw that he was in earnest. And his eyes, there was not a hint of subterfuge carried in their cool, blue depths.

"Good day," she said, her voice wavering on those two short words. "Oh, wait!"

He stopped before he left the kitchen. Sophia settled George more comfortably on her lap and began to extricate the gold pocket watch from his drool-soaked fingers. "Here, you mustn't forget this."

But Lord Haughton shook his head, even raising a hand against her in protest. "Let him keep it. It belonged to my father, to his grandfather. Perhaps it's only right that he should have it."

Sophia didn't say thank you. She didn't say anything, but listened in dumbfounded silence to his footsteps as he walked out of the cottage, shutting the door firmly behind him.

Chapter Eight

The ballroom was a press of too many bodies and too little air. Candles burned in every sconce, dripped from chandeliers above the heads of dancers who moved through patterns Finnian suspected had been specially choreographed to drive a man mad. Even the music reflected the repetitive nature of the steps, the quartet—carefully secreted behind a painted screen, lest anyone's delicate senses be offended by a vision of the working class—sawing away at their instruments in a manner that would have sent the original composers back to their graves, should any of them have been gifted with a chance at resurrection.

It was late in the evening, or perhaps early in the morning. Finnian reached into the pocket of his waistcoat, his fingers ready to grasp the smooth circle of his watch, but then he recalled that particular item's current location, approximately three hundred miles north, no doubt already well crusted over from grubby fingers and bearing numerous teeth marks from a chubby, nine-month-old boy.

He passed from one room into the next, the ballroom holding the majority of the overheated, over-perfumed guests. There were the remains of that evening's supper in one chamber, and in another several guests—many of them more advanced in years, and so had no need to parade themselves up and down the length of the ballroom in search of a marriageable partner—played at various games of cards. He lingered there for a few minutes, enjoying the muffled quality of the music this lack of proximity lent to it, but he chose not to take place at any of the assembled tables.

The truth of the matter was, Finnian had experienced some difficulty with paying attention to any single matter since his return from Northumberland six days earlier. He had attended to his business matters with some small amount of success, but when left to carry along with the remainder of his day's routine, to leave himself to his own thoughts and musings...

No, that was when it all went to hell.

At first, he wanted nothing more than to blame it on having been away from his London home for several days. It had unsettled his mind, all those hours of damp, miserable travel. The truth of it, though, and something he had no wish to admit to himself, was a bit more corporeal.

Sophia Brixton had got into his head. He wasn't certain how she had managed it. Never before had he permitted anyone, of either sex, to distract him to such an extent. Even his brother's libertine behaviors were best treated as another business matter, merely one of which he didn't wish for the public to obtain more than a cursory knowledge. But Mrs. Brixton...

She had succeeded in unnerving him. He liked to believe that he was capable of forming an accurate portrait of a person's character within the first few minutes of conversing with them. But Mrs. Brixton had surprised him at nearly every turn, from the first time he'd set foot in her home.

He'd recognized anger in her, in the flash of her hazel eyes and the bloom of colour in her cheeks, highlighting the sprinkle of freckles that decorated her skin. But he'd also seen fear, and strength, and humour. And far more intelligence than he was used to facing against in most others of his acquaintance.

He returned to the ballroom, skirting the main area of the floor where dozens of couples moved through a simple country dance. The wallflowers and matrons kept to chairs tucked beside potted plants or near tables set with crystal bowls filled with what Finnian could only imagine was a ghastly sort of punch or lemonade. A whiskey would have suited him quite well, but he doubted he would find any such refreshment in a room full of gimlet-eyed mothers and cosseted daughters.

The women—both generations—kept an eye on his progress around the edges of the room. He felt their attention, like the buzzing of an unwelcome insect. He shouldn't have come here, but he had wanted a distraction, any distraction, and a ball had seemed like a good enough idea. Well, at least it had at the time.

Before him, there stood a wall of white. White lace, white flounces, white satin gloves and white strings of pearls around white, slender necks. Sisters, he realized. And all of them unmarried, he also realized, but a moment too late. Their mother, a most stalwart woman dressed in a vibrant orange silk creation that drained the last vestiges of colour from her daughters' complexions as she stood beside them, shifted forward at his approach.

"Why, Lord Haughton!" she cried, and snapped her painted fan shut with a flick of her wrist. "How long it's been since you've graced our humble home with your presence!"

Our home? His mind leapt back to the invitation on his desk, the one on top of a stack of hundred others.

"Mrs. Carruthers," he said, recalling the name a second before he bent over her proffered hand. "How kind of you to invite me."

"Oh, well!" She waved an arm in a broad, sweeping gesture that nearly boxed the ear of her eldest daughter. "You can be a bit of a recluse, you know. I take it you're like my Richard, always poring over his ledgers and cantering about the countryside, measuring canals and pastures and—oh!—I don't know what it is that some of you men get up to in your own time. But I'm always sure to send a card your way, though it's a rare thing to see you in a ballroom, I must say!"

She laughed, high and loud, and his glance swept across the faces of her assembled daughters—four, in all—as their tired smiles became a little more pained at the edges.

"Quite rare," Finnian agreed, but without humour. Already, his gaze had traveled beyond the ring of women before him, towards the doors, and in his mind's imaginings, a straight path that would lead him back to his own dark, quiet townhouse.

"Oh, but you must have a dance!" Mrs. Carruthers said, her hand wrapping like a vise around his forearm. Though her eyes remained bright and her speech overflowing with exclamation points, her fingers tightened around his arm as she steered him towards one of her daughters, a small thing with pretty blonde curls and an unfortunate tendency to cringe every time her mother opened her mouth. "Brigitte? Stand up straight, girl! No one likes to see a slumping set of shoulders in a brand new gown!"

Brigitte mended her posture admirably, though her chin remained tucked against her chest as her cheeks burned with spots of red and pink.

"Here, you'll do for each other!" Mrs. Carruthers slapped her daughter's hand onto Finnian's arm and began waving towards the screen where the musicians were tucked away. "Ah, there we are!" she trilled as they struck up another song. "A shame dear Briggy cannot waltz yet, but a gavotte will have to suffice!"

Finnian led the poor girl out onto the floor. She was a shy thing, barely capable of making eye contact with him as moved through the patterns of the dance. Not a surprise, he mused, considering both Brigitte's mother and her place in the line-up of sisters. Being neither the oldest nor the youngest, she seemed to have settled into an existence of doing as little to be seen as was necessary.

He attempted to make conversation with her, to draw her out in some way, but her gaze continually flicked back to where her mother stood, and when Finnian glanced over his shoulder, it was to see that woman miming directions to her second youngest child.

"I'm sorry," he said quietly, as the dance wound to a close.

"Oh, no," she said in a faint whisper. "You are a fine dancer, my lord."

"No, I mean I'm sorry I must return you to your mother."

She raised her chin at that, and a touch of a smile graced the corners of her mouth. She was a lovely girl, he realized. Too quiet and reticent by half, but perhaps she would improve if she ever found her way out from beneath her mother's wing.

"Are any of your sisters married?" he asked as he walked her around the circumference of the ballroom, taking as long a route as possible before he relinquished her to her parent.

Brigitte shook her head. "Not yet," she said, still in that breathy whisper he was beginning to believe was not an affectation, but rather her true voice. "I think Mother... Oh, I don't think she realizes how she drives them away!"

"Beaus, you mean?"

A sharp nod, which sent her fair curls bobbing around her head.

"It will get easier," Finnian said, though he had no idea what drove him to offer some words of comfort to this slip of a girl. Most likely, they would never cross paths again. "Once one of your sisters is safely wed and your mother feels her burden begin to lessen, it will become easier for the rest of you."

"Oh, I do hope so!" Brigitte gazed up at him, a fresh spark of hope lighting up her brown eyes. That she didn't look up to him as her savior, ready to sweep her off her feet and carry her posthaste to the nearest church told him that there were some brains in the girl's head. She understood that their dance had been nothing more than a small gift, both a respite from her mother's incessant attentions, and also a signal towards other eligible young men in the room that the Carruthers Sisters were worthy of notice.

As he finished depositing young Brigitte at her mother's side, he caught a glimpse of a dark head moving through the crowd. At first, he hoped his eyes had taken to playing tricks on him, especially considering the assault his head endured from the combination of noise and lights and the miasma of odors all around him. But when he blinked and looked again, he was sure he recognized the profile of his brother, David.

"Excuse me," he blurted out to Mrs. Carruthers, while that lady was in the middle of an attempt at extracting a promise from Finnian that he should call on Brigitte and take her for a drive in the park the next day. He abandoned them without another glance and moved at a swift pace through the wall of bodies that seemed to have sprung up before him.

"You," Finnian hissed in his brother's ear as he came up beside him. He placed a hand on his arm, gentle but persuasive. "I would like a word, if you please."

David turned around, his face lighting up with an almost beatific glow at his elder sibling's sudden appearance at his side. "Finn! Is this some sort of joke, eh? Seeing you at a ball? Never thought I'd live to witness the day!"

Finnian's fingers tightened on David's sleeve. "Outside. Now."

David put up no resistance and allowed his brother to guide him toward the pair of doors that opened onto a well-lit terrace. Several other people strolled through the gardens, couples mostly, a few of them more than likely seeking out the less illuminated regions among the mazes of shrubbery and the privacy they would afford.

David leaned against the balustrade, one leg crossed over the other, his shoulder cocked as he gazed back in the direction of the ballroom. There was a smirk on his face, an expression Finnian had learned was a near-permanent fixture of his brother's features.

"What are you doing here?" he asked his little brother, and was rewarded with a dazzling grin in return. At least, it was an attempt at dazzling. Finnian had long found himself immune to his sibling's charms.

"What, here? Merely sampling the delights of town life," David remarked, before his mouth stretched open in a yawn. "Mrs. Carruthers and her passel of daughters are insufferable, but I did hear of her fondness for cards. She always takes to setting a few rooms aside for those who would prefer to derive some enjoyment from their evening, which I doubt anyone would find while galloping about the floor with some mewling virgin." He directed a pointed look at his brother. "What about you, eh? Come here in search of your future bride?"

Finnian ignored the question. "I suggest you avoid all games of cards, or any sort of recreation in which betting plays a rather large part, even if your wager entails little more than a handful of matchsticks."

David tipped his head back, showing off the overwrought and meticulous folds of his neckcloth. Most likely the very height of fashion, but Finnian thought the neckcloth—along with the ridiculously high points on his collar, and the violet lining of his coat—made him look like a fool. A fool who also undoubtedly had in his possession an innumerable collection of bills from his tailor. "Is that the whiff of an order I catch in your words, Finn? I wasn't aware the crown had gifted you with the power to lay down any sort of ultimatum concerning your brother's recreational habits."

"I have the power to cut off the rest of your allowance," Finnian said, the words spoken in a clear and direct voice. "At least, what little there is left of it."

David straightened up to his full height, which was still several inches shorter than his brother. "Which wouldn't satisfy a pauper. How am I supposed to live when I cannot even keep up with daily expenses?"

"Perhaps if your expenditures didn't include losing a thousand pounds at the faro table in a single evening—"

"Still having me followed, then?" David interrupted, his voice rising along with his anger. "Interesting that along with your various pontifications about how I should behave, you send one of your nursemaids after me to tattle on all of my doings. If you insist on treating me as a child, I don't understand how I'm able to continually fall below your expectations."

Finnian closed his eyes as the strains of a waltz floated out from behind them. "This has nothing to do with what I wanted to speak to you about." He sighed. "Do you happen to recall any and all encounters with a young woman from Yorkshire?" Another meeting with Winston after his return from Northumberland had gifted him with the knowledge of Mrs. Brixton's and her sister's whereabouts before their departure for Stantreath. "One by the name of Miss Lucy Penrose?"

David's anger deflated immediately as he tapped his chin, his eyes narrowed in thought. "Penrose...Penrose... And did you say Yorkshire? Damn, that must have been well over a year ago."

"Eighteen months," Finnian provided, after rapid calculation.

"That long?" he said, apparently unconcerned by Finnian's ability to conjure such a specific number out of the air. "Well, it would have to be. It was two seasons back that Jaunty and I had our little trip along the coast. But Yorkshire? Did we go that far north?" Another minute passed, and David's eyes flickered. In that instant, Finnian knew he remembered.

"Ah, Lucy." His brother heaved a wistful sigh. "Oh, she was a beauty, and wonderfully round in all the right places. Not like the tall, willowy things they're parading about as the current fashion." He sighed again. Then, his blue eyes, a more muted shade than his brother's, narrowed again. "Why do you ask? If you're looking for a tumble, I can't imagine you'd need to travel all the way to that godforsaken place for one."

Finnian resisted the urge to grind his own teeth down to powder. "I want to know if she's made any attempt to contact you since you last saw her."

David scoffed. "Good God, man! Do you think I'm a fool? I never use my real name. At least not when I'm sober enough to remember. But a fine coat, clean fingernails, and that's usually more than enough for them. They can imagine I'm some wayward duke, traveling in disguise. Or even—"

Finnian held up a hand. "Enough." Behind them, the waltz wound its way to a conclusion. "So you're certain you've heard nothing from her?"

His brother shrugged. "Not a whisper."

"All right." He rapped his knuckles against the balustrade and turned his back on the garden. "Where are you staying?"

David grinned again, wide enough to display a dimple in his left cheek. "Why bother asking? Shouldn't your hired nursemaid already know?"

"I'd prefer to hear it directly from you."

"Well, I could tell you now, or I could wait until you arrive back at your house, ready to settle down in your study for a few hours of tedious bookkeeping, and find yourself with a new houseguest."

Finnian drew in a sharp breath. "When did you arrive?"

Another shrug. "About an hour or so ago. My valet should still be sorting out my clothes."

"I'm surprised you can afford a proper valet," Finnian muttered.

"All right, *your* valet. That is, if you'll be good enough to lend him to me every evening once he's finished with you."

The smile was still affixed to David's face as he strolled away from his brother, across the terrace and through the open glass doors that led back to the ballroom. Finnian remained outside, needing the chill of the midnight air to temper his irritation. He would have to alert the servants to lock up every valuable that wasn't nailed down, or risk his silver disappearing in order to settle one of his brother's blasted debts of honor.

He glanced towards the ballroom, at the shifting silhouettes of couples dancing on the floor. Perhaps his brother would find himself an heiress, someone who... But, no. That wouldn't do. As much as Finnian wished to be rid of David's profligate ways, he couldn't find it within himself to curse some poor woman with such a shiftless, selfish burden.

Chapter Nine

Sophia uttered a whispered reprimand and gently batted George's hand away as he attempted to tug on the strings of her bonnet. All around them were the sounds of feet shuffling into place, of skirts being arranged, and of various coughs and utterances hidden behind handkerchiefs and gloved hands. Someone banged their knee on the edge of a pew, a sound swiftly followed by a muffled curse and capped by a hushed scolding for daring to use such language where the Lord could hear them.

Sophia bit her lip to keep from smiling. George sat on her knee, his grasping fingers making another reach for her bonnet as the last of the parishioners settled into place and Reverend Fenton signaled for them to take up their hymnals. Everyone stood, a full minute passing as the bodies that had shifted into their seats creaked and groaned their way back to their feet, and the singing began.

The music distracted George long enough for Sophia to shift him onto her hip while she thumbed through the pocket-sized hymnal with her other hand. The song was halfway over by the time she found her place, but she joined in with enough enthusiasm to hear her voice carry up to the church's vaulted ceiling.

She sat in the back of the church, quite near to the door and its drafts. Only one other person shared her row, Mr. Ludlow spending so many of his days in close proximity with his pigs that no one cared to sit too close and unintentionally draw a portion of his particular odor onto themselves.

Once the hymns had been sung, the congregation returned to their seats. The shuffles and coughings began anew as Reverend Fenton stepped up to his pulpit and nodded serenely until the last of the whispering trailed into silence. Sophia found she could not look at him for more than a few seconds before the smug superiority contained in his expression set her heart to beating more rapidly. And so she tucked George against her side, rubbed her hand up and down his back as he pushed his fingers into his mouth, and allowed her gaze to wander over the heads of the parishioners sitting before her.

There were the same bonnets and powdered wigs as always, belonging to the same faces with the same chins that always tipped upwards an extra inch when she happened to be nearby. She spotted Lissy and her mother, Mrs. Granger, several rows ahead, and Mrs. Kirkland—that pretentious purveyor of fine teas and things—sat beside her portly husband in a pose that would have caused a figure of Crown Derby porcelain to feel inferior in her presence.

As Sophia rubbed George's back, her gaze continued to roam until it arrived near the front of the church, where the front rows were occupied by the town's betters: namely Lady Rutledge and the Reverend's own family.

She was about to allow her attention to return to George's head—a head that had taken up a heavy and blessedly somnolent residence on her shoulder—when Josiah Fenton turned slightly in his seat, enough to glance behind him and catch Sophia's gaze with his own. At first, she thought that, like herself, he was simply taking a moment to relieve a bit of boredom and peruse the expressions of those around him. But his grey eyes found her through the forest of snoring fathers and twitching children, his expression inscrutable as he dipped his chin, a small nod in her direction.

Stymied as to how else to respond, she returned the slight nod, though her gaze soon searched the faces of those around her to see if anyone had witnessed their silent communication. As far as she could tell, no one had, but she could not suppress the apprehension she felt at having been so blind to Mr. Fenton's attention until now. Lady Rutledge had warned her of the young man's interest in her, so it could not be argued that he had been cautious enough to ensure that no other person became aware of his intentions towards her.

His intentions...

She swallowed, loudly, a gulp of sound that seemed—to her ears, at least—to shatter the relative silence of the congregation as they listened to the Reverend's dry sermonizing. Would Mr. Fenton go against the wishes of his own family? For she was sure that no one in that family would care to see their eldest son and brother aligned with someone who, in their eyes, bore the weight of idle gossip as if it were truth.

No. Sophia shook her head as she pressed her lips to the top of George's head. Josiah would never defy his father in such a way. And she... Well, she harbored no feelings, romantic or otherwise, towards Mr. Fenton. Even if she did, the thought of gaining someone such as the Reverend Fenton and his wife as her in-laws... A shudder passed through her. Spending the rest of her days as a pariah, raising her sister's illegitimate child in a cold, drafty cottage less than two miles from the sea was a fate infinitely preferable to being forced to take Sunday tea with the elder Fentons for the foreseeable future.

As the final prayer and benediction sounded through the church, other noises were added to the Reverend's voice, until it was a chorus of mutterings and groanings that carried the stiff and thankful parishioners out of their seats and through the open doors. Sophia waited until nearly every other person had passed by her pew before she stood, careful not to shift George back into wakefulness, and followed the rest of the townspeople outside.

Her intention, as on every Sunday immediately following the service, was to return home, settle George into his crib for the remainder of his nap, and set about fixing a small meal for herself before taking on a few of the smaller chores she'd neglected during the week. She understood that Sunday was to be set aside as a day of rest and reflection, but she suspected the authors of said rule had never found themselves running a household which contained a babbling infant as one of its occupants.

With one hand securely wrapped around George's slumbering form, she adjusted her bonnet with the other and ducked her head before setting off in the direction of the stone and iron-wrought gate that encircled the churchyard. Before she had traveled more than a dozen paces, a hand on her arm halted her progress.

Sophia drew in a breath to speak, then found her words dissipate as she turned and looked into the wizened face of Lady Rutledge.

"My dear," the older woman said, her voice lowered as dozens of other people still occupied the churchyard around them. "You appear to be a tad bit out of sorts this morning."

Sophia shifted George in her arms, who snored softly as he turned his head and settled his bottom more heavily on her hip. "I am..." *well*, she wanted to say, but faltered into silence instead. Unbidden, her gaze darted towards Josiah Fenton, who stood near the entrance to the church, flanked by his mother and the Reverend. Lady Rutledge, who was too quick by half to miss the change in Sophia's attention, easily traced the direction of her glance.

"Ah, I see." Lady Rutledge nodded, a poorly stifled grin twitching at the corners of her thin lips. "I warned you about that one, you know. Following after you like a particularly lovesick breed of puppy. I suspect it's the reason why the Reverend holds you in such great dislike."

Sophia blinked. "I beg your pardon?"

"Ever since you and your sister arrived here, the boy hasn't looked at another young woman. That cannot be pleasing to a father who already had several potential wives chosen out for him." She looked again at Sophia. "But nevermind about him. I had a more interesting bite of news to share with you. It has to do with that viscount you mentioned the other day. What was his name? Haughton?"

Sophia's spine stiffened. "I-I'm not sure I recall..."

Lady Rutledge studied her. "Well, according to gossip, and you know how much I covet my share of the stuff, Lord Haughton himself was here in Stantreath, gracing our dull little backwater of a town with his lofty presence."

"Oh, well." Sophia wrapped her arms more tightly about George and glanced towards the churchyard gate, wishing suddenly that she could make a mad dash through it and race all the way back to the cottage without catching the notice of another soul. "That must be what Lissy was talking about. She must have heard... I mean, as you said, gossip and all, and... well..."

A tight group of parishioners passed by, nodding deferentially towards Lady Rutledge, while also managing the feat of pretending that the noblewoman stood all by herself, treating Sophia as one who had mastered the skill of turning herself invisible at will.

"Was he here because of young George?" Lady Rutledge asked once the people had passed beyond earshot.

Sophia's mouth opened a little, then snapped tightly shut. The fact that she could make no immediate reply was enough to give herself away, she knew. But still, she attempted to school her features into something that would resemble a calm and unfluttered demeanor, at least for anyone who might happen to glance their way at that particular moment.

"I'm not blind," Lady Rutledge continued, her own gaze making a brief sweep of those around them, scanning for eavesdroppers and gossip-mongers. "But twice now this Lord Haughton has come up in conversation, and twice I've seen you wrap your arms around that boy as if you expected a vulture to swoop down from the sky and snatch him from your grasp."

In response to her words, Sophia loosened her grip on George. "Yes, there is... some connection between them."

Lady Rutledge leaned forward, her chin dipping down as her eyebrows climbed halfway up her forehead. "Is he the father?"

Sophia shook her head. "He's... Well, I'd rather not discuss it here."

"Tea, then?" Lady Rutledge straightened up and gripped her cane with both hands. "How does two o'clock sound? I can send the carriage around to collect you, if you wish."

"No, it's a beautiful day, and I'd much rather take advantage of the exercise."

"Because you don't already wear yourself down raising your sister's child," Lady Rutledge scoffed, half to herself. "But if that's your decision, I'll not force my own upon you. Now, two o'clock, mind you. And I *will* send the carriage out to look for you if you're more than ten minutes late."

After a spate of brief farewells, the two women parted and Sophia set her course back towards home. The day was indeed a lovely one, the sky a startling blue broken only by a few small clouds clinging to the horizon. Sophia tried to derive as much pleasure as she could both from the weather and the walk, but the memory of Josiah Fenton's attentions, along with the uncertainty brought into her and George's life by the arrival of Lord Haughton repeatedly sent her eyes down to the ground, her chin pressed against her chest as she slipped deep into a mire of anxiety about the future.

Certainly she'd not seen nor heard the last of Lord Haughton. If she believed he would allow her to simply continue with her quiet life, raising George and tending to her kitchen garden, then she was a fool. He may have granted her a slight reprieve by departing from Stantreath, but there was no doubt in her mind that he was not finished with her entirely.

The cottage stood out to her as she approached, a beacon of calm and normalcy, with its thatched roof and the tangle of climbing roses and ivy crawling over every available surface. She pushed through the gate, strolled up to the door, and was about to step over the threshold when George huffed against her shoulder, raised his head, and let out an earsplitting cry of complaint.

So her plan of accomplishing a bit of work around the house while he finished his nap had now rapidly altered. Cradling a red-faced and squirming George against her, she passed through the house to the kitchen, her bonnet still tied beneath her chin as she struggled to dig for a bit of biscuit to quiet the recalcitrant child. As soon as he began to gnaw on the treat, she shifted him to her other hip, drew her gloves off with her teeth, and twisted out of her shawl before tossing the items onto the kitchen table. She was tugging at the strings of her bonnet with her free hand when a knock sounded on the front door, drawing a fresh bout of cries from George and a sharp groan from the back of Sophia's throat.

A shiver of fear passed through her as she marched back towards the door. Perhaps Lord Haughton had already taken it upon himself to return, perhaps to take charge of the child once and for all. But while the image of the tall, arrogant viscount gained clarity in her mind, she grabbed the latch on the door and pulled it open to find herself faced with brown hair instead of black, and grey eyes instead of blue. And though her visitor was tall, the kind softness of his shoulders and jaw were the antithesis of Lord Haughton's sharply aristocratic features.

"M-Mister Fenton," she stammered, and the vision of the obnoxious Haughton was swept from her thoughts in less time than it took her to blink. The Reverend's son stood on her doorstep, his hat already in his hands, his fingers turning the brim around and around between his fingers in a nervous, fidgeting manner. "What brings you here?"

Josiah cleared his throat, while his fingers worked more quickly around the brim of his hat. "I was wondering, Mrs. Brixton, if you were free for a bit... Well, for a few minutes, at least. There's a matter of some importance... I mean, I don't wish to give you any cause for concern, it's only..." He looked up at her from beneath raised eyebrows, his expression anxious.

"Would you care to come inside?" Sophia stepped back while George continued to squall between mouthfuls of soggy biscuit.

"Yes, of course. Thank you." Josiah stepped past her, and Sophia closed the door behind him. Her hand lingered on the latch while she shut her eyes and drew in a breath that was meant to fortify her, but still her heart pounded out an uneven tattoo inside her chest as she turned and followed Josiah through to the parlour.

The air in the room was unbearably close. George squirmed to be let down, but she held him tight against her as she gazed at Mr. Fenton's broad back, his shoulders rounded forward slightly as he hesitated between two armchairs.

"The garden, perhaps." She spoke suddenly, and without preamble, causing Josiah to spin around at the sound of her voice.

"I beg your pardon?"

The poor man, she thought. He looked so young, though she was sure he was her elder by at least two years. Perhaps it was the softness of his features, lending an air of youth to his face. But she knew, deep within herself, that it was no childish errand that had brought him to her doorstep. A voice in the back of her head sounded an alarm that he had come here to propose marriage to her, though George's fussing and the fact that she still wore her infernal bonnet was enough to distract her from such thoughts as she gestured towards one of the parlour windows.

"It's such a lovely day today," she continued, her voice much higher than usual. "We could go into the garden. I'm sure George would much rather be outdoors on an afternoon like this."

"The garden," he said, echoing her words. "Yes, of course. That would be charming."

She led the way through the kitchen, pausing only to snatch a few more biscuits for George, and stepped out into the small square of lush greenery and colour that had become her sanctuary over the last few years. She heard Josiah's footsteps behind her, the soft catch of the latch as the door swung shut, but she stood still, long enough to draw in a deep breath, this one imbuing her with at least a small measure of strength.

Various paths cut their way through multiple beds, demarcating the fruits from the vegetables, the savory herbs from the more sweet. As she walked, the hem of her skirt brushed against a patch of lavender, and the air was suddenly filled with the scent of it, momentarily clearing her head as she made for the small wooden bench near the raspberry brambles. In her arms, George fussed at her until she set him down on a soft patch of grass and clover.

Josiah was not far behind. As Sophia settled on the bench, and finally removed the bonnet that had been clinging sideways to her head since Mr. Fenton's arrival, he took up a post beside her, still standing and twisting his poor hat between his hands.

"Mrs. Brixton," he began.

Sophia could not look at him. She bent down instead towards George, who had busied himself with tearing clumps of grass out of the ground and dumping them over his head, and plucked a few blades of greenery from out of his mouth.

"Mrs. Brixton," he repeated, his voice louder, as if he were attempting to speak over his nervousness. "I understand your... your grief at the loss of your husband must still be great. And your parents, I understand, also passed away some years since. I am not certain as to the manner in which such things should be handled. You've no guardian to whom I could apply for permission in requesting your hand, if indeed such a course of action should be necessary. And yet, I come here today, a humble creature, asking you..." Suddenly, he lowered himself to one knee beside her, his hands struggling to maintain a grip on his hat while also seeking out one of her own hands to grasp. "I beg you, Mrs. Brixton, to relieve me of my sufferings. Please," he said, his hat falling to the ground as he took her fingers within his own. "Please consent to be my wife."

Sophia could not speak. Though some part of her had known, and dreaded, that this would be the purpose of his visit, she had not allowed herself to fully believe that he would go so far as to express a wish to marry her. Her, of all people.

She tore her eyes away from George long enough to look at Josiah, at the brilliant light in his eyes, at the hope that faintly glowed from his flushed face. He was infatuated with her, for whatever reason he believed himself to be in love with her. Perhaps because she was so different from anything his family would want for him in terms of a wife, or simply because he was drawn to her, for a reason she could not even begin to fathom. But she knew, as she looked down at him, his knee in the damp grass, his hat by his foot—the brim now being gnawed on by an especially avaricious George—that she could not accept him.

"I am flattered by your particular interest in me," she said, choosing her words carefully as he continued to hold her hand. "And I do believe that you are a good man, and will make a fine husband one day. But..." And here, she drew in another breath. "I do not think we are a good match."

He opened his mouth to speak, but she raised her hand—the one not still in his possession—and continued.

"I am a widow," she said, her voice catching slightly on the last word of the lie. "Raising a child on my own. And my sister, as you know, has been gone for these three months. I do not know where she is or when, or even if she will ever return."

Mr. Fenton's eyes widened, but he did not make any move to interrupt. She noticed, however, that as she spoke, his hands only tightened around her fingers, as if attempting to lend her strength as she worked her way towards refusing his suit.

"As long as my situation is such a precarious one..." She paused, while an unbidden of image of Lord Haughton returned to vivid life in her mind. "I cannot bring myself to think of marriage or... Well, any such thing. George is my first concern, and as long as he is in my care, he always will be."

Guilt stabbed at her for using George in her refusal, but that much, at least, was not a lie. As long as George was with her, and Lucy missing, and arrogant Lords roaming around the countryside offering their aid in exchange for her silence, her own needs and desires could not be considered. If she were not such an outcast in the eyes of the town, and if she were not also worried about the taint her situation might pass on to the Reverend's son, then perhaps she would entertain the idea of marriage to him, if only for the protection he would bring her. And he was a kind young man. It had not been an exaggeration when she'd spoken of her belief that he would one day make a fine husband.

But he was a fool, a love-blind fool, if he assumed that marriage to her would result in anything but catastrophe. Aside from the fact that his parents would most likely perish from the shock of it, she bore the weight of her sister's indiscretions on her shoulders, and she would never ask him to take on a portion of that burden for himself should the full truth of her situation ever come to light.

"Perhaps I was too hasty," he began, his gaze now focused on her hand, her own slender fingers still resting in his palm. "If you were given some time to finish your mourning. A few weeks, maybe. Or months. Years, even. Mrs. Brixton..." His grey eyes returned to her face. "I will wait for you."

Oh! If only she loved him. Then she might see the world in the same gilded haze. "I am sorry, but whether days, or weeks, or years, I do not think my answer would change."

He nodded once, and shifted back, her hand finally slipping out of his. He stood, bare-headed, and glanced down at the tips of his boots, bearing streaks of dew and blades of grass adhered to their tops. "I... I will not become a nuisance, then. But know that if you need me for anything, anything at all, I will always be more than willing to assist you."

"Thank you." Sophia bent down and plucked Mr. Fenton's battered hat from George's grubby fingers. "I wish you all luck in your future endeavors, and I do hope you will find someone worthy of your love and devotion."

"Mrs. Brixton." He tipped his head to her, and took his hat from her grasp. Sophia thought he would say more. But then he struck a small bow, bent down to give George's pale hair a gentle fluff, and turned on his heel before leaving her in the garden.

Sophia remained on the bench for some time, long after Mr.

Fenton had gone back through the house and, she assumed, returned to his own home. George continued to crawl through the grass, pulling at small weeds, stuffing leaves in his mouth before she gently prised them from his gums.

Her first marriage proposal, she realized. She settled down on the ground with George, watching him as tore a clover leaf to pieces and then fussed when the stem stuck to his drool-soaked fingers. Her first marriage proposal, from a man she did not love. A man who had no idea the difficulties attached to courting someone such as herself.

Her first marriage proposal, and more than likely her last.

Chapter Ten

Finnian arrived at Denton Castle, his country estate in southern Derbyshire, quite late in the afternoon. He'd sent word to his sister notifying her of his imminent arrival, but considering the state of the roads and the weather over the course of the journey from London, he would not be surprised to find that his arrival had preceded any message sent from his own desk.

As the coach turned through the gates, he leaned back in his seat, his gaze directed heavenwards, though he saw nothing more than the red satin interior of the roof. It had initially been a relief to leave London and his brother behind, his townhouse having been rapidly usurped by David and his cronies, but as soon as he'd left Watford, a new set of worries had begun to take hold.

He'd left his brother in his home, where all sorts of silver and paintings and various family valuables were kept. Of course, he'd given word to the servants to lock up the costliest items and keep a close eye on the rest, but still the unease settled over him, the same he'd feel if he left a child home alone with a cricket bat and a cabinet full of the finest porcelain.

The coach came to a stop outside a grand, stone building, complete with crenelated walls over tall windows that seemed to take up more space than the stones used to fashion the place. It was nothing more than a showpiece, built in the early seventeenth century by its first owners as a grossly conspicuous demonstration of their wealth. Today, the building was in need of a great deal of repairs, and though he was often tempted to sell it and place the burden of remodelling—or demolition—on someone else's shoulders, his sister would not allow it, and he suspected she had decamped for the castle four years earlier especially so he would not sell it out from under her.

He waited for the coachman to descend, for the door to be opened and the steps lowered. By the time he stepped down onto the gravel drive that curved around the outer walls of the house, his sister had already come out through the front entrance to meet him.

"I received your letter this morning," she began without preamble. She tilted her cheek up to him to be kissed. "And I knew you would not be far behind. You are terrible about giving one proper notice of your comings and goings, Finn. It is a habit that no woman of any sense will tolerate in a husband."

"You are tolerant enough of it," he replied gruffly, and reached up to rub a kink out of his neck as they walked into the house.

"But I am not your wife," she pointed out, her pert mouth curving upwards in a smile as they passed through the entrance and into the foyer. "A fact for which I am forever grateful. I may love you both dearly, but I think I would rather abscond to a convent before setting up house with either you or David. Which brings me to another point," she said, plowing over any attempt he may have made to insert a word into the conversation. "What did you wish to speak to me about concerning our prodigal brother? Your letter was incredibly vague and contained a frustrating lack of details, and I could only solace my curiosity with the fact that I knew you would be arriving before the day was out."

They wandered into the drawing room, after Finnian had divested himself of his coat and hat. His sister rang for tea, while he proceeded to pace about the room, his limbs restless after so many hours spent folded inside a coach bouncing over roads rutted and pock-marked with puddles from the recent rains.

Bess settled on a chair and picked up a bit of embroidery that he would have sworn she had been working on the last time he'd paid her a visit, three months earlier. And yet she didn't appear to have made any progress. "Are you going to stomp about the rooms all afternoon, or are you going to speak in something resembling a civilized manner?"

Finnian ceased his pacing and glanced over at her. She still had that infernal smile teasing her mouth, and her eyes glimmered in a vexatious way he suspected only a younger sister could master. "David is in London. He's taken up residence at Haughton House."

"Well, I gathered that much." Bess picked at a few of her stitches, her nose wrinkling at the botched job she'd made of a rose. Or perhaps it was a bird. "And that is enough to chase you all the way up to Derbyshire? Are you going to become like father, simply turning a blind eye to his less savoury activities? I never would have thought as much from you."

"The last thing I'm doing is ignoring his behavior," Finnian grumbled, and paused in front of the window, one that looked out on a fine expanse of the garden. The grass was lush and green after the recent rains, and he knew that he men would be out with their scythes and trimmers, attempting to tame the wild greenery. "In fact, I was just in Northumberland a few weeks ago, trying to attend to one of his...messes."

"Oh, dear." Bess looked up from a tangle of red thread. "What has he done now? Surely not more gaming debts, is it? Or has he gone and purchased another passel of horses that he cannot afford? I remember the last time—"

Finnian held up a hand, silencing his sister before she could wander off on one of her tangents. "It is neither," he said, turning his attention away from the window, back to the muted blues and creams of the drawing room. "He's gone and sired a son."

"Of course he has," Bess said on a sigh, while the embroidery returned to her lap, the rose or bird having acquired an extra petal—or perhaps a third wing—in the last several minutes. "And who is the poor girl, hmm? Some little thing he no doubt charmed and flirted with until she could not resist him or anything he said to her." She sighed again, and tossed the embroidery onto the ottoman beside her. "You know, I always knew he would be too handsome for his own good. He's well aware of how others see him, all goodness and charm etched in the details of his face. A wink and a smile and he thinks all will be forgiven."

"Because it was any different when he was a child?" he pointed out. "We gave him everything, and now he expects things to continue that way despite the fact that he's grown."

"Father spoiled him," Bess said with a slight shake of her head.

"Can you blame him? David was his youngest child. And with Mother gone..."

Bess spread her hands out in her lap, her gaze directed at the rug until she cleared her throat and raised her chin again. "But you said David has a son? Have you seen the child? And what of the mother? What sort of woman is she? Will you help her?"

Finnian sorted through the plethora of questions and did his best to tackle them in their order of having been asked. "Yes, he has a son. His name is George, and he is... Well, there is a strong resemblance, so I cannot imagine David making any attempt at denying paternity."

"And the mother?" she asked again.

He sighed. "The mother... Unfortunately, I have not yet had the pleasure of making her acquaintance."

Bess's blue eyes narrowed, while her dark brows knitted together. "Ah, there is a tone underlying those words. I cannot imagine that anything you are about to say will be pleasant."

"The mother is gone," Finnian said. But before he could elaborate, and while Bess's eyes widened in distress, the tea arrived, and so they waited in tense silence while the maid brought in the tray and set it on the table beside Bess's chair.

"What do you mean 'gone'?" The question burst out of her as the door clicked shut behind the maid. "Is she dead?"

He strode over to the tray and poured himself a cup of tea, then poured enough cream in it to nearly turn it white. "The mother is gone. She left, and no one knows where she is. Apparently, she's a flighty thing, and very much like someone who would fall under David's spell."

Bess eyes Finnian's cup with obvious distaste as she fixed her own tea. "And so where is the child now?"

"As I said, he is in Northumberland, in a small coastal village, living in a damp, crumbling little cottage with his aunt, the mother's sister."

"Well, I do hope *she* is not a flighty thing." Bess stirred her tea, tapped the spoon against the rim of the cup, and then took to stirring it again. "I assume you've met her, or at least seen her. Is she like her sister? Does she take good care of the child? Oh!" She suddenly straightened up in her seat, the teaspoon dripping on the edge of the lace doily that lined the tray. "How old is the child? I cannot believe I didn't think to ask it before. Is he still quite a small thing?"

Finnian gulped down a large swallow of tea, cooled to near room temperature with the amount of cream he'd dumped into it, and watched the change of expressions on his sister's face over the edge of his cup.

Bess had been married, once. At the age of nineteen, she'd fallen in love with a gentleman twice her age, a bachelor who shared the wishes of his new, young wife to settle down and raise a family. And then the man had died less than a year after they'd exchanged vows, his heart having given out during a hunting excursion in Scotland.

And so at the age of twenty, Bess had donned her widow's wardrobe, declared that she had no intention of ever marrying again, and left London at their father's invitation to set up house at Denton Castle.

But Finnian knew she still harboured a keen desire to have children. If ever there was an announcement of a birth, or if she happened upon a nanny pushing her charge in a pram through the park, her face always took on the same, wistful glow. She would deny it, of course, and brush away his comments with a torrent of conversation meant to distract and divert him, but he knew his sister. Ever since she'd been a child herself, she'd wanted to be a mother. So no wonder she was demonstrating such a marked interest in this particular foundling.

"He is not yet a year old," he said carefully, and watched Bess's smile broaden. "But he is old enough to crawl and to play and to create quite a racket when left to his own devices."

"How wonderful!" She set down her cup, it seemed, for the sole purpose of clapping her hands together in excitement. "So he is healthy? What wonderful news! But, Finn! You still haven't told me about the sister, the one who is caring for the boy. Tell me that she is good, that she is kind and that she loves the child most sincerely."

He swallowed the last of his tea and returned the cup to the tray. Bess was still gazing up at him with that unnerving look in her eye, and he suddenly began to fear that he'd ventured into dangerous territory.

"She is the older sister," he said, keeping to the barest of facts as well as he could. "Their father was a gentleman, a solicitor, I believe, but when their parents both died, they were left with a pittance of a living."

"How awful," she whispered under her breath. "But again, you're avoiding the point. What is she like? Is there something terrible about her? You seem to be going out of your way to avoid speaking of her, when I'm sure you must have met with her. Did you take her into dislike for any reason? Oh, please tell me that she is not uncommonly cruel or neglectful!"

"Mrs. Brixton is a fine and competent guardian," he ground out, before taking to another circuit around the edges of the room. "I saw no signs of neglect, and I must admit, she does appear to care for the child."

It was an understatement, he knew. Should anything threaten the health or welfare of that boy, he had no doubt that Sophia Brixton would gird herself in armor and, like a modern Boadicea, cut down any enemy to cross her path.

"*Mrs*. Brixton?" Leave it to Bess not to miss a thing. "Is she married, then?"

"Well..." Finnian cleared his throat. How much of Mrs. Brixton's true history did he have a right to tell his sister? Of course, without thinking he'd already revealed that Mrs. Brixton was not the mother of the child. And if they were going to do this right, he couldn't see perpetuating a lie that might later prove detrimental to one or all of the parties involved. "She puts herself forward as a widow, in order to raise the child and care for her younger sister without fear of creating a scandal."

"Oh, goodness." Bess placed a hand to the base of her throat. "What a thing to do! Can you imagine? What sacrifice on her part!" Her gaze wandered to some far corner of the room, while her head shook back and forth. "And you say she is the daughter of a gentleman?" She spoke again, her gaze snapping back to his face. "Well, she must be tolerably educated then. Was she well-spoken, do you recall?"

He recalled all too-well the things Miss Brixton had spoken to him. "I could find no fault with her mind or manner of speech." Aside from the fact that almost everything she said had been designed to infuriate him beyond anything his little brother had been able to achieve.

"Then I cannot see why we should not invite her and the child here," Bess said, her hands clasping and unclasping before her as if the matter were already as good as settled. "In fact, I will say that you must! The house is so dreadfully quiet this time of year, and to be quite honest, I think the halls are in need of some laughter, for goodness knows, I'm not about to hear a gurgle of mirth from your quarter."

He should have known, he realized, that Bess would so smoothly steer the conversation towards this, its ultimate destination. He wondered if, perhaps, this had been his intention in sharing the news of David's folly with her, that she would then set him on a path that would prove impossible to turn away from. But he shook his head at such a foolish notion. Of course, he didn't want anything more to do with Mrs. Sophia Brixton of Stantreath or her well-sharpened tongue.

"I will not entertain David's illegitimate offspring along with their families on some heartfelt whim of yours to play the part of aunt," he said, but before he'd even finished speaking, he saw a spark, the beginning of a fight he had already lost, illuminating the depths of her eyes.

"Because you are busy providing the family with so many children yourself, hmm? Heaven knows, the mantle has already fallen from my shoulders to produce another generation, so if David is the only one to sire a child, illegitimate or no, then I will acquaint myself with this infant and dote upon him to my heart's content."

Exasperated, he spun on his heel and returned to the window, his hands held tightly behind his back. "She will not accept your invitation, you know."

He heard the clatter of dishes behind him. Bess must be pouring herself a second cup of tea. "Tell me, Finn. When you approached her for the first time, in Stantreath, what did you say to her? Because if I'm familiar with your tactics when it comes to dealing with your fellow members of the human race, then I suspect you have gone and offended her in some way. Am I incorrect in thinking so?"

Of course his little sister would leap with all haste to the conclusion that he had been the one to offend, and not the other way around. "I did nor said anything that should have caused offense. I simply—"

"Oh, dear," Bess interjected with a slight shake of her head.

"—made a quite generous offer of a suitable annuity and also assured her that all expenses towards the boy's education would be provided."

"And?" Her dark eyebrows rose significantly.

Finnian spread his hands apart, his palms turned upwards. "And she turned me down. Most vehemently, I might add."

"Hmm." She toyed with the edge of a jam tart on the tea tray, breaking off a corner of it before popping it into her mouth. "No doubt your presentation left something to be desired. So!" She dusted the crumbs off her fingers and once again allowed a brilliant smile to grace the lower half of her face. "You will write to her, and you will apologize for your prior conduct, and you will invite her and the infant to come and stay here."

"I will not—"

"And if you do not," she spoke smoothly over him. "Then I will. So I suggest you proceed with some haste, for I would very much like to meet the child before he has been introduced to trousers."

Between David and Bess, though the both of them were opposite in every conceivable way, he wondered that he had any sanity left to him. He pushed one hand through his hair, the only overt sign of irritation he'd displayed since his arrival.

"I will write to the infernal woman," he muttered, and turned back towards the window. "I will write, and she will refuse, and then this entire matter of visits and becoming better acquainted will be at an end."

"Of course, Finn," Bess said from her place on the chair, her smile even audible in her words. "As you say."

Chapter Eleven

"A letter," Sophia cried triumphantly. "Six weeks of silence. And now, he's sent a letter."

Lady Rutledge dismissed her butler with a wave of her hand after he'd divested Sophia of her bonnet and shawl. "A letter, from Lord Haughton?" she asked once the door had snapped shut behind the butler and they were alone in the drawing room of Rutledge Hall.

"Just this morning," Sophia declared, and set George down on the floor before reaching into her reticule and retrieving the missive in question. She unfolded the letter, scanned the first few lines, and began to read. "'*Mrs. Brixton...*'...dum dum dum... '*...apologize for the circumstances of our last meeting in Stantreath...*' ...da da da... Ah! Here we are: '*I am issuing an invitation for yourself and George to visit Denton Castle, my country estate in Derbyshire. My sister currently resides there, and looks forward with great anticipation to a visit from both yourself and our young nephew.*'" Sophia raised her chin and flicked the edge of the paper with her free hand. "Now, what do you think of that?"

Lady Rutledge looked up from George, who sat dutifully at her feet, munching on a bit of marzipan she had slipped to him from beneath her handkerchief. "It sounds like a kind and well-worded invitation. Does he mention how long your stay will be?"

"How long my...?" Sophia exhaled heavily and lowered herself onto the settee across from Lady Rutledge. "You don't actually expect me to accept, do you?"

"And why wouldn't you?" Lady Rutledge wiped a smudge of marzipan-laced drool from George's chin. "He apologized for his previous behavior, and perhaps he now wishes to make amends. He did make mention of his sister. Maybe she's worked some redeeming influence on him over the last few weeks."

Sophia bit back the urge to scoff at such a suggestion, and instead allowed her gaze to drift over the letter for no less than the seventeenth time since it had been delivered into her hands. "Were you ever acquainted with his sister?"

Lady Rutledge shook her head. "As I said, I knew their parents, but I've been cloistered for too long between these four walls for any of the younger generation to have made an impression on me. I do believe she is a widow, if memory serves. But beyond that, I could not tell you anything else about her."

From another portion of the house, there was a bustle of sound, a clatter of some sort, and Sophia wondered if Lady Rutledge had already made the call for tea before she'd even been admitted into the drawing room.

Six weeks earlier, she'd sat in this same spot and told Lady Rutledge everything. About George's parentage, about the reason for Lord Haughton's visit to Stantreath, and Sophia had even laid out—with remarkable clarity—the tone of every comment to pass between the two of them.

And she had also confessed to receiving a proposal of marriage from Josiah Fenton. Lady Rutledge had heartily agreed with Sophia's decision to turn him down—while also despairing over the young man's fate of being punished with such interminable parents—but Sophia realized concerning this matter, Lady Rutledge's opinion was not going to be in agreement with her own.

"It does not make a whit of sense," Sophia said, as she began to crumple the edge of the letter between her fingers. "Six weeks ago, he came here ready to settle a large sum of money on us in exchange for our silence, ensuring that no one would ever discover George's connection to his great and illustrious family. And now he's inviting us to his home, to mingle with his sister and make banal conversation about the weather over tea and light refreshments?" She shook her head. "I simply cannot fathom what has worked this supposed alteration in his behavior."

Lady Rutledge slipped a bracelet from her wrist and held it out to George, who crawled quickly over to her side and babbled excitedly as she dropped the bauble into his grasp. "You suspect all is not as it seems?"

"Well, I certainly don't believe he was visited by angels on the road to Damascus. I simply..." She exhaled heavily as her shoulders slumped forward in a most unladylike manner. "George has been in my care for his entire life. Even when Lucy was still here, she never... She always treated him as a burden. And I do understand how she could think such a thing. Children are not easy creatures to care for. They are maddening and exhausting and consume your entire life in a frightening amount of time. But even so..." She closed eyes that had suddenly become watery. "I don't want to lose him."

For a moment, there was nothing but the jangle of Lady Rutledge's bracelet and the satisfied sounds of George as he attempted to shove the sapphire concoction—along with a great deal of his fist—into his mouth.

"And you believe Lord Haughton will take him from you?"

Sophia blinked several times and looked across at Lady Rutledge. "I don't know. A part of me wants to think he'll spirit George away forever as soon as I enter his home. But another part of me—a much smaller part, I must admit—hopes that he is truly penitent and wishes to...I don't know, create some sort of compromise that will benefit George."

"One in which you don't lose access to him," Lady Rutledge pointed out.

As George crawled his way towards her part of the drawing room, Sophia reached down and removed the bracelet from between his teeth. When he began to fuss, she merely tickled him under his arm until his cries turned to damp-cheeked giggles. "Or that involves him lording his control over me with a few coins," she said, her fingers lightly teasing George's plump chin.

"More than a few coins, if your description of his offer was accurate."

"Quite accurate," Sophia said, her eyebrows raised at the memory. "Perhaps it was foolish of me to turn him down, but I could not like the idea that I was somehow being purchased, like a horse or a bolt of silk."

A moment of silence passed between them, apart from the steady thump of George's knees and hands as he crawled across the floor.

"So you will accept his invitation?" Lady Rutledge asked, though the question seemed to have already begun to resemble something more of a statement of fact.

Sophia watched George as he reached for the edge of the settee and slowly, shakily, pulled himself up into a standing position. He turned his head and grinned at her, as if fully aware of the level of his accomplishment, then let out a high-pitched squeal of delight before he released the furniture and dropped back down onto his bottom with a thump. "I suppose I will. After all, if I decline, I risk enduring Lord Haughton's return to Stantreath. And as you suggested, perhaps his sister has worked some change in him."

"Perhaps." Lady Rutledge inclined her head.

"But it will be strange, I think," Sophia continued. "To stay in some great house, a castle, where no doubt the servants will be more finely attired than George and myself."

Lady Rutledge waved a dismissive hand. "You will be fine, and the state of your dress is no matter. You are going all that way to procure a connection with George's family, and nothing more. And if they are ready to turn their noses up at you simply because your dress is a few months—"

"Years," Sophia muttered under her breath.

"—out of fashion, then you'll know once and for all if these are the sort of people you want exercising their influence over your dearly beloved nephew."

A connection with George's family. A connection with Lord Haughton, to be more precise. It was not something she particularly cared to think about, the prospect of sitting at a vast dining table to endure the glowering of those ice-blue eyes of his over a tureen of turtle soup.

"So it's to Cheshire, then?" she announced, as she shifted forward in her seat and stood up. "Then I hope you will excuse me. I do believe I need to return home in order to compose a letter to a certain Lord Haughton, who is awaiting my reply."

"Why, there's no need for you to walk all the way back to your cottage simply for a letter. I've a surplus of paper and ink, due to the fact that I loathe correspondence and my fingers protest the moment I wrap them around the tip of a pen."

Sophia went to the desk indicated by Lady Rutledge and found the professed surplus of writing materials stacked neatly inside a wide drawer. "And you'll keep an eye on George as I write? It should only take a minute or two, not more than that."

"Of course," Lady Rutledge said, and reached for the dish of marzipan at her side as she beckoned to a gleeful George.

***

Sophia disliked travel. It wasn't due to a disinterest in seeing new places or experiencing a bit more of the world beyond the confines of her own home. No, her aversion stemmed from the hours spent trundling over pockmarked roads in a creaking coach, its cushioned seats providing no additional comfort from the bumps beneath her after the first ten miles of her journey slipped away.

And it was a great deal more than a mere ten miles before she arrived at Lord Haughton's estate in Derbyshire. Over 200 miles rocked and bounced beneath the wheels of the carriage Lady Rutledge had insisted on hiring for the trip.

Sophia thought she might lose count of the number of inns at which they stopped, in order to change the horses, so that she could stretch her legs and have a hot meal with George before a fire, though the meals were often disappointing and the beds provided for her at night had to be thoroughly checked for both damp and fleas.

The final leg of her journey could not come soon enough, and yet as the edges of Lord Haughton's property came into view, a feeling of trepidation took over from the aches and jostlings that had plagued her for the last several days.

For the first time, she would be encountering Lord Haughton on his territory, in his home, his place of strength. She couldn't help but worry how much of an advantage it would give him over her. And what sort of woman would his sister be? Would she be as stern and imposing as her brother? Would Sophia take her first step down from the coach and find herself immediately outnumbered?

She pressed her head back against the seat, but as the carriage creaked and turned onto a gravel drive, Sophia pushed the curtain back and peered out the window. A few more trees, a small rise as they traveled over a stone bridge that crossed a winding brook, and there stood Denton Castle.

The long drive that curved from the gates led the coach to the front of the house, its face bearing a mixture of long, large windows flanked by various statuary perched on the cornices, and the lot of it all nearly hidden by a flood of ivy that had begun to creep around from the side of the building. The house's entrance stood at the top of an imposing staircase, and before the coach had even drawn to a complete halt, Sophia looked out to see both doors flung open before Lord Haughton himself stepped out onto the landing.

There was a flurry of activity as the door to the coach was opened and the step unfolded for her descent. She tore her eyes away from the window long enough to make certain that her bonnet was still in place, and she quickly tugged on her gloves before again gathering George into her arms and rising from her seat.

She intended to step down on her own, George clutched securely at her side, but a hand appeared in the narrow doorway, long-fingered and masculine, and she knew without a doubt that Lord Haughton had already reached the side of the coach.

She placed her fingers in his. His grip was immediately firm, and as she set her foot down onto the fine white stone that comprised the drive, his other hand came to rest on her elbow before he guided her towards the stairs.

Her gaze remained fixed on the doors, outside of which now stood another person, this one a woman, and so like Lord Haughton in both looks and carriage that there could be no question she was his sister. Sophia ascended the stairs carefully, fully aware of how bedraggled and threadbare she looked in comparison to this beautiful creature standing poised and ready to welcome her.

Sophia shifted George to her other hip, freeing her right hand, which she assumed was all that would be necessary when greeted by Lord Haughton's sister. But before he could make any sort of introduction, indeed before Sophia had hardly cleared the last step, the woman rushed forward and pulled her into an embrace that succeeded in squeezing the breath from her lungs.

"Bess," he warned gently from behind Sophia, and the woman suddenly stepped back, her eyes bright, an expression between a smile and a grimace on her face.

"Oh! I do apologize! And here I've nearly crushed you and this darling child!" The woman ducked her head, putting her eyes on a level with George's. "Goodness, he does look like David, doesn't he? All but for the hair. Not a single one of us ever had anything but dark hair since the day we were born. But I assume he gets this fairer colouring from your family?"

Sophia didn't know what to say. Still stiff and sore from her journey, still in awe of the grand house before her, her mouth did nothing more than open and close several times before she managed a small, "Um."

"Bess," Lord Haughton spoke again, this time stepping halfway between the two women, the better to prevent his sister from leaping forward and smothering Sophia in another embrace. "This is Mrs. Sophia Brixton, the sister of Lucy Penrose, George's mother. Mrs. Brixton," he turned towards her, his blue eyes hooded. "Allow me to introduce you to my sister, Mrs. Finchley."

Sophia's breath caught at the realization that he had already revealed the truth of George's parentage to his sister. Had he also disclosed the fact that she was not even a widow, but had only paraded as such in order to claim George as her own, legitimate son? She swallowed hard and raised her chin an inch. At this point, she could not see how heaping more lies onto an already difficult situation would be of any use to anyone. And Bess, it seemed, did not care a whit that Sophia cradled a baseborn child in her arms.

"H-How do you do?" Sophia managed, before Bess threw a withering glance at her brother and neatly stepped around him to take Sophia's arm.

"Enough with all these dull formalities," Bess said, a fresh smile creating a dimple in her left cheek. "You're already acquainted with Finn, so I'm sure you know how dry a stick he tends to be when left to his own devices."

Finn? Sophia wanted to glance over her shoulder and look at this man referred to as "Finn" and a "dry stick" by his own family, but between Bess's pressure on her arm, and George beginning to fuss at not being set down after so many hours in carriage, she could do little more than allow herself to be tugged along through the doors and into the foyer of Denton Castle.

She was immediately struck by the utter vastness of the place, of high ceilings painted with dark scenes from mythology and a wide staircase that split into two halfway up, creating a gallery that wound around them. The floor beneath her feet was marble, a checkerboard of grey and white, and when Bess again began to speak, her voice rung out and echoed through the enormous space.

"I'm sure you'll want a tour of the place at some point. Heaven knows I feel as if I'll lose my way without a map, and I've lived here for over a year now." She stopped at an open door that appeared to lead into a brightly lit sitting room of some kind. "Now, don't permit me to overwhelm you when I'm certain you're about to faint with exhaustion. Finn tells me I can be quite *too much* at times, so you must let me know when you want nothing more than to sit and nibble at cakes and sandwiches in front of the fire."

Sophia blinked, feeling stupid and gauche before this elegant woman in her fine blue silk and delicate seed pearls adorning her ears and throat. Again, she was disconcerted by Bess's resemblance to Lord Haughton, though his sister seemed always to have a smile on her face and a glint of laughter in her eyes. "Um, tea," she managed to say as George let out a terrific wail. "Though I'm sure George is in need of a change." She gave his full bottom an exaggerated pat, so Bess would understand.

"Ah! Silly me!" She took Sophia's arm a second time and instead steered her towards the staircase. "A bit of a rest in your room, some time to change and make yourself more comfortable, and then perhaps a small meal in the drawing room? Nothing formal, of course. And then it will off to bed with you, before Finn gives me another of his *looks*, hmm?"

She allowed herself to be led up the stairs, Bess chattering the entire time about the house, about the paintings that graced the walls, about the weather and the gardens and how much George would enjoy a stroll to the stables in the morning. Sophia was then propelled into a large bedroom, the walls and trim done in pale shades of green and yellow, and the furnishings—all in white and of the most current fashion—more than enough to fill the entirety of her cottage back in Stantreath.

"I thought to put you in here," Bess began, as she swept forward into the room, the air she left behind filled with the lingering scent of her perfume. "Of course, if you don't like it, please don't hesitate to speak up. But I've always loved the light on this side of the house, and it's quite near to my own rooms should you need me at any time."

The room was indeed awash with a brilliant amount of light, despite the clouds that had lingered in the sky for the final leg of Sophia's journey. She walked towards the center of the room and set George down in the middle of a rug woven in pale colours that matched the other hues of the bedroom. She glanced at the bed, an enormous thing that appeared in need of a small ladder in order to climb into it. But it was what stood beside the bed that caught her attention once her wonder at the excellence of the furnishings had begun to wane.

"Is that a cradle?" It was a silly question, as the small bed was no doubt made for anyone else than a child. Sophia had assumed George would be put in a nursery, left under the care of an old nurse who would know nothing of his wants and needs.

"Unless you want to bring him into the bed with you," Bess said, oblivious to the note of astonishment in Sophia's voice. "But Finn did tell me how you dote on the child, and I knew you would not wish him to be banished to the nursery his first time away from home."

"It is very thoughtful of you." Sophia drew in a deep breath, wishing to say something more, but then George found a porcelain figurine of a shepherdess on a low shelf. He was about to smack it against the floor before she swept in and rescued the lovely—and most likely incredibly expensive—figurine and placed it on a higher shelf, one that was hopefully well out of his reach.

Bess smiled down at George, her expression suddenly wistful. "Oh, how much he reminds me of David. There's something in his eyes, a glint of some mischievousness that makes me wonder how much of a handful he'll be as he gets older." She looked up at Sophia. "Did you ever meet our David?"

"No, I never had that..." She bit her lip. *Pleasure* had been the word about to spill from her lips, but she knew there was little that was pleasant about the repercussions of David's activities on their family. Aside from George, she mused. But even the shadow of his illegitimacy would always follow him.

"I am sorry," Bess said, for the first time, her expression devoid of its usual mirth and excitement. "I cannot even begin to fathom what you must think of us, what you must think of our family. David is... Well, he's always been a bit careless. The curse of the younger son, most likely. Raised with all he could want at his fingertips, and without any of the responsibility that Finn bears. It is partly my own fault, I'm sure. We all coddled him, praised him over every little thing. We never wanted him to think we blamed him."

Sophia's eyebrows lifted in question. "Blamed him? For what?"

"Our mother died while giving birth to David. The last thing we wished was for him to bear any guilt or to think he was in any way responsible for taking her away from us. And so..." She tilted her head to one side, her shoulder lifting in an unladylike shrug. "Here we are."

It was a great deal of information to take in. Sophia gave herself a moment to think as she tugged at the hem of her skirt and kneeled down on the rug beside George. The babe immediately crawled over to her, nuzzling her shoulder before he attempted to bite her sleeve. "As easy as it would be to do so, I would not have you place the blame for my sister's predicament on your brother's shoulders. My sister is not... She is young," she amended quickly. "And not always one to think before she acts."

While seated on the floor, Sophia removed her bonnet and gloves, both of which became playthings for George before she then tackled the small buttons of her pelisse. As she shrugged out of the snug jacket, she looked up to find Bess regarding her in a curious manner.

"My apologies," Bess said, lowering her gaze as another grin tugged at the corners of her bow-shaped mouth. "It is only that you remind me very much of Finn."

Sophia raised her head so quickly she almost gave herself a crick in her neck. "I beg your pardon?"

Bess laughed, a lovely tinkling sound Sophia suspected no one but the female members of the aristocracy could master. "See? Now I've offended you. It is, I think, why Finn claims he cannot take me anywhere. My tongue moves faster than my thoughts on most occasions. It is one of the difficulties of marrying young, you see. Why adhere to proper etiquette when you're courted and wed before the age of seventeen? A full season in London, and perhaps I would've learned to play the blushing coquette, all shy smiles and fluttered eyelashes while allowing a prospective husband to drone endlessly about a fine bit of horseflesh." She sighed, and while the smile remained on her face, her eyes took on a brighter, more watery light. "Unfortunately, my Mr. Finchley loved to hear me prattle about anything and everything, and now I find it is most difficult to break myself of the habit."

Sophia found herself blinking at the end of this speech, delivered at such a rapid pace that she was forced to review portions of it in her head before the full of it made sense to her exhausted mind. She wanted to return to Lord Haughton—or Finn, as his sister insisted on calling him—and how she could believe the two of them had anything in common. But Bess had already moved on to other subjects, talking about Sophia's trunks and whether she would prefer to have tea in her room before joining them below for dinner.

"And remember," Bess said as she walked towards the door, her dark curls bouncing around her ears. "Anything you need, don't hesitate to ask. I've been waiting to meet you and little George since Finn first informed me of your existence, and now, I find I cannot wait to become better acquainted with you, Miss Brixton."

"A-And you," Sophia said, her voice sincere. "Mrs. Finchley."

"Oh, call me Bess! Mrs. Finchley makes me sound like an old dowd, and I'm still several months from my twenty-third birthday."

"Well, then. Bess," Sophia tried out the name. "And you must call me Sophia."

Bess's lovely face lit up with a renewed grin. "Splendid! Now, a bit of a rest, and I'll see the two of you at dinner, hmm?"

Sophia nodded. It was the only reply she could make before Bess stepped out of the room, a whirl of blue silk and dark hair and long, elegant limbs. She, however, remained on the rug, George half-crawling, half-climbing his way around the edges of the room, exploring this new world before him.

"Oh, darling." Sophia released a sigh she felt as if she'd been holding since setting foot in Lord Haughton's carriage three days before. "Dinner, with a viscount and his sister. And here I thought the only thing to worry about was how to change your linens over a stretch of bad road."

Chapter Twelve

Finnian stood by the fireplace, keeping well out of the way while his sister fussed and fretted over the table and the placement of the napkins and whether or not the glasses displayed any evidence of not having been buffed to a brilliant enough shine.

They were to eat in the drawing room, which had been cleared of most of its furniture so that a dining table—one much smaller than what currently stood in the actual dining room—could be brought in for their evening meal. Bess had claimed it was all to make Mrs. Brixton feel at ease. Finnian wondered why all the work necessary to make a guest feel at ease was doing nothing but making him feel decidedly ill-at-ease in his own home.

"What do you think?" Bess came up beside him, the jewels at her ears and throat glittering in the firelight. "Is it too much? Oh, I do believe I am overthinking this! And my gown!" She brushed her hands down the sapphire blue and silver of her dress. "The brown silk would've been a more suitable choice, but I do wish to make a good impression on her. Will she bring the child down to dine, do you think?"

"I think," Finnian began, before his sister could delve into another litany of questions and worries. "That we should have employed a nurse of some kind for the boy. I don't think I am being callous when the prospect of dining with a creature who has yet to learn that food goes in his mouth and not on the floor is unappealing."

"And how would you have presented such a situation to Mrs. Brixton?" Bess said, looking appalled. "The moment she arrives, you snatch the babe out of her arms and hand him off to a complete stranger?" She rolled her eyes heavenward. "Really, Finn. No wonder you have yet to find a woman who will agree to take you on as a husband. Now," she said, and gestured towards the table. "Will it do?"

Finnian ran a finger beneath his neckcloth and glanced back towards the fire instead. "I do not understand why you feel the need to go to all this trouble to impress a woman who isn't even the mother of David's child."

"Because I want her to like us," Bess stressed. "I like her already. She carries herself well, it is readily apparent she loves the boy, and from the little I conversed with her, I can already sense she has a good, steady head on her shoulders. And she really is quite lovely," she added, with a brief look in Finnian's direction. "Have you noticed?"

A noise issued from his throat, one he hoped couldn't be interpreted as either an assent or a denial. What did it matter if Mrs. Brixton was lovely? And what, especially, did his sister care what his thoughts were on the matter of the woman's beauty?

But before she could attempt to interrogate him further, the door to the room opened, and in stepped Mrs. Brixton herself, and only Mrs. Brixton, Finnian noticed, marking the absence of any infant on her hip.

She hovered near the door, her gloved fingers pulling at one another in an apparent state of anxiety. Her hair had been braided and neatly pinned about her head like a crown, and her dun travelling gown of earlier had been exchanged for a pale green frock, trimmed with white ribbon in what Finnian assumed had been an attempt to infuse some new life into the tired gown.

Her gaze found him first, then darted quickly away and instead settled on the fireplace behind him. He wondered what she had seen about his person that brought such a brief look of disapproval to her face, but before he could muse further about why her censure should bother him, Bess stepped forward and reached out to their guest with open arms.

"Oh, Sophia!" she began, instantly diverting Mrs. Brixton's attention from the fireplace and Finnian himself. "You look much improved now you've had a chance to settle in, and that colour is quite becoming on you! Now, after so much travel, and with the care of little George so much on your mind, I hope you will forgive my presumption in thinking this would be a more comfortable atmosphere in which to dine."

Finnian watched as her gaze swept over the table, the green of her eyes seeming to pick out the light reflected by the china and silver displayed there. He entertained a discourteous thought that she had most likely never dined at such an elegant table, then brushed it away before he could feel thoroughly guilty for it.

"But where is George?" Bess exclaimed before Mrs. Brixton could provide an opinion on the settings, one way or another. "I take it the poor thing has already been tucked into his bed for the night?"

"I doubt I will hear a peep out of him before sunrise," Mrs. Brixton commented, as Bess took her arm and led her nearer to the fireplace, and nearer to Finnian.

"Is he an early riser?" Bess asked.

Mrs. Brixton nodded. "If he sleeps past six in the morning, then I should consider myself extremely grateful."

Bess tilted her head back and laughed. "I'm afraid I cannot drag myself from my bed before ten, and not until I've had a cup of chocolate and at least four slices of toast. But Finn is always up with the sun," she said, turning towards her brother in order to include him in the conversation. "Perhaps he can be the first to take you and George on a tour of the house tomorrow!"

There was no chance for him to protest. The door to the sitting room was opened by a footman, signalling the beginning of dinner. The three of them—himself, Bess, and Mrs. Brixton—made their way towards the table, Finnian pulling out the chairs and seeing to it that both women were seated before he took his own place at the round table.

As the first course was laid before them, he chanced a glance in Mrs. Brixton's direction. She sat directly across from him, and with the diminished size of the table and only three people dining together, he knew there would be no way to avoid conversation with her. And if their previous meetings were any indication, he could not imagine that anything good would come from the two of them speaking with one another, especially before such an avid audience as his sister.

He watched her, taking in the rich shades of auburn the fire brought out in her hair, set off by the pale green and white of her gown.

Her eyes, though, were what held his attention. He had forgotten the brilliancy of their colour, the way the green seemed to change beneath the light reflected into them. She looked towards his sister, who had said something that demanded her attention, and his gaze traced the lines of her cheekbone and jaw, before settling on her mouth, her full lips moving as she spoke something in reply.

She was a beautiful woman, he realized. No, that was not quite correct. He had realized it the first time he'd set eyes on her, at her cottage in Stantreath nearly two months before. He wanted to tell himself that her contrary nature only diminished her looks, but instead, he recalled the flush in her cheeks when she'd stood against him in her small, humble kitchen, the glint of fire in her hair and the change of colour in her eyes when she'd ordered him from her home.

It was while he continued to study her features that she suddenly turned to look at him. Finnian would not allow himself to quail. He could have looked away, pretended not to have been staring at her at all, but instead he held her gaze, and even tipped his head in her direction as a slight furrow carved a line between those changeable eyes.

"I trust your journey here was not unpleasant?" he asked, during a brief lull in the conversation.

She looked away from him long enough to pick up her fork and stab at the fish on her plate. "As pleasant or unpleasant as such journeys can be," she said, and again raised her eyes to meet his. "There were both good roads and bad, poor meals and hearty, damp beds and dry. In my experience, it was what was to be expected."

"It was very kind of Lady Rutledge to provide a carriage for you for the trip!" Bess said between bites of fish. "If she had not, then Finn would have insisted on sending his own for you."

"I thank you for your consideration," Mrs. Brixton said, her gaze again lifting from her plate to meet his own eyes. Her words, he noticed, had come out with a sharpened edge, as if she wished to insult him but could not find a more adequate way to do it in front of their present company.

"You are most welcome," he told her, and watched her mouth tighten. His gaze, he realized, remained on her mouth for much too long, and it was with a low grunt of irritation that he returned his attention to the food before him. "This... Lady Rutledge," he began, eager to change the subject. "Does she make her home in Stantreath?"

"She does," Mrs. Brixton said. At first, he thought she would say nothing more on the matter, but another bite, another sip of wine, and their guest continued. "She was a great friend of my grandmother's, while they were in London together years ago. She remained a close acquaintance of our family, and after the loss of our parents and the... the difficulties surrounding George's birth, she invited us to come to Stantreath, and offered us the use of her cottage."

"How kind of her!" Bess chimed in. "What a great lady she must be! I must say, isn't it always those who come to your aid in the most trying of times who prove themselves the greatest of friends?"

"Yes," Mrs. Brixton agreed, and gifted his sister with a small smile. "I am beginning to believe that as well."

Finnian sat back and let Bess carry the bulk of the remaining dinner conversation, most of it consisting of mundane tidbits about people with whom he did not share an acquaintance, nor likely would in the future, if his ability to avoid the various balls and routs of the ton continued. He sank into silence as he pondered what Mrs. Brixton's arrival here would do to his future.

Yes, his intention had been to allow her to come here so that Bess could meet her nephew, and nothing more. No comment had yet been made about how long Mrs. Brixton was expected to be a guest at Denton Castle, but he could not imagine her staying for more than a week, perhaps two. As much as Bess cooed over their visitors, it did not alter the fact that he still needed to settle the child's future. Mrs. Brixton had refused his offer before, but could there be another option, perhaps one more palatable to her, that would finally convince her to fall into agreement about what was best for George's future?

And that brought him to another question: What *was* best for the child? To remain in Stantreath, raised by his aunt, subjected to the sidelong glances and ridicule of the townspeople because of the rumors of his illegitimacy, no doubt fueled by a certain oily reverend? What would happen if he were to remove the infant from that tiny backwater, perhaps even acknowledge his existence as David's son?

Illegitimate children were not a rare occurrence among members of the aristocracy. Of course, they could not inherit titles or carry on the family name, but more and more often they were raised along with the other children of the family, sent to school, even had fine fortunes settled on them and were even accepted into society—depending on who had sired them in the first place, more often than not.

Finnian looked towards his sister. She was only twenty-two years old, but since her husband's death, she'd shunned London society and taken up what looked to be a permanent residence in the country. Would the appearance of this new family member, this child, be enough to draw her out of her self-imposed cloistered existence? She had already shown an inordinate amount of interest in both the babe and his aunt, so perhaps...

After dinner, Bess offered to take tea with Mrs. Brixton in the drawing room. Finnian, eager to find himself some solitude while his mind worked through the tangle of what to do with David's offspring, excused himself and retired to his study. He would work, he told himself, as he always did when the rest of the household went to bed for the night. He would sit at his desk, he would take up his quill and his bottle of ink, and he would attend to business.

Because, in the end, what else had he been raised to do?

Chapter Thirteen

Sophia woke to a strange sensation of comfort. Everything around her was warm and soft, and there was a deliciously sweet smell that seemed to waft up each time she moved. She rolled onto her side, the experience of that simple change in position like sinking deeper into a cloud. It was all so luxurious...

Her eyes flew open. This was not her bed, in her mousey little cottage in Stantreath. Her hands scrabbled for the edges of the bed clothes as she pushed the covers down to her waist and sat up.

Oh, of course. She pressed the heel of her hand to her forehead and attempted to force some of the fog from her mind. She wasn't in Stantreath, and hadn't been for several days. This morning, she was in Derbyshire, at Lord Haughton's country estate. She had eaten a wonderful dinner the night before, then sat and talked with his sister, Bess, for several hours.

She wondered that someone like Lord Haughton could have a sister of such a kind and charming disposition. But then she had to remind herself that David, the man who had compromised her sister and left her with a babe, could also be counted among their siblings. And when she dared to compare herself to her own sister, Lucy....

Well.

The cradle still sat in its place beside the bed, and inside, George began to stir into wakefulness. Sophia glanced at the windows, the sheer drapes suffused with a pale grey light. It must be early, she thought, and a moment later, the chiming of a clock, marking a quarter until six, confirmed her suspicions.

She threw back the covers the rest of the way and padded, barefoot, towards the chair beside the bed. She shrugged into her robe, tied the belt around her waist, and was thus clad when the first cry sounded from George's mouth.

She picked up the babe and held him against her chest, his fingers disappearing into his mouth as he rubbed his face into her shoulder. Despite her opulent surroundings, Sophia fell into as close an approximation to her usual morning routine as she could manage. While holding George on her hip, she sought through the wardrobe—sparsely filled, though it contained every article of clothing she owned—for a gown, and a chemise, and soon she had all she would need gathered into a small pile on the end of the bed.

She lowered George to the floor as she tugged at the tie on her robe, but before she could slide the garment from her shoulders, a light knock sounded on the bedroom door.

"Yes?" she uttered, a second before a slight maid opened the door a few inches and popped her head through the gap.

"Oh, ma'am! It was Mrs. Finchley sent me to tend to you this morning," the girl said in a great rush, a bit of a Scottish lilt underlying her words. "That is, if you be needing me?"

Sophia stood frozen in place, her hands still holding her robe closed as the young maid bobbed in the doorway. "Um, I've never... I mean, I should be fine on my own. Thank you."

The maid took a small, tentative step into the room. "My name's Gemma, ma'am. And I could dress your hair for you, if you like. Mrs. Finchley says it's my talent, and I must admit, I've never seen hair as pretty and red as yours is, ma'am."

Sophia hesitated while George batted and pulled at the frayed sash of her robe. "All right," she finally acquiesced. "Just allow me to get dressed, and—"

"Well, let's have a look at your gown, then." Gemma bustled into the room, the door snapping shut behind her as she strode briskly towards the bed. "Oh, this colour doesn't suit you at all," she said, picking up the faded pink muslin that Sophia had taken out of the wardrobe only a few moments before.

Sophia had to admit, she was a bit offended. The pink was one of her favorite gowns, which explained its washed-out colour and the numerous repairs she'd made to its hem and seams over the years. But it had held up well, and despite the fact that it had actually been made for Lucy—who had declared it ghastly after one wearing and tossed it unceremoniously to the floor before kicking it beneath her bed—it fit her better than most of her other dresses.

"Ladies of your complexion should never be seen in pink," Gemma declared, and with the gown over her arm, turned towards the wardrobe.

Left by the bed, Sophia raised a hand to her face. She thought of her fair skin, of the smattering of freckles that decorated the bridge of her nose and her cheeks. Her sister had used to taunt her for them. Lucy, who had been blessed with their mother's golden blond hair and creamy skin.

But she had never taken the opportunity to fret over her appearance before now. When their parents died, Sophia had quickly taken over as head of the household, a household that had suddenly been demoted from a fine townhouse to a leaking house on the borders of Yorkshire. And then Lucy had gone and gotten herself into trouble, they'd taken Lady Rutledge up on her offer to relocate to Stantreath, and Sophia found herself caring less and less whether or not she'd even bothered to brush her hair properly before pinning it up on top of her head.

"Now this is a lovely one," Gemma said, and pulled out a gown of pale yellow. There were some aged stains around the hem, if one bothered to look closely, and a small hole in the sleeve that Sophia hadn't had time to mend yet, but it would do, she thought. Which was about as much as could be said of anything in her wardrobe. "I'll fix the hole," the girl went on, her keen eyes immediately narrowing in on the tiny faults peppered around the edges of the gown. "While you do your washing up. Oh, but would you like me to take the little babe down to the kitchen for his breakfast?" She knelt down on the rug and began to make faces at George, who squealed and tried to smack the poor girl in the face.

"I wouldn't want anyone to go to any trouble," Sophia said. To be honest, she was feeling a bit reluctant to let George out of her sight, though an evening spent in Bess's company had made her previous fears that Lord Haughton would attempt to take the child away from her, and from under her nose, seem a bit silly.

"It's no trouble at all, ma'am," Gemma assured her, before giving George a little tickle under his arm. "I'm sure Cook has something perfect for a growing boy his age. I can pop him downstairs and then come back to help you with your toilette."

Gemma was so eager, and George seemed to have already taken such a liking to her...

"Yes, of course."

Gemma grinned and swept George up from the floor as easily as if she'd been caring for babies for her entire life. "He's such a sweet one," she said, and nuzzled his ear. "I've three little brothers and if any of them were half as good as this one, I don't think I'd have been so quick to take up work away from home! Now, I'll be only a minute," she said, and carried a smiling George out of the bedroom.

Sophia stood where she had been for the last several minutes, between the bed and the wardrobe. She picked up the yellow gown, a simple cotton thing, one of the last gowns to be made for her before her parents' deaths. After that had come the inability to find it within their annual budget for such fripperies as new gowns and gloves and lace-trimmed bonnets.

All things that belonged to a world of which they were no longer a part.

She had never bothered to admit it to herself, but Sophia knew, even before Lucy's indiscretion, that she would never marry. Her concern had been Lucy, and when her sister had given birth and quickly handed over the responsibilities of raising a child, her attention had shifted towards George. He would always be in her care, in one way or another, until he was grown. And by that point, the combination of her age and her lack of fortune would make her completely ineligible as a choice for a wife.

A memory of Josiah Fenton's proposal flitted into her mind, but she quickly brushed it away. She would never have accepted him, even if a dozen of the arguments against it—her care of George, having the Reverend Fenton as a father-in-law, the town's opinion of her, to name a few—had not existed. She did not love Josiah Fenton, nor did she even care for him beyond his place as a common acquaintance in her life. She could not marry someone she did not care for, or respect, or esteem. And she certainly could not marry someone she did not love.

By the time Gemma returned, Sophia had washed her face and other parts of her body, and begun to brush out her hair. The girl immediately set to work on mending the hole in the pale yellow gown, and even began tacking on a small bit of lace from her workbox around the cuffs and the neckline.

"It's just a scrap leftover from one of Mrs. Finchley's gowns," the girl assured her when Sophia began to protest. "She'll give us some of her tidbits and things, and even let us have the pick of her gowns when she no longer wants them."

Sophia changed into her stockings and chemise, and Gemma helped her with her stays, though Sophia had undertaken the task for long enough on her own that the assistance was not absolutely necessary. Then she helped pull the gown over her head, and turned Sophia towards the bevel glass as she fastened the buttons along her upper back.

"Now, see? That's a lovely colour against your skin," Gemma said, while fluffing the bits of lace added to the garment. "It does such a wondrous thing to your eyes."

Sophia tried not to let the compliments go to her head as she took her seat and allowed Gemma to make a second pass over her hair with the brush.

"There's quite a curl to your hair," Gemma pronounced as she began performing a fantastic amount of twists and braids to catch all of Sophia's long, thick locks. "I'm surprised you've not thought of wearing it short. I heard from Mrs. Finchley herself that it's quite the thing in London."

Sophia didn't feel inclined to point out that she had scarce knowledge of what and was not popular in London fashions. And so she sat still and silent as the maid pinned everything into place, foregoing the usual plain bun that had been Sophia's only morning hairstyle for the past... Oh, goodness. She'd already begun to lose count of the years.

When Gemma had finished, Sophia sat and admired the girl's handiwork. It was nothing elaborate, only a few fine braids around her head, finishing with the ends of her hair pinned into place where her simple bun usually took up residence. The maid was correct in her observation that her hair possessed quite a bit of curl, those soft red locks curling and twisting from beneath the yellow ribbon she'd tied around them.

"You're like a fresh spring flower, ma'am." Gemma stepped back, pleased with the contribution she'd made to Sophia's toilette. "Like them daffodils that bloom all down along the river. Lovely things, they are."

Sophia wasn't sure she'd go as far as to compare herself to a bit of blooming plant life, but she would at least admit to not looking as drab as usual. Though everything in the house still outshone her, at least she no longer felt like someone who resided at a level beneath the servants.

"Well, then." She smoothed the front of her gown with hands that threatened to twitch. "Is the rest of the household already awake?"

"Oh, no, ma'am. Mrs. Finchley will be sleeping for a while yet, and as for Lord Haughton, he's not terribly strict about the sort of hours he keeps. Some days, he's in his study from sunrise to sundown, bent over his desk with work. But I'll occasionally see him go off for a ride, first thing before the grass is even dried."

"I see," Sophia muttered, while hoping this would be one of the days Lord Haughton chose to bury himself in his work. "Thank you, Gemma. I believe I'll go down and check on George, and make sure he's not creating too much work for anyone."

"I wouldn't worry about him, ma'am," Gemma assured her as she began picking up the various odds and ends that had been scattered around the bed and the dressing table. "I think the cook about lost her heart to him the moment she laid eyes on him. Said she was going to bake up a special batch of apple dumplings and cream, just for him. And don't worry about him being in the way. The boys men were in from the stables, finishing up their breakfast, and one of them was already fixing to make a little plaything for him out of some leather and bits of wood."

"Oh, I see." Sophia said, her hands leaving her dress to hang loose at her sides. "I guess there's nothing left for me but to get my own breakfast."

"It's already been laid in the dining room." Gemma looked up from putting the last pieces back in her workbox and smiled cheerfully. "Now, is there anything else you'll be needing, ma'am?"

Sophia shook her head. "Thank you, but... No, I cannot think of anything else."

The two of them left the room together, Gemma walking towards the back of the house, where the servants' corridors no doubt were, and Sophia towards the front of the house and the main staircase. The hall, she noticed, was suffused with a soft glow of morning sunlight shining through the many tall windows. In the warmer light, she glanced down at her gown, at her work-worn hands, at the toes of her slippers that peeked out from beneath her hem with each step.

She wondered why she should suddenly care so much about her dress, and how Lord Haughton and his sister perceived her. But, of course, she knew the answer. If her dress was shabby, if her hair was unkempt or anything about her appearance less than pristine, she knew it could count against her as an appropriate guardian for George. Illegitimate he may be, but he was still related to them by blood, and as a consequence, they may not find her, or her damp, drafty cottage as good enough for their nephew, the son of their overly coddled and petted brother.

At the bottom of the stairs, a footman stepped forward and directed her towards the dining room. She thanked him, proceeded towards the door, and went inside.

She had expected to find the room empty. And indeed it was, for the most part. A sideboard, set against one wall, held all manner of silver-domed platters and dishes, and she could smell the rashers of bacon and ham, the scrambled eggs and toast, her mouth watering instinctively as she paused to take another deep breath. But her attention was quickly diverted from the food when she noticed Lord Haughton already seated at the table, a cup of coffee set before him and a copy of The Times shielding most of his upper body from view.

Another step forward into the room must have alerted him to her presence. One corner of the paper drifted down, and then he pushed his chair back and rose to his feet. A stiff bow, and his bright gaze seemed to fix on her with a most alarming intensity.

"Mrs. Brixton," he said, his voice more gruff than normal. Or perhaps that was simply her imagination along with her nerves playing tricks on her. "Good morning."

She paused before walking towards the sideboard and its delicious-smelling offerings. "Good morning, my lord," she returned the greeting with a small nod of her own.

The niceties done away with, she returned to procuring her breakfast while he remained standing by his chair, his newspaper still clutched and folded in his hand. She noticed he was not all in black and white today, his coat rather a dark shade of blue, contrasting nicely with the buff shade of his breeches.

He continued to watch her as she picked up a plate and lifted the lid from the first platter. As if to make up for his earlier hesitation upon her entering the room, he dropped his paper on the table and walked up beside her, his hand extended, palm upturned as he offered to take her plate from her.

"Allow me," he said. "Please."

She drew in a breath. To protest, she knew, would be nothing short of petty. And so she passed the plate into his keeping, and calmly and succinctly told him which items to add to it as he moved down the length of the sideboard.

"Thank you," she said when he had finished. She meant to take the plate from him, but he insisted on returning with her to the table, setting down her food and pulling out her chair for her.

She was incredibly hungry, she realized. Picking up her knife and fork, she plunged into the meal without worrying about making conversation with the man across from her. Indeed, Lord Haughton had no difficulty returning to his own seat and resuming his perusal of the newspaper.

A few minutes passed however, and she began to feel a prickling around the vicinity of her collarbone. She looked up from her now half-finished breakfast, and noticed his gaze upon her, only his eyes and the bridge of his nose visible above the fold of his newspaper.

"I'm sorry if I intruded on your privacy," she said, and toyed with a bit of potato on her plate. "One of the maids informed that breakfast had already been laid. If I had known you were the only one down here..."

His mouth twitched. Was he fighting the urge to smile or to frown? Considering what she knew of him, no doubt it must be the latter. "If I had wanted privacy, I would've remained in my room and ordered my meal to be brought up to me." He gave his paper another shake, though his attention did not return to it. "You are a guest in this house, Mrs. Brixton. I would not wish for you to feel unwelcome at any time."

She said nothing to this, but popped her potatoes into her mouth and chewed for longer than was necessary.

"And why, may I ask, am I a guest in this home?" She set down her utensils and dabbed carefully at the corners of her lips.

Lord Haughton's gaze found her again, only this time, he folded his newspaper in half, then again, and tossed it onto the table before him. "I beg your pardon?"

Sophia drew herself up in her chair. She was alone with him. When she would have another chance to speak with him in private, she did not know. The last thing she was going to do was waste such an opportunity.

"The last we saw of each other, we did not part on anything even closely resembling equitable terms. Then, nothing for weeks. Until I receive a letter, containing both an apology and an invitation to come here, with George, to stay in your home for an unspecified amount of time." She kept her voice low, calm, as if they were discussing nothing more than the state of the weather outdoors. But the tension that had built inside of her since arriving at Denton Castle—No, she must trace it even further back, to when Lord Haughton had first entered her home and offended her so terribly—was beginning to rise to the surface. She paused to take another breath, and smoothed the tremble of both nerves and anger from her voice.

"Little more than six weeks ago, we were an embarrassment to you. Something to be paid off and forgotten, as if we were not even worth your attention beyond ensuring we received our money each year. And now?" She spread her hands, taking in not only the room around her, but the entire situation in which they found themselves. "I only wish to understand this change of heart you seem to have undergone in so short a time. If it is sincere, then I am glad. But if there is some other motive fueling your kindness..." She licked her lips. Her voice had lowered to almost a whisper, and as she watched him, watched the glint of steel in his eyes as he listened to her, she almost wished he would become angry enough to interrupt her before she could continue. "I hope you will be honest and come out with it. I'd much prefer to deal with the man I met in Stantreath than someone who is going out of his way to be false."

Lord Haughton shifted forward in his chair. There was something about the way he moved, she noticed. How he always seemed to be fighting to remain in complete control. She wondered why he worked so hard to remain so, when it did nothing but make him appear a hard and unfeeling man.

"Mrs. Brixton," he began. His voice was rough. With anger? Oh, of that she had little doubt. And now she hoped he understood her feelings from several weeks ago, and how perfectly their positions were now reversed.

He moved as if to say more, but the door to the dining room opened and Bess swept into the room.

"Goodness!" she exclaimed, her dark curls bouncing around her ears. She was dressed in a gown of lavender muslin, with long sleeves and a high neckline that only accented her long, slender throat. "How do others manage to begin their day at such an early hour? I doubt I could even correctly spell my name when I first opened my eyes and found that it wasn't yet seven o'clock!"

While Bess continued to talk and dither over how many slices of toast she wanted on her plate, Sophia glanced up at Lord Haughton. He was still looking at her, and she wondered if he had even spared a look for his sister since she'd come into the room. She noticed it in his eyes, a glint that told her without any words that their previous conversation was by no means at an end.

"Well, since I am up so bright and early this morning," Bess said, and sat down beside Sophia, her plate heaped with nothing but breads and scones and anything that possessed a crust of some sort. "I can relieve Finn of his host duties, and take you on a tour of the house and grounds myself. And perhaps George will be finished with his own breakfast by then and can join us?"

Sophia finally turned away from him and graced his sister with a genuine smile. "That would be lovely. Thank you."

There was a scrape as he pushed back his chair and stood up.

"Since I am no longer needed, I will not burden you with my presence." He bowed to both of them, but when he raised his head, his gaze was for no one but Sophia. It wasn't until he strode from the room, shutting the door behind him, that Sophia realized she'd been holding her breath since he'd risen from his seat.

"There now," Bess announced, and began munching on a wedge of buttered toast. "Just us ladies. And so much more pleasant because of it, don't you think?"

Chapter Fourteen

Finnian kept himself to his study for the rest of the morning and most of the afternoon. He quickly found that simply because he'd left London several weeks before, it didn't mean that his business remained in town as well. There was the running of the estate to manage, along with all of his other properties—aside from Haughton House in London and Denton Castle, there was a small bit of land up in Scotland which had been favored by previous generations for hunting, and also a pile of stones in Kent that was in dire need of refurbishment. Not to mention the countless investments his father had begun that he was desperate not to see fail under his watch.

And, of course, there was David. It was a bit like having a servant on the payroll, one who continually pilfered from the family coffers and ran up bills that always managed to find their way into Finnian's hands.

Their last confrontation had ended in a shouting match. No, that wasn't precisely true. David had shouted, and kicked things, and thrown various breakable objects across the room. And all because Finnian had made the suggestion that he use what allowance he had to settle his debts with tradesmen—tailors, hostlers, bootmakers, and the like—before worrying about any of his supposed 'debts of honor', which were all gambling debts and money owed to friends and fellow members of the aristocracy.

David had thrown a fit, behaving no better than a child, as he'd shouted that no one would allow him into any of the clubs, that he'd never be able to show his face at any decent fighting hall. To which Finnian had responded it would do him well to avoid those places anyway.

And then David had stormed out, probably to lose a few more hundred pounds on a game of cards, and Finnian had begun preparations to set out for Derbyshire the next day.

He leaned back in his chair, pushed his hands through his already tousled hair, and tugged at the knot in his neckcloth. He would need to go upstairs and change for dinner soon. As much work as he had before him, he knew that Bess would not forgive him if he attempted to excuse himself from the meal over mere paperwork, as she termed it.

The prospect of another meal with Mrs. Brixton did not excite him. He found himself becoming increasingly frustrated in her presence, and then this morning, when she'd told him she'd rather he continue to be an offensive boor than to make any attempt at fooling her...

Well, those hadn't been her exact words, but the point was clear enough.

She disliked him. Intensely. And yet she had accepted his invitation to come here, to travel hundreds of miles beyond the boundaries of a town she called home, and all because...

He couldn't figure her out. Did she merely wish to create some sort of connection between George and the rest of his family? After their brief acquaintance in Stantreath, he couldn't have imagined her ever wanting to set eyes on him again. But the letter containing her acceptance of his invitation had been swiftly received.

She claimed to distrust his sudden change of heart in the matter of what to do with the child. But should he have any reason to distrust her?

As he retired to his rooms to dress for the evening, he resolved to speak to Mrs. Brixton after dinner. Before she spent another night beneath his roof, he would lay out his plan for George's care and upbringing before her. And if she refused it?

No, she would not refuse. Not this time. Though she seemed willing to fight him each step of the way, there would have to be a point when she would step back and see what was best for the child.

She loved the boy. He knew that. And he had to hope that she loved him enough to make the wisest choice for him.

He washed and shaved and dressed with care, his valet fussing about him as if he were about to attend one of the greatest *ton* balls of the season, rather than a quiet dinner with his sister and a guest from the country.

As he walked downstairs, a frisson of something swept through him. Unease, perhaps. But, no—that wasn't precisely correct. It was different than that. It almost had a tinge of excitement to it. But he couldn't imagine how a small dinner with two other women would affect him in such a way, unless the business matters he'd buried himself in over the last few months made him look forward to even a few moments of distraction.

Dinner would be in the dining room this evening, Bess had informed him before he'd gone upstairs to dress. But he went to the drawing room first, where he knew the ladies would be gathered before going in to dine. They were both there, his sister clad in a stylish gown of deep red silk that suited her status as a widow while still adhering to the most current fashions, and Mrs. Brixton stood there, too, her own gown of blue muslin as plain and simple as something he would expect the servants to wear to Sunday services.

But still, his gaze lingered on her. Her hair shone in the golden light from both the candles and the fire, and her skin...

Freckles were not fashionable. He knew this, and yet his eyes always seemed to seek them out, first the dusting of them across her nose and her cheeks, and then the ones that decorated the extraordinarily fair skin of her arms and chest. And his attention dipped as she drew in a deep breath upon his entering the drawing room, towards that slight swell of her bosom, towards that shadow between her breasts...

He cleared his throat as he dragged his gaze back to his sister. "Bess," he said, and cleared his throat a second time. "Mrs. Brixton."

They both greeted him in turn, Bess with her never-ending smile and Mrs. Brixton with a tightness at the corners of her mouth and a flicker of defiance in her eyes.

He wanted to continue to look at her eyes, to determine what colour they had chosen to be tonight, but his sister spoke and he was forced to turn away.

"I was beginning to doubt you would join us," Bess said, her tone carrying a slight reprimand as she reached up and tugged at a fold of his neckcloth, as if she were his mother and not his younger sister by nearly a decade. "Sometimes I wonder what it is that you do in that study of yours all day. Should you not have a secretary of some sort, someone to take care of the more tedious bits of business and allow you more time for yourself?"

He had employed a secretary at one time, a weedy young man who had done his job tolerably well, but Finnian had spent so much of his time checking and double-checking the man's work that in the end, the secretary had quit and taken himself off to Chester to work for his uncle. He had always thought about seeking out another person for the position, but he had always preferred to take care of things himself, to make sure they were done exactly as he wanted. That, and the less people in his employ, the less money laid out for their wages, and the fewer who would be privy to David's various deeds and misdeeds before they could be swept beneath the rug.

"I'll look into it in the summer," he said, hoping to placate her despite the vagueness of his reply. "And might I ask how you and our guest amused yourself for the duration of the day?"

Bess's smile brightened. "Well, I daresay that Sophia now has as great a knowledge of the house and its history as my own, if not better. I declare, her memory is sharper than I believe any person I've ever met—even yours, Finn!—and I would definitely not wish to find myself against her in any game of wit."

Finnian watched a slight blush as it spread across Mrs. Brixton's cheeks before she lowered her eyes to the floor, her head shaking slightly as she did so.

"And Mrs. Brixton," he said, her name on his lips drawing her gaze upwards again. She looked at him through thick lashes, brown tinged with the slightest hint of red. If she had been attempting to act the coquettish miss, the angle of her face and her eyes meant to charm and entice him, she could not have been more accomplished. But everything about her was utterly artless, and before he could experience that same tightening in his abdomen as had afflicted him when he'd descended from his room, the old glint of fire and steel returned to her eyes, the warmth of his sister's compliment giving way to her evident aversion towards him. "What did you think of the house?"

She studied him, and then she tipped her head to one side, though her gaze never left his. "I find it to be a beautiful building, and possessed of a tremendous amount of character. I like it very much."

Her approval should not have mattered to him. She was the daughter of a gentleman, yes. But she had also fallen from that meagre position both upon the death of her parents and because of her sister's indiscretions. The entirety of her current home could fit snugly into the gallery of Denton Castle, and with room to spare.

In both dress and manner, she should've paled in comparison to his sister, who had been one of the most celebrated beauties of her first—and only—season before her marriage to Mr. Finchley. And yet he found himself continually seeking her out with his gaze, a behavior that had afflicted him even all those weeks ago while he'd been in her kitchen in Stantreath. Except that now, he recognized what it was about her that drew his eye.

He wanted her.

He had fought it, he realized, for quite some time. Perhaps even since he'd first found himself in her presence, since she'd spit fire at him and nearly escorted him from her home by his ear, he had been attracted to her.

And now she was a guest in his home. She and their illegitimate nephew.

Their conversation remained on banal topics until the call for dinner. He escorted both women into the dining room, one on each arm, and took the seat at the head of the table while Bess and Mrs. Brixton placed themselves across from one another. And still, they continued to converse on matters that irritated Finnian, though he acquitted himself well over discussions of a new canal to be constructed near the edge of their property.

As the meal drew to a close and Bess suggested they all retire to the drawing room for the remainder of the evening, Finnian snatched at a moment to step up beside Mrs. Brixton and whisper a few words in her ear.

"I wonder," he began, his hand touching her arm above her glove. "If you would share a private word with me, in my study?"

She pulled away from him enough to turn and regard him. Her gaze scanned his face, and then something in her own expression changed, as if she understood that the discussions about George's future were due to begin again.

She nodded once, and said nothing more. Finnian told his sister that they would join her shortly, and then again placed his hand on Mrs. Brixton's arm, his grip more firm this time as he escorted her to the other side of the gallery and into his study.

The servants had kept the fire built up during his absence, no doubt because they believed he would return after the meal to continue with his work. Mrs. Brixton paused in the doorway, then took herself to a large, leather armchair quite near to the fire. He followed her, but chose to remain standing several feet away from her.

She sat straight and tall, her hands held loosely in her lap. In the light of the fire, her own hair seemed to be the colour of flame, flames that had been expertly braided and curled around her head. She watched him, waiting for him to speak. A sudden wave of self-consciousness overtook him. And then his gaze strayed to her mouth, where the pink edge of her tongue slipped out to moisten her bottom lip.

She is beautiful...

He pushed the thought out of his head almost as soon as it had appeared. He did not need this, to suddenly discover that he harbored an attraction for a woman with whom he was about to discuss such a serious matter. Why his feelings had decided to make themselves known on this evening of all evenings, he couldn't begin to comprehend. But here he stood, gazing down at her, and suddenly hating himself for what he was about to say.

"I am not, of course, going to make any repetition of the offer I made to you in Stantreath. You made it very clear that you found it most distasteful and insulting, and so I consider that particular matter to be ended. However," he continued, and resisted the urge to clear his throat again for a third time that evening. "It is imperative that something is done to ensure the child's future care and education. Should anything happen to you, or your sister, or even myself or his father..."

Mrs. Brixton squeezed her hands together once before placing them on her thighs, palms down, her fingers spread apart and visibly tense. "You would make sure that he is secure, unlike what my parents did for my sister and I."

Finnian nodded. He hoped this would be easier than he feared. "As George is illegitimate, he has no claims on any title or fortune. But I do not wish to see him struggle simply because my brother cannot exercise either common sense or restraint."

"So what do you propose?" she asked. She drew in a breath, but appeared unable to release it again until she heard his reply.

"My sister, as you know, was left a widow several years ago, and childless. She expresses no wish to marry again or have children, but I believe she would enjoy the presence of a young child in the house."

He was about to continue, but he saw Mrs. Brixton's eyes narrow as she regarded him keenly.

"Do you mean *this* house?"

He glanced away, but he could not stay as resilient as he wished beneath her fierce gaze. "I think it would be best for the child to be brought up here. He would be given all the best advantages, the best nurses, tutors, everything. He would learn to ride and to hunt and to dress as if he were indeed legitimate. This would be his home, where his ancestors lived before him."

Again, she licked her lips. His eyes flicked down to her mouth and then back up again. "And where would I be, during this grand tutelage?"

"Of course, you could return to Stantreath, to your own home, if you wished."

He spoke too quickly. It was the wrong answer, and he realized it before even the final word had cleared his lips.

"I see," she said. She shifted forward in her chair and stood up. Easily, gracefully, without any of the country clumsiness he had wanted to apply to her since their first meeting. Because no matter her circumstances, no matter the state of her gowns, or the shabbiness of her tiny cottage buffeted by the winds coming off the ocean, she was born and bred as a gentleman's daughter, and he had been a fool to treat her as anything less than such.

"So your sister will take over the care of George while I, the poor relation, will be sent back to my hovel to mend my linens for the dozenth time and wait for the occasional letter enlightening me as to my nephew's progress, is that correct?"

As beautiful a figure as she made in her simple blue gown, lit both by the fire and by some passionate anger that seemed to glow from within her, Finnian had not ceased to find her completely infuriating. If she would simply allow him to finish...

"I would never attempt to keep you from the child, if that is what you mean. I am not a monster."

"No, you are a man too aware of his own importance, and that is much worse." She gave him one last look, imbued with a healthy amount of venom, before she took to pacing the length of the study, taking care, he noticed, not to pass too near to him. "But I should be solaced by the fact that George would be reared by the finest caregivers available for purchase, his character molded in the same manner as his father before him."

He grit his teeth at the way she spoke the word "father". She *would* refer to David, of course. And he could not find it within himself to blame her. But he also knew that many of the deficits in his brother's character were from mistakes made by himself, his sister, and the previous Lord Haughton.

"You make it seem like you would no longer have any influence over the boy," he said, but she spun on her heel to face him, her eyes flashing fire and her nostrils flaring as she inhaled sharply.

"What do you expect? You would relegate me to the level of mere visitor, and compared to you and your sister and..." She faltered then, her hands flailing at her sides as she tried to draw all of the house around her into that futile gesture. "I would be nothing more than some simple, poor aunt to him. And I do not think I could bear that."

Behind him, a log split and tumbled into the fire, sending up a shower of sparks that flooded the room with a flash of brilliant illumination. The light was enough to show him her expression, the pain etched in her face, and the shine of moisture that pricked the corners of her eyes.

"What if you lived here? You and the child both? Then you would lose no measure of influence over him. You would—"

But she held up her hand to silence him. "No," she said, her head already shaking from side to side. "To live here, under your rule?"

He blew out a breath, exasperated. "I will have you know I spend most of my time in London."

"But this is your home," she explained. "Not my own. My tiny little cottage may not seem like... like anything to you, but it is mine, a gift from Lady Rutledge. And I have lost so much these last few years, I cannot..." She closed her eyes and turned her face towards the floor, away from him. "I'm sorry, I cannot accept your offer. I will not give George over to you to be raised by strangers, and neither will I live here, to exist off your charity until George is grown and you've no further need to placate me."

She stood in the shadows of the room, the colour of her gown making her almost seem like a shadow herself. But for her hair and her eyes, he realized. Those continued to glow, despite the shades of grey that seemed to have descended over her face.

"I beg you to make my apologies to your sister," she said, drawing herself up again, her brief show of exhaustion disappearing as quickly as it had appeared. "I find I have a headache, and I have no wish to spend any time in the drawing room chatting and laughing and..." She swallowed. "Goodnight, my lord."

She turned and walked towards the door. There was no hesitation from her, no pause or look back before she passed through the doorway and into the corridor beyond.

Finnian still stood in his same place before the fire, one hand on the mantelpiece while he beat his other fist against his thigh.

He was a fool. He was a damned fool, and yet he could not bring himself to go after her. He would speak to her in the morning, most likely over an awkward breakfast with his sister straining to hear the words that passed between them.

But at that moment, he realized the damage caused by merely copying his late father's behavior. Since the death of the former Lord Haughton, he had continued to do everything within his power to hide any and all of his brother's misdeeds, in some misguided and outdated attempt to not allow a single speck of scandal besmirch the family name.

Well, he'd already offered to allow his brother's bastard son to be raised in the family home, and made a belated offer to the child's aunt to reside here as well.

And now he found himself no better off than where he'd been before he'd even learned of the child's existence. Except that he'd managed to offend a beautiful woman two times over the course of a single season.

He stalked over towards a large tray of glasses and decanters, and picked up a rather heavy bottle of scotch and held it up towards the light. It had been his father's favorite drink, but Finnian had never harboured much of a taste for the stuff.

He poured himself a large glass, returned to the armchair that Mrs. Brixton had so recently vacated, and sat down. He took one sip of the scotch, swished it around in his mouth, and nearly choked as it burnt a trail of fire down his throat. But as it settled in his stomach, he understood why his father and others of his ilk took to drinking so much of it in the evening hours.

Another sip, and then another, and he began to feel a pleasant sensation spreading out from his abdomen towards the tips of his fingers and his head. One more sip, and he wondered how much he would have to imbibe in order to forget what had transpired between him and Mrs. Brixton only minutes ago.

Chapter Fifteen

Sophia surveyed her belongings spread out on the bed before her.

It didn't amount to much. One trunk was all she needed for both her things and George's, though she imagined that Lord Haughton and his sister were of the sort to require an entire coach for their luggage alone when they chose to travel.

She picked up the first of her gowns and laid it in the trunk. She knew, of course, that a maid could be called for such a task, and one who would most assuredly finish the job with greater skill and in a timelier manner, but Sophia glanced at the bell pull with reluctance. She didn't want to alert anyone to her flight, at least not until her bags were packed, her bonnet secured to her head, and George duly fed and watered for the journey ahead of them.

But it couldn't be a true escape, since someone would have to call for the carriage to be brought around, and then there would be such a fuss, she was certain…

She tossed a shawl into the trunk and followed it with a pair of gloves. It had been a foolish decision to come here, to accept Lord Haughton's invitation and place both herself and George beneath his roof. Had she honestly believed that the infuriating man had changed his ways since he'd first barreled his way into her cottage in Stantreath? And his sister had been all that was gracious and kind, and yet the entire time they'd been merely plotting another way to extricate George from her possession.

Except that George wasn't really hers in the first place, she realized, and slumped down onto the edge of the bed.

Here they were, the aunts and uncle of this child fighting over who would raise him and where he would be brought up, and all while the babe's own parents gallivanted about the country, without an apparent care in the world for the turmoil left behind them.

Sophia picked up another glove and slid the satin between her fingers. Despite the faint stains at the cuff and a small hole near the thumb, it had been a fine accessory in its day. In fact, it had belonged to her mother, she remembered. The cream-coloured satin had matched well with her mother's ball gown of pink and ivory silk.

Those had been the days of balls and assemblies, of standing in the doorway of her parents' bedroom with Lucy, watching their mother dress for another evening of cards and music at the house of a neighbour. Those had also been the days when Sophia had still dreamed of having a season in London, of wearing new gowns and learning to dance and perhaps finding a husband to marry and with whom she would eventually start a family.

She folded the glove along with its mate and tucked them into the trunk. Six years had passed since the death of her parents. A fever, swift and inimical, had taken them both, and only a few hours separating their last breaths. Then, while still buried deep in her grief, she had endured the reading of the will, the dispersal of the house and the lands and her family's fortune, the majority of it passing to a distant cousin in Wales no one had ever met. And a few weeks after that? She and her sister found themselves searching for a new home while subsisting on a mere fifty pounds a year.

A knock on the bedroom door pulled Sophia out of her reveries. She stood up, smoothed her hands down the front of her skirt, and sniffed. "Come in."

Bess's dark head appeared in the doorway. Her smile faltered as she eyed the clothes strewn about the room, before her gaze settled on the open trunk beside the bed. "Ah, I thought I might find you thus." She opened the door further and let herself inside. "One of the maids told me you'd been up since quite early, and that you'd begun to pack once George was taken down to the kitchen for his breakfast."

Sophia glanced down at the trunk, then at the door and the

portion of wall above it. She didn't want to have this conversation now. She didn't want to have this conversation at all, but there was no way to avoid it before she and George made their return to Stantreath.

"I apologize for not giving you greater notice, but I believe George and I have trespassed enough on your hospitality. I thank you for allowing us into your home, but—"

"Does this have anything to do with what Finn said to you last night?"

Sophia opened her mouth to speak and then closed it again. Turning around, she picked up a gown from the bed and folded it over her arm, the movement giving her time to think over her next words. "So you know what he said? That one of his suggestions was to take George from me?"

Bess took another step into the room and closed the door behind her. She wore a simple white gown embroidered at the hem with small blue flowers. She wore no jewelry but for the wedding band on her finger, and her dark hair was dressed in a simple bun on the top of her head. Sophia had never seen her look so… so unadorned, and the lack of accessories and glamour only heightened the expression of pure irritation that drew creases into Bess's normally cheery face.

"I spoke to him this morning," Bess said, her tone clipped. "*After* I'd been dragged from my bed and told that our guests were about to leave, and *after* I found Finn stalking about his study like an animal caged."

Sophia lowered herself back down onto the edge of the bed. For a short while, she had allowed herself to think that perhaps Bess and Lord Haughton had planned this together, to remove George from her care. But as she watched his sister walk towards the window, her hands clasped in front of her, her nostrils flaring delicately on each breath, Sophia realized she wasn't the only one upset with Lord Haughton and his tactics.

"I suspected something had occurred between the two of you last night after Finn returned to the drawing room, relaying some paltry excuse about your retiring early due to a headache. Of course, an inordinate amount of time in his company could make anyone think themselves ill, but when I was told that you were preparing to leave, I made a point of seeking him out." Bess turned her back to the window and unclasped her hands. Immediately, her fingers began fidgeting with the lace at the edge of her sleeves. "I demanded he tell me every word he spoke to you last night. He didn't, but I was able to glean enough from what he did say to understand what would make you want to leave so suddenly."

She walked over to the bed and sat down beside Sophia. "I will tell you now that I will never—*never*—make any attempt to separate George from you. I've no doubt Finn believes he has everyone's best interests at heart, but... Well, sometimes I think he takes the role of eldest brother with a touch more seriousness than it demands."

"A touch?" Sophia blurted out the words before she could stop herself. "I'm sorry, it's only... Your brother and I have never seen eye to eye about anything, and I don't think we ever will."

Bess patted Sophia's hand, while a spark of her former humour illuminated the blue of her eyes. "Don't fret. He's terrible with people, and always has been. Pappa used to say he was like a horse with blinkers on, constantly moving forward without an idea as to what was occurring beyond his range of sight."

Sophia thought Bess's description to be nothing less than an understatement of ridiculous proportions, but she was not about to correct her. "So I take it you've come here now with the intention of begging me to continue my stay here?"

"Indeed, I have," Bess's smile grew. "Of course, if you choose to depart, I will not stop you. But I will, as you put it, beg you to stay. I must say I've already grown quite fond of having you and little George in the house, and I would never forgive myself if I allowed your visit to be cut short by Finn's inability to communicate with another human being."

A moment, Sophia thought, was what she needed. A moment to

close her eyes and draw in a breath and approach her thoughts with a clear head and a calm demeanor. She looked towards the window, at the weak light that had yet to burn through the rest of the morning mist that clung to the gardens.

If she left, if she returned to Stantreath...what then? Lord Haughton, she knew, would always have some sort of presence in her life, in George's life. He was not the sort of person to allow himself to be so easily displaced, and then there was Bess...

Sophia genuinely liked Bess, and it would be a cruel thing to come all this way, dandle George and the prospect of newfound family beneath her nose before scampering back to Northumberland.

"I will stay," Sophia said slowly. "If you are in earnest, and truly do not find George or I to be a burden—"

"Oh, not at all! How could you even entertain such a notion?" Bess leaped up from the bed, clapped her hands together, and allowed her smile to broaden to its full extent. Sophia had to admit that it was a dazzling sight to behold. "Now, once this dreadful fog clears away, I think we shall have a picnic. I'll tell Cook to fill a basket with all sorts of lovely things, and George can crawl around the edges of the blanket until his knees are absolutely streaked with grass strains!"

She moved towards the door, a vision of white and lace, and eyes that sparkled with delight. "And perhaps I can even convince Finn to join us. That is, if his presence with us would not reignite your desire to leave us." Her words were spoken in apparent jest, though with enough sincerity that Sophia knew should she wish it, Bess would do everything in her power to keep her and Lord Haughton out of one another's sight.

"It is not my place to hinder where your brother may come and go within his own home," she said, though she didn't say that she hoped Lord Haughton would have some tremendously pressing business that would keep him occupied for the majority of the day.

***

Bess was proved correct in her assumption that the mist would fade beneath the morning sun, leaving a blue sky streaked with wisps of clouds. Sophia, however, had not benefited from her wish that Lord Haughton would find himself too preoccupied with the business of the day to join them on their excursion. Balancing George on her hip, she glanced out of the corner of her eye to see him trudging across the lawn behind them, a large basket on his arm and an indiscernible expression on his face.

Ahead of her, Bess cut a path through the manicured grass, a heavy blanket folded over one arm while she shielded her eyes from the sun with the other, despite the wide straw brim on her bonnet.

"How about over there?" She pointed across the lawn, towards an ornamental lake that boasted an equally ornamental island in its center, complete with an artificially crumbling folly. "Not right next to the water, of course. I wouldn't want to have to worry about George tumbling in. But perhaps on the slope behind it? The one that leads towards Mamma's rose garden?"

Without waiting for a word of assent from her companions, Bess strode onward, her skirts fluttering around her ankles. Sophia switched George to her other hip and gently pulled his hands away from the strings of her bonnet. She heard Lord Haughton behind her, or rather, the muffled tinkle of the dishes in the basket clattering against each other as he carried their lunch for them.

She wondered why he didn't task a servant with lugging the basket halfway across the lawn, but she wasn't allowed to give the matter much thought, as George chose that instant to squeal at a swan that flapped its wings several times before taking off from the surface of the lake.

"Here we are!" Bess stopped a dozen yards from the edge of the water and unfolded the blanket before spreading it out on the grass. She kneeled down on one corner before patting the space beside her, indicating where Sophia should sit. "Just place it there," she told Lord

Haughton, before her brother lowered the basket to the ground and reached up to give a surreptitious tug to his neckcloth.

Sophia hadn't spoken to him since the previous evening, when he'd so generously offered to remove George from her care in order that he might be raised in the bosom of his family.

She sighed and ran her fingers through George's hair before he crawled from her lap and planted himself on the edge of the blanket, the better to tear up handfuls of grass. Sophia knew she was being unkind to Lord Haughton, no matter what Bess had said in his defense or whether he truly had the best interests of everyone at heart. But she needed someone at which to direct her ire, and Haughton, with his inability to conduct a conversation that didn't conclude with him telling her what to do, was the perfect recipient for it.

"I'm sure there's some lemonade in here." Bess began rifling through the contents of the basket, pulling out dishes of cakes and sandwiches and fresh berries with cream. She served each of them, heaping ample portions onto each plate and taking on the chore of feeding George bits of bread and fruit all by herself. Sophia picked at her food until Bess chivvied her to eat more, and Lord Haughton spent an inordinate amount of time gazing at everything but the three figures sharing the blanket with him until his sister patted his knee and rose gracefully to her feet.

"I think George and I will go for a walk," she announced, and reached down to pick up the infant just as his nimble fingers had found their way into the dish of clotted cream. "Perhaps he'll enjoy feeding some bread to the birds, or getting his chubby little feet wet!" She laughed as she bounced George onto her hip and headed in the direction of the lake, without another word to Sophia or her brother.

Sophia sipped at her lemonade, her lips puckering at its tartness. She followed Bess's departure with a longing glance, but knew that she couldn't stand up and accompany her without abandoning Lord Haughton, who had opened his home to her and her nephew.

His nephew, too, she reminded herself. And took another sip of her drink.

He made no effort to speak, and neither did Sophia. She watched Bess's attempts to wrangle George and prevent him from trying to crawl towards a particularly irritable swan, her entire posture cutting Lord Haughton from her line of sight. But when he moved, reaching into the basket for another sandwich, she was immediately aware of where he was, his proximity to her, and how strange it was that the blanket on which they sat seemed smaller now that two of their company had departed for the water's edge.

"My sister says I should apologize," he began without preamble, his mouth still working around a bite of bread and smoked ham as Sophia turned her head to look at him. "I'm not good with apologies." He wiped a bit of mustard from his bottom lip with a napkin. "But in this case, I do believe she's correct. I am sorry, Mrs. Brixton."

Sophia nodded, simply because she couldn't think of what to say.

"In my defense," he continued. "This entire situation is without precedent for my family. Believe it or not, but when the previous Lord Haughton breathed his last, I wasn't left with a list of instructions on how to deal with the matter of illegitimate children coming to light."

She plucked at a blade of grass and spun the narrow leaf between her fingertips. "Should you ever discover such a list, I'm certain it would prove useful for more than only yourself." At his questioning look, she took a deep breath, swallowed over a small lump in her throat, and pressed on. "You at least have the luxury of a title, of a fortune and connections and status to temper any sting of scandal set against your family. My sister and I, however, do not. We were already forced to leave our childhood home due to the weight of disapprobation leveled against us, and it did not take long for the rumors to follow us to Northumberland, aided by Lucy's inability to hold her tongue concerning personal matters."

He nodded. Neither of them spoke for another minute, Lord Haughton finishing off his sandwich and brushing the crumbs from his lap with an exaggerated amount of care. Sophia again let her attention wander to Bess and George, the both of them having worked their way towards a small copse of trees where his sister held up the child and allowed him to grab at leaves on the branches.

"My sister is ruined," Sophia continued, and blinked away the sting of tears at the corners of her eyes. "And by association, so am I. Of course, with your family's...*patronage,*" she said, pronouncing the word with a hint of distaste. "George will have more opportunities than anything I alone would be able to provide. So, for that, I must offer my gratitude."

"Your sister..." The pause that followed his words was long enough to draw Sophia's attention back towards him. "Will she return, do you think?"

It was a question Sophia had asked herself countless times. Every day since Lucy's departure she had expected her sister to come back, to barrel through the front door of the cottage in a flurry of ribbons and lace and flounces, her chatter bouncing off the walls and the low ceilings of the place. But not even a letter marked her absence. Aside from the note Lucy had left before she'd left, Sophia had no proof at all that her sister was even still alive.

"I believe she will," Sophia said, putting all of her faith into those four words. "When she grows bored of her current situation—wherever that may be—I do believe she will find her way back to Stantreath."

"But she will not stay."

Sophia opened her mouth to argue, but faltered before she could give life to a single syllable. She knew, of course, that Lucy would not return for good, if indeed she ever dared to cast her shadow across the streets of Stantreath ever again. Should her younger sister come back, it would probably be for no more than a few months, at the most. And then she would flutter away again, attaching herself as a companion to a friend on the other side of the country, perhaps the other side of the world, for all Sophia knew of Lucy's jaunts and where they took her.

"No." She shook her head. A dull pain lodged itself in her chest and the back of her throat. She hurt for George, she realized, even more than for herself. "No, she will not. But I do wish..." She closed her mouth and lifted her chin, all too aware of the man on the opposite end of the blanket. "I fear George will not know his own mother the next time he sees her."

"I see." Lord Haughton leaned back until he was resting on his elbows, his long legs stretched out in front of him. Sophia blinked several times at seeing him in such a relaxed pose, a contrast to the image of a staid and unyielding gentleman overseeing the cares of his family and estate. He tipped his head back, eyes closed against the sunlight, and she thought he looked younger, more handsome now that he wasn't glaring at her with a critical eye. If only for a moment.

"But is it such a terrible thing for his mother to become a stranger to him?" As if sensing how his words could be received, he sat up again, the familiar rigidity returning to his posture. "What I mean is..." He cleared his throat. "If your sister is determined not to be a fixture in her son's life, perhaps it is better if he not become attached to her. I think it would only be more difficult for him each time she takes it upon herself to disappear."

He was right. She knew this before he even bothered to put it into words. Lucy did not want to be a mother. She had warmed to the idea of it before George had been born, her hands resting on her oversized stomach protectively as she talked about what a delight it would be to have a babe to feed and to dress and to love. But Sophia suspected that what Lucy had expected from motherhood and what had been thrust upon her were two markedly different things.

"I am curious," he began, his gaze fixed on the edge of the blanket beneath them. "And you have every right to dismiss my curiosity as boorish, if you so choose."

"If I so choose..." Sophia echoed his words as a small smile raised one corner of her mouth. "Very well. What do you wish to know?"

He sat up, crossed his legs in front of him, and leaned forward until his elbows rested on his knees. "Brixton. Where does the name come from? Since I assume your real name is still—"

"Penrose," she finished for him. "Like my sister, yes." Another awkward smile, and she pulled in a deep breath for fortitude. "Brixton was my grandmother's name, her maiden name. It was Lady Rutledge's suggestion that I take it on, seeing as how they had been such good friends in their youth. But in truth, I am still poor Miss Penrose, no matter how kind you and your sister have been to continue with the ruse."

She watched as his dark eyebrows knitted together. "But why did your sister not take on the role of grieving widow? Seeing as how she is George's mother, why would the task fall to you?"

"If you were a young woman, not yet eighteen years of age, do you think you would take kindly to playing the widow while subjecting yourself to a year's worth of drab colours and modest behavior?"

Lord Haughton nodded in apparent understanding. "And so you..."

"Yes." Her smile became a grimace. "Lucy refused. What choice did I have?" She gave a small shrug before opening her mouth to speak again, but the words died on her lips when she looked up and saw a man striding towards them across the lawn, from the direction of the house. He wasn't a servant, the cut and colour of his clothes marking him as nothing less than a gentleman.

He noticed the direction of her gaze and turned his head. "Damn it all," he muttered, and quickly stood. "Perhaps you and George should return to the house. Immediately."

"My lord?" Sophia looked again at the approaching gentleman. Who was he to have suddenly filled Lord Haughton with such tension?

"It's my brother, David," he said when Sophia failed to move. Another curse slipped out of him, and his jaw set. "George's father," he announced from between gritted teeth. "Now, if you'll excuse me, the prodigal son has returned." And with that, Lord Haughton stalked off towards their newest guest.

Chapter Sixteen

Finnian resisted the temptation to hoist his brother up by his ridiculously sharp collar points and toss him into the lake. His hand curled into a fist at his side, but he beat his knuckles against his thigh rather than David's face as he waylaid his brother's progress across the lawn.

"Goodness gracious, a picnic?" David smirked, though beneath the brim of his beaver, his eyes looked tired and rimmed with red. "Tell me you've not gone rustic on us? I thought not even a call from the Heavenly Host would be enough to tempt you from your study and your constant counting of coins."

"What are you doing here?" Finnian looked directly at his brother. If he glanced back at Sophia and Bess to see if either of them had returned to the house, he knew it would only succeed in drawing more attention the ladies—and the child, *David's* child—behind him.

David's easy grin faded a little. "And such a welcome as that? I doubt our father would care to hear you use such a tone on our ancestral lands. But nevermind all that!" He stepped around his brother and made for the blanket and the abandoned picnic. "I see our sister, but who is this other young lady? Don't tell me you've been entertaining prospective wives while I've been away!"

"David." Finnian snagged the edge of his brother's sleeve between his fingers. "Are you drunk?"

"This early in the day? What do you take me for?" He yanked his arm from Finnian's grasp. "Hungover, I may be. But drunk? I do have some scruples, my good man."

Finnian swore under his breath as he followed David towards the blanket. Sophia had packed up the food, and Bess, seemingly unaware of the danger of the situation, returned from the lakeside with George still balanced on her hip.

"Good afternoon, ladies!" David tipped his hat to each woman in turn. Finnian noticed that his gaze lingered on Sophia, and he had to tamp down the rage that threatened to curl his fingers into his palms again. "Bess, m'dear!" He stepped forward and kissed his sister once on each cheek. A glance at George was all the attention he gave to the infant before his eyes turned once more towards Sophia. "But I'm afraid I've not yet been introduced to this young lady."

Sophia glanced at Finnian, her brow furrowed. How much should they reveal? As little as possible, he thought, and cleared his throat before beginning the introductions. "This is Mrs. Brixton. A friend of Bess's, come to stay with us for a little while."

"Mrs. Brixton." David dipped his chin and held out his hand. Sophia, having no other recourse, placed her hand in his.

He watched as his brother placed a kiss on the tops of her fingers, before he slid his thumb across her knuckles in a way that made Sophia's mouth tighten. "I'm pleased to make your acquaintance," she said between gritted teeth.

"I don't recall seeing you in town, Mrs... Brixton, was it?" David's eyes narrowed, as if he were trying to connect something about her face to a faint memory in the farthest recesses of his mind. But whether because he was still fighting the effects of a recently inebriated state, or if he simply couldn't remember having seen anyone who resembled her before, the thoughtful expression faded. A crooked smile took its place, and he leaned in towards Sophia once more. "Of course, if I had ever been given the pleasure of making your acquaintance, I doubt I would soon forget."

Sophia did not smile. But while his brother's attention was fixed on her, Finnian nodded to Bess and indicated with a gesture that she should return to the house with George. Once their sister was halfway across the lawn, he stepped forward to interrupt David's attempted flirtation.

"Come along, David. There's a matter I wish to discuss with you." He could not think of anything he needed to speak about with his brother, but all he could think about was getting him away from Sophia.

David easily sidestepped Finnian and graced Sophia with a wink. She did not appear to be amused. "And I will see you at dinner tonight? Perhaps I can even convince Bess to play some music and you will grace me with your hand for a gavotte!" Another smile, and David finally turned away as Finnian steered him towards the house.

Finnian breathed a bit easier once they were inside and both Sophia and George were out of sight, but the fact that they were all together under the same roof did little to calm his nerves.

"So who's the woman?" David said once they were both ensconced in Finnian's study. His brother proceeded to flop into a chair, swinging one leg over the arm while he sucked at his teeth. "You say she's a friend of Bess's?"

Finnian made a noncommittal sound and did a quick inventory of the various items scattered about the room. It wouldn't be unlike his brother to pocket something of value when he thought no one was looking.

"Has Bess taken on charitable work in her spare time? I can't imagine her meeting someone like that among her usual circle of acquaintances. Did you see her gown? I've seen back-alley lightskirts dressed in greater finery. Where on earth did she find her?"

Finnian counted backwards from ten while wondering if his sister would forgive him for throwing their little brother through a window. "I will not have you speak so disparagingly of a guest in this house," he said, his voice so taut he thought it might snap. "Bess approves of her, and that is enough for me. And it will be enough for you as well if you care to spend another minute under this roof."

David swung his other leg over the arm of the chair and leaned back against the opposite side, making a sort of bed for himself. He bounced one booted leg idly as he reached above his head and toyed with a brass gyroscope on the table behind him. "Leaping to quite a defense of the fair maiden, aren't we?" He chuckled and tossed the gyroscope from one hand to the other as he would a mere toy. "And here I thought I'd be seeing an announcement in the papers about your forthcoming marriage to that soppy chit you paid such attention to in London."

"Miss Carruthers," Finnian corrected him, his eyes squeezed shut as he pinched the bridge of his nose between his thumb and forefinger. "Miss Brigitte Carruthers."

David rolled his eyes. "Well, as long as you're not planning to chain the dreadful girl to me..."

Finnian scoffed. "Why would I force such a punishment on the young lady? You're undeserving of nearly every well-bred woman to have passed through town in the last twenty years."

"Perhaps Bess's new companion will have to do, hmm?" David sat upright again and carelessly dropped the gyroscope onto the table. "I've never been partial to redheads myself, but in a pinch, she might prove entertaining. And you said *Mrs.* Brixton, eh? Married or widowed, that lessens the chance she'll sink her hooks into me."

Finnian moved faster than he would've given himself credit for. His fist connected hard with David's jaw, sending his brother backwards with such force that he, along with the armchair in which he was seated, toppled onto the floor.

"What the devil...?" The words came out slurred as David struggled to his feet, stumbling once over the chair and then again because of his own lack of balance. "You... You hit me! You son of a bitch! I can't believe you hit me!"

Finnian flexed the fingers of his right hand and wondered if their cook had any ice down in the kitchens. "I will allow you to stay here for one night. Eat, bathe, get some rest, and then I want you gone in the morning."

"You're a brute." David worked his jaw for a minute before running his tongue over his teeth to ensure they were all still attached. He looked at his brother from the other side of the fallen chair, deep lines carved into the skin around his red-rimmed eyes. "This is about that woman, isn't it? Your Mrs. Brixton. She's not merely a friend of Bess's, is she?"

Finnian cursed himself. If he'd been able to hold his temper in check, David's interest in Sophia would've soon faded the moment something more enticing came along. But now because of how he'd reacted to his brother's comments, he'd done nothing more than shine the brightest of lights on Mrs. Brixton and her presence at Mowbray Hall.

"One night," he repeated. "If you've not left the premises by breakfast, I'll drag you to the edge of the property myself."

David rubbed his face and spat on the floor. "Bastard. You know you're nothing at all like our father. He'd never have dared to treat his own flesh and blood in such a shabby manner."

"Coming from you, I'll take that as a compliment," Finnian said. He bent forward in a mock bow, and turning on his heel, walked out of the study.

***

Finnian stood inside his sister's sitting room, one hand still on the doorknob as he took in the scene before him. He hadn't thought to knock or announce his presence in any way, his recent interview with David still buzzing like a swarm of irritated insects inside his head. And so he'd stomped upstairs, down the hall, ready to complain to Bess about the behavior of their infernal sibling.

But instead of Bess, he found Sophia. She sat on a delicate settee, surrounded by pink upholstery and pink cushions and more lace and fringe than should have been permitted to exist in a single space. She held George against her chest, the infant's head resting on her shoulder, a small bead of drool soaking the muslin sleeve of her gown as a soft snore escaped from the child.

Why such a tableau should arrest his progress into the room, he couldn't fathom. She sat with her cheek on top of the boy's head, her eyes closed and lips slightly parted. He might have almost thought her asleep as well if he hadn't noticed the gentle movement of her hand, slowly stroking the child's back, the rhythm of her caress matched by the soft song, as quiet as a whisper, that slipped from her mouth.

He was struck then by the privacy of the scene, between this woman and the child in her care, and he had a terrible desire to both retreat without interrupting them and to better place himself where he could observe them without being seen. Because he knew if Sophia noticed his presence, the delicate song would cease, and her demeanor would change, and the lines of tension and weariness would fan out around her eyes.

But in this moment, he could see her. Not the facade she put in place for him and for others, but only her, and how she truly looked and behaved when she thought no one was watching.

His hand tightened around the doorknob as he took a step back, pulling the door nearly closed before he scuffed the heel of his boot on the floor and cleared his throat, loud enough that she would be certain to hear him and so adjust her posture in preparation of his entry. He knocked lightly, and waited for Sophia's voice to draw him into the room.

"Mrs. Brixton." He bowed his head as he strode into the sitting room. But before he'd dipped his chin, he noticed the rigidity already funneling into her shoulders and arms, and the hand on the infant's back was still. "Where is my sister?"

"In the kitchens, I believe. Something to do with sorting out dinner preparations now that your brother has arrived."

Finnian's jaw clenched. "He will not be dining with us, I assure you."

Sophia drew her bottom lip into her mouth and glanced towards the windows. "Does he know?" Her arms tightened around George's slumbering form. "Does your brother know he is residing beneath the same roof as his son?"

"I don't believe so. He was much too focused on…" *You*, he almost said. "… other matters," he finished haltingly, and took another step into the room. "He'll be leaving in the morning. Until then, I pray he'll remain in his rooms, hopefully to sleep off the rest of the drink he undoubtedly imbibed before he arrived."

"Will you tell him?" She turned the full force of her gaze on him, and he saw the worry that constantly shadowed her expression.

"No." He shook his head. He could not stop watching her, the way the light came in through the lace of the curtains, how it illuminated the gold in her hair and accentuated the shadows beneath her cheekbones, the slight smudge of grey beneath her eyes. Had he noticed her tiredness before and simply disregarded it, too worried about his own troubles to spare a thought for someone else's trials and tribulations? "Not without your permission, at least."

She nodded and lowered her eyes again. Her chin brushed the top of George's head and the tips of her fingers teased the fair hair at the nape of the boy's neck. "You doubt his capabilities as a father?"

Finnian scoffed. "I doubt his capabilities as a grown man." He took a few more steps into the room and settled in an overstuffed armchair, the upholstery reeking of something that might have been lavender. "He is not the sort who does well when faced with responsibility."

"Not many of us do," Sophia said, low enough that he wondered if he'd been meant to hear. She straightened up, arching her lower back slightly as a grimace tightened her mouth. When he shifted forward to offer her aid, she waved him away without disturbing the sleeping figure on her chest. "He'll soon be too heavy to use me in place of his cradle," she said, her expression taking on a bittersweet edge. "And to think that one day he'll stand taller than me."

He looked down at the boy, this child for whom she had sacrificed everything. Something twisted in his abdomen, a sensation that made him uneasy. Jealousy, perhaps? No, that couldn't possibly be it. But as Sophia's hand moved to straighten a bit of the infant's clothing,

Finnian found his gaze tracing the line of her fingers, then her wrist, up to the curve of her shoulder and the arch of her neck.

It was a sudden need to protect her, this woman who had stood before the censure of society, giving up her her chance to marry well, to be anything more than an outcast with a gentleman's bastard on her hip and no other family to come to her aid.

The sudden appearance of his brother, he realized, must have exacted this change in him, awakened his protective nature towards Mrs. Brixton.

Mrs. Brixton? He passed his hand over his face, as if he could wipe away any expression that might give away his current thoughts. He hadn't referred to her as Mrs. Brixton—at least not within the confines of his own mind—since the night before, when he'd become aware of his attraction to her. And there she sat, oblivious to the turmoil inside his head, holding a child who would not have an easy life if he did not step in to help.

But it would have to be on her terms. He understood this now. All his years of conducting the business of the various houses and estates passed down to him from his father had trained him well in matters of business, but the woman before him and the babe in her arms... They were not business. They were not things to be bought and sold, or to be silenced with the promise of a generous annuity.

"Mrs. Brixton." He slid forward in his chair, his elbows on his knees, his posture taking on an air of supplication. "Whatever you may want from my sister and me, whatever you may need...it is yours. You have only to ask, and I will make sure my nephew and *you*," he added quickly. "are always provided for."

She did not tense, as he had expected. Instead, her shoulders sagged, her eyes closing as she released a sigh. "I have no wish to become an object of charity."

"And nor would you be," he said, injecting some of his former sternness into his words. But when her gaze flicked towards him, he dared a wry grin. "You are family. Should you even wish to one day make Denton Castle your home—" He paused when her eyes widened a fraction. "—I've no doubt Bess would welcome your company with open arms. And should you find my presence intolerable, I assure you that I spend the majority of my time in town or elsewhere. I've left Denton for my sister, to run as she sees fit."

If the glint in her eyes was from tears, Sophia blinked them away too quickly for him to be certain. "Thank you," she said, after a full minute had slipped away. "Now, do not take my gratitude as a firm acceptance of your offer, but I will consider it."

"Please do." He stood up from his chair and began to move towards her. A part of him wanted to take her hand, to brush his lips across her knuckles, as if he were a practiced rake and the woman in front of him was simply another conquest. Fear, however, held him back. She did not trust him. He knew this. And no doubt she would scorn such an overture from him, seeking to win her friendship and affection through an affectation of charm and honeyed words. "I will leave you and George to your rest. Please inform my sister, should you come upon her before I do, that I was seeking an audience with her."

"I will, of course." Her smile was a fleeting thing, but it lasted long enough to illuminate the flecks of gold amid the green in her eyes. "And again, thank you."

A nod of farewell, and he turned on his heel and strode towards the door. Again, the sensation of unease afflicted him. He wanted to stay there with her, and yet he knew that to spend more time with her, to give in to the nascent desire he had for her was nothing more than the most utter foolishness. She was the last woman who would welcome his advances, and he would do well to regard her as nothing more than the guardian of his nephew.

It would do well for all parties involved, he told himself. And for a moment, he almost believed it.

Chapter Seventeen

In the end, Sophia remained at Denton Castle for another ten days after David's departure. Lord Haughton had taken his leave as well, returning to London only a day after seeing his younger brother off the estate. Of course, Bess had brought out her best arguments for the occasion, declaring that they could send for Sophia's things and have them brought out to Derbyshire without her having to experience the inconvenience of traveling halfway across the country and back again. But Sophia was adamant. She would return to Stantreath. She was not yet ready to give up the independence of living alone, though a niggling voice in the back of her mind reminded her that everything about her existence—and George's—would be more free and easy once they had settled themselves at Denton Castle and she agreed to allow Lord Haughton to help with the cost of George's upbringing.

Sophia stretched her legs out in front of her as best she could, the toes of her slippers peeking out from beneath the hem of her gown as she tried to shift into a more comfortable position. Beside her, George slipped in and out of a fussy, restless sleep. Sophia knew another tooth was about to make an appearance in his mouth, and so she had been a companion to his drooling and his cries for the entire journey back to Northumberland.

He fussed again as he shifted, his legs tucked beneath him as his mouth sought out his fingers in his sleep. She reached over and placed a gentle hand on his back, the quick thrum of his heartbeat sounding out a rabid rhythm under her fingers.

Her George. But not her George, not really. And yet she was making the decision to remove him from Stantreath, to take him more than one hundred miles inland, and all with the hope that Lord

Haughton's name and resources would allow him to grow up without the stigma of "bastard" casting a shadow across his future life.

She would make no secret of her departure. In a town as small as Stantreath, it would be near impossible for her to abscond to another part of the country without its meagre population discovering it before she'd completed her first leg of the journey. Even now, she knew the gossips were most likely already masticating over the gristle she'd thrown to them by accepting Lord Haughton's initial invitation and leaving her cottage for several weeks. Only Lady Rutledge had been privy to her whereabouts, but Sophia did not doubt that the truth of George's parentage would one day become the most popular topic over Mrs. Fenton's teapot.

George let out another soft cry as the carriage struck a particularly deep rut that marked their return to the outskirts of Stantreath. Sophia picked him up and cradled him against her chest, despite his efforts to squirm and escape from her embrace. The sight of Lady Rutledge's carriage trundling through the town would catch everyone's attention, she was certain. And then to see it make the turn towards her cottage...

A cloud passed in front of the sun as soon as the door was flung open and the step lowered down. A gloved hand appeared in the narrow doorway, one of Lord Haughton's men ready to help her out of the carriage. Both Bess and her elder brother had insisted on the additional help to Lady Rutledge's servants during her journey, and she knew she would have to pen a note of thanks to them for their generosity.

She held tight to George as she maneuvered down without stumbling or tripping over the hem of her dress, and as she walked up the path to the house, a flurry of activity began behind her as her belongings were removed from the carriage with an astonishing amount of efficiency. The weeds and the grass beyond the step, she noticed, had flourished in her absence and were in desperate need of a trim. As she fumbled in her reticule for the key with which to let herself inside, the door she was about to unlock swung open on creaking hinges. A young woman stood there in a proprietary pose, her fair hair in ringlets, her gown of yellow muslin far too sophisticated for its backdrop of an old cottage with a step in need of repair.

"Oh, Soph! How good it is to see you at last!"

Lucy skipped down to the path, her golden beauty only enhanced as she stepped out of the shadow of the house and into the sunlight. Sophia remained where she was, her mouth working over a response that wouldn't materialize before her younger sister could wrap her arms around her in a tight embrace.

"I cannot begin to describe how much I have missed you!" Lucy took a step back, and her blue eyes alighted on George, who squirmed and fussed in Sophia's arms. "And my darling boy!" Without another word, she swept the child into her arms, ignoring his cries as she peppered his face with kisses. "Now, you must come inside at once! We'll have tea and cakes, and I'll tell you everything that is new and wondrous in Bath. Oh, my beautiful boy!" She placed another kiss on George's cheek before he squeezed his eyes shut and let out a piercing yowl. "Come along, Soph!"

Sophia watched her sister disappear into the cottage with George, the latter kicking and screaming his discomfort the entire way. As Lord Haughton's men came up with her things, she found her voice long enough to direct them inside and inform them where they should deposit her trunk. Once the carriage departed, Sophia made her way into the sitting room, where she found Lucy attempting to bustle over a tea tray while George sat in the middle of the floor, making his discomfort known to all and sundry.

"You must tell me where you've been!" Lucy began, speaking over George's cries as if he weren't howling loud enough to shake the dust from the rafters. "Here I return from Bath, all covered in dust and exhausted from travel, with expectations of enjoying a warm welcome from my sister and my son, and what should I find but an empty house! Locked up and cold as a grave, without a note or a single clue as to where I might begin to look for you!"

Could her sister be so obtuse as to not realize how well her words applied to her own behavior? Sophia pressed her lips together as she picked up George from the rug and placed him on her hip, where he immediately began to quiet.

"And whose men were those? Certainly nothing the likes old Rutledge can afford?" Lucy flounced onto an armchair and tossed her curls over her shoulder. "Here I thought I'd be the one living a life of some interest, and I return to the sight of you stepping down with the aid of someone dressed in enough finery to look after a duke!" She bit into a cake and chewed noisily. "Do, tell!" she prompted, a bit of icing still clinging to the corner of her mouth.

"So you were in Bath all this time?" Sophia said, ignoring her sister's interrogation. She would not allow the girl to disappear for several months and then return again as if she had only been gone for morning calls. "A letter would have been appreciated."

"Oh, really!" Lucy rolled her eyes and huffed out a breath. "And this is the welcome I receive? Perhaps I should not have returned at all!"

No, Sophia would not bite on her sister's hook. Lucy wanted an argument, wanted people to flatter and praise her until she calmed down again, but Sophia would not fall for it this time. "If you'll excuse me, I need to feed your son. And unfortunately cakes and sweets will not suffice."

She could not help being rude. Each word sharpened itself to a point before flying out of her mouth, but Lucy's sudden appearance on the doorstep had shaken her. Already exhausted from the journey home, her mind awhirl with thoughts of packing up and taking George to live with Bess at Denton Castle, she could not now turn her attention to her wayward sister's sudden decision to once again make an appearance in their lives.

In the kitchen, she set George on the floor, handed him a wooden spoon and a cast iron pot with which to bide his time while she searched through the jars of canned fruits and vegetables for something to prepare for him. Lucy followed her, as Sophia knew she would. If there was anything her sister abhorred, it was being left without an audience.

"So is it a gentleman?"

Sophia spun around, the jar of peach preserves she held nearly tumbling out of her grasp. "I beg your pardon?"

"Your journey, silly! And those lovely footmen!" Lucy laughed, and in the light that came through the kitchen windows, her beauty lacked some of the freshness that Sophia remembered. The bloom that used to colour her cheeks was already beginning to fade. "Have you finally found yourself a beau after all these years?"

The superiority in her sister's tone set Sophia's teeth on edge. "He is not—" She stopped the movement of her tongue before she could say something she would regret. Abandoning her search through the shelves for a jar of something suitable for George to eat, she turned her attention to the few potatoes still lingering in their wooden box set back in the darkest corner of the kitchen.

"I cannot imagine who would develop a tendre for you," Lucy continued, unaware of the dark expression taking root on Sophia's face. "The only man who has ever paid you a bit of attention that I can recall is poor Josiah Fenton. Goodness, how he used to follow you around like a lovesick mongrel!"

Lucy's laugh cut through the last of Sophia's patience. With a wrinkled potato in one hand and a paring knife in the other, she bit back the snappish retort that sprung to the edge of her lips and took a deep breath before daring to speak again. "If you must know, the footmen belonged to Lord Haughton of Derbyshire," she said in a calm, measured voice. In front of her, the peel of the potato dropped into a bucket with a soft thunk. "He is also George's uncle, on his father's side." She glanced at her sister to see if she was listening. "That is, if I am not mistaken."

Lucy's pretty mouth turned down in a frown. "Oh, him? Well, that's nothing to crow about. He's so dull, you know. David used to tell such awful stories about him."

"I'm sure he did," Sophia replied. Another peel went into the bucket, and she reached for a second potato. "I met his sister as well. Bess? She was all that was kind and hospitable." She chanced another look at Lucy, who did not appear to be enjoying the conversation as much as before. "Did you know he had a sister? Your David, I mean."

A huff of breath marked the beginning of Lucy pacing from one end of the kitchen to the other. "No, I did not... Well, he might have mentioned her in passing, I suppose."

Sophia said nothing more. She could practically hear the various thoughts and questions spinning around in her sister's head. All she had to do was practice a few minutes' worth of patience.

"And how..." Lucy cleared her throat and shook a few lines of displeasure from her face with a quick toss of her head. "Did Lord Haughton introduce himself to you, or...?"

"He sought me out," Sophia said as she reached for a third potato. Behind her, George squealed and kicked his heels against the floor before banging his spoon on the bottom of the pot. Lucy winced at the noise, but Sophia had long since failed to be bothered by the sounds of his play. "He simply arrived on the doorstep one day, searching for the mother of his brother's child."

"And he believes it's you? Oh, jolly good!"

Again, Sophia chose to say nothing to that. Instead, she placed her peeled potatoes in a pot, stepped outside to fill it with water from the pump, and returned to build a fire in the stove. As she worked, Lucy continued her amble around the edge of the kitchen, her attention firmly fixed on anything that did not pertain to her son.

"And what did he have to say?" Lucy ventured to ask as Sophia hovered in front of the stove, feeding kindling to a growing flame. "I cannot imagine he came all the way to Stantreath just to speak with you."

Sophia sniffed at the slight and picked up a small piece of

firewood. "As a matter of fact, he did come all the way here to speak with me. Or to speak with you, to be more precise. But as you weren't here, he accepted me as a suitable replacement." An edge began to creep back into her words, along with a desire to rage at her sister for having abandoned them several months before. But another breath slid in and out between clenched teeth, and another chunk of wood went onto the fire. "He knows, Lucy, that you are George's mother, and not I. It would have been impossible to keep up the ruse for long, as he knows his brother's preferences better than anyone."

Lucy let out an indelicate snort. "Oh, no! I could never see David with the likes of you!"

Sophia allowed the remark to pass and continued. "He came to discuss George's upbringing. His wish is to make certain that George will want for nothing. His education, the cost of his upbringing… He wants to pay for everything. In fact…" Sophia paused, her throat nearly closing around the words that were sure to provoke a volatile reaction from her sister. "He would like George and I to live at Denton Castle with his sister, Bess."

Lucy drew in a sharp breath. "Well," she said in a huff, but Sophia interrupted her before she could throw herself into a full tizzy.

"Of course, now that you've returned, we must discuss everything and come to a decision as to what is best for—"

"What gall the man has!" Lucy ceased her pacing and stomped her slippered foot on the hardwood of the kitchen floor. "Such a pittance of an offer. No, if he wishes to give assistance of the pecuniary kind, then he'll do the proper thing and give us a house of our very own, not shove us into a cupboard behind the servants' quarters."

Sophia tossed her last piece of firewood onto the flames and turned around. "Lucy, I don't think—"

"And servants, of course!" Lucy clapped her hands together, her eyes lighting up with avaricious glee. "A maid for each of us, and a cook, and a housekeeper, and a butler, and—Ooh! Footmen! Do you know how much I've longed to preside over a household complete with footmen? And we must tell him that we want tall, attractive ones. I will not accept a handful of short, aging men with thinning hair and pockmarked skin!"

"Lucy!"

Her sister's mouth closed with a snap. Sophia had not intended to speak as sharply as she did, but she resisted the urge to give in to the quiver of Lucy's bottom lip.

"I do not believe this is the time to discuss such matters." Wiping her hands down the front of her skirt, she turned and reached for the pot of potatoes still resting on the table. "I am weary, George and I both are in need of a hot meal, and if you could keep an eye on the potatoes while I go upstairs to change my gown, I would be much obliged."

Sophia walked out of the kitchen before her sister could protest. A glance over her shoulder showed that George still sat in the corner, banging on his pots and pans, in-between moments spent gnawing on the edge of the wooden spoon until his chin and collar were soaked with drool.

Lord Haughton's men had been good enough to deposit her luggage in her bedroom, rather than assuming she possessed a servant who would be left to haul the battered trunk up the narrow stairs. Her things had gone through the normal tumble and shifting during the last leg of the journey, and she snatched up a plain, grey muslin that appeared to boast the least folds and wrinkles. She would unpack the rest of everything later, once everyone had eaten and George—if the restless sleep he'd had in the carriage hadn't ruined his chance of a decent nap later in the afternoon—was tucked into his cradle for an hour or so before dinner.

And Lucy...

Of course, her sister would choose the one time she was away from Stantreath to make her return. She could have thought the coincidence a suspicious one, but quickly pushed the thought out of her mind. Lucy couldn't have known that Lord Haughton had decided to show an interest in George.

Could she?

Sophia shook her head and quickly slipped out of her dusty and travel-worn gown. She had other things to worry about, aside from welcoming her sister back into the household after too many months away. And if she tarried for much longer, no doubt Lucy would allow the potatoes to burn.

Chapter Eighteen

Sophia stepped into Lady Rutledge's drawing room and shivered as the warmth from the fire brushed the last of the evening chill from her shoulders. Lady Rutledge sat in her favorite chair, her walking stick resting against the outer arm of it. The elderly gentlewoman reached out towards a dish of sweets at the center of the table beside her, but her movement was arrested when she gave her guest a look that reached from head to toe.

"And where is George this evening?"

"At home," Sophia said. "In the care of my sister."

Lady Rutledge's fingers pulled back from the silver dish filled with marzipan and fondant. "Really?"

Sophia grimaced at her tone, but could not find it in herself to blame Lady Rutledge for her reaction. "Yes, really. Lucy complained of a slight headache this afternoon, bading me to send her regrets for not joining us this evening. And then, before George rose from his afternoon nap, she offered to remain home with him in order that she might acquaint herself better with her son, as she put it."

"Hmm." Lady Rutledge's mouth drew into a thin line. "Are you certain this headache of hers has not addled her wits?"

"No, though she did complain about our lack of wine, as she claims it to be the only remedy of any use when her head pains her."

"Of course it is," Lady Rutledge murmured beneath her breath. After clearing her throat, she gestured towards the sofa on the other side of her chair. "Now, sit here and give solace to an old woman who has been bereft of your company for far too long. I read your letters, but ink and paper can be so confining. I much prefer to watch the change of expression on a person's face as they speak. It provides far greater entertainment than the words that come out of their mouth."

Sophia pressed her lips together against the urge to smile. She took the offered seat, adjusted her skirts, and folded her hands in her lap. "And what is it you most wish to know?" The question was superfluous. She could already guess the topic at the forefront of Lady Rutledge's mind.

"I gathered from your missives that your stay in Derbyshire with Lord Haughton and his sister went tolerably well. But what was it you mentioned about their offer for you to go and live with them?" Lady Rutledge's grey eyebrows pinched the dry skin of her forehead into several deep lines. "Surely you cannot mean to move there permanently!"

"We have not gone over all the details," Sophia began, weighing each word carefully. "But... Lord Haughton's sister, Mrs. Finchley, made it quite clear I was welcome to make Denton Castle my home, even into the years when George goes away to school."

Lady Rutledge narrowed her eyes. "And Lord Haughton? Does he share this generosity of spirit?"

Sophia's mouth quirked. Now they were to the point of it. From what little she had been able to ascertain from Lady Rutledge's letters to herself, the gentlewoman's curiosity about Lord Haughton was not going to be satisfied by the few descriptions of him Sophia had put into her letters. "I believe he wants what is best for his nephew," she said with utmost sincerity. "And, to tell the truth, it was his idea that George and I make our home in Derbyshire."

"Was it?" Lady Rutledge's eyes gleamed as she reached over to the silver dish, picked out a particularly large piece of marzipan, and began munching on the corner of it. "How good of him to take such an interest in George's upbringing, and your life as well," she added, the light in her eyes only shining brighter. "But from what I understood, he proved to be rather difficult at the beginning of your acquaintance. Were you wrong then, in the unflattering portrait you sketched of him?"

"Oh, no!" Sophia assured her. "No, he was difficult, to say the least. We were always at odds with one another, and there was a time when the mere thought of him made me uncommonly angry. But now... Now, he... " She paused to lick her lips. Her mouth had gone dry, and she wondered how much longer until the bell for dinner when she could moisten her tongue with a spoonful of soup or a sip of wine.

An awkward minute of silence passed during which Sophia could not think of what to say. Lady Rutledge, however, finished her last bite of marzipan and brushed the crumbs from her fingers as she leaned back in her chair. "Remarkable that the man is not married yet, don't you think?"

Sophia looked up sharply from her hands, still clasped in her lap. Lady Rutledge's eyes still shone, and she made no attempt to hide her smile. "I do not know what you were insinuating," Sophia said, though she knew precisely what her friend insinuated. "Any interest he has in me is due only to the fact that George has been in my care for some time, that he even supposed me to be his mother upon our first meeting. He does not... I am not..." She cleared her throat and raised the back of one hand to her cheek, which she feared was warm with a blush. "He does not like me, I am sure. At least not in that way. And besides, he already said he does not spend much time in Derbyshire, that it is primarily his sister's domain, so I doubt we will but rarely see one another. And..."

"What is Lucy's opinion of this scheme?" Lady Rutledge asked suddenly, changing the subject before Sophia could become more flustered or discover why the conversation had made such a tumble of her thoughts.

A sigh slipped out of Sophia's mouth as her shoulders sagged. "Should my sister have her way, she would demand a large annuity, a house, a carriage, a butler, multiple footmen, all other manner of servants, and most likely a new wardrobe for every season. And that is not to mention any funds put towards George's future education and his own wants and needs."

"And what of your wants and needs?" Lady Rutledge reached out for her walking stick, her gnarled hand grasping the silver handle as she began to shift towards the edge of her chair. "Who is to say Lucy will not flit off again the moment another shiny bauble draws her a hundred miles away? You are the child's mother, the only mother he truly knows." She leaned forward. "What do you want?"

Sophia drew her bottom lip into her mouth, her teeth worrying the tender flesh. What did she want? Her glance darted from one corner of the room to the other, to painted screens and ivory figures and silver boxes collecting layers of dust. Trinkets and things... No, she wanted none of that. Nor did she desire a large home, or a passel of servants to wait at her beck and call. And fine clothes? A carriage? Jewels to string around her neck?

"I want to be safe."

Lady Rutledge let out a soft sound, not quite a sigh, as her head nodded twice.

"And George, of course. I want nothing more than to be able to keep him safe, as well."

"Just so." Lady Rutledge rose from her chair, shakily at first, until she straightened to her full height and pushed her shoulders back beneath the delicate lace of her shawl. "You will make the right choice. I'm sure of it."

The door opened then and dinner was announced. Sophia took Lady Rutledge's arm, the older gentlewoman leaning on her more than she would've liked. As they passed into the dining room —an absurd tradition to eat in there though it was only the two of them, yet Lady Rutledge insisted—Sophia thought of her sister and hoped this burgeoning interest in caring for her son would signal a change in her behavior. A change for the better, she hoped, and helped Lady Rutledge into her seat.

***

Of course, Lady Rutledge insisted that Sophia take the carriage home. Clouds earlier in the day were enough to convince Lady Rutledge that a deluge could begin at any minute, and Sophia was too exhausted to argue with her. It was a brief journey through Stantreath to where the cottage lay, tucked back from the road as it was. Sophia waited for the step to be lowered, for the hand of one of Lady Rutledge's servants to appear in the open door, and she stepped down onto the rough stones of the path that led to her front gate.

A drop of rain struck the edge of her bonnet as she closed the gate behind her. Two more spattered on her arm as she neared the front step. As she reached for the door, something struck her as wrong—terribly wrong. Behind her, Lady Rutledge's carriage still stood in the road, the horses stamping their hooves in the dirt. Sophia tugged at the hem of her skirt as she turned around, raced back down the path, and waved her hand to catch the driver's attention.

"Would you be so kind as to wait a moment? Just a moment?" She glanced back at the house, at the darkened windows upstairs. A horrible chill swept down the length of her spine. She could not account for why she should feel so uneasy, when everything about the outside of the cottage appeared as she had left it a few hours before. "I need to check something. Will you please wait until I return?"

Before the driver had finished giving his assurance that he'd wait as long as she needed, she ran back into the cottage, the front door slamming open against the wall as she moved hurriedly from one room to the next, her throat threatening to close in panic as she noticed various items that had been moved or were missing entirely. In the sitting room, their last few pieces of silver—a candlestick, a dish their mother used to keep her rings in—were gone. In the kitchen, the wooden box in which she kept a few spare coins for emergencies was also nowhere to be found.

The noise she made as she rushed through the downstairs would have woken the dead, she knew. So it was with a heart pounding fast enough to burst out of her chest that she went upstairs, first to Lucy's room, and then to her own, where George's cradle stood beside her bed, cold and empty.

"Oh, Lucy. No."

She returned to Lucy's room for no longer than it took to search through a wardrobe and beneath her bed for clothes and bags that were no longer there. At the doorway, she paused, thinking she might be sick on the floor at her feet, but she swallowed down the fear and the illness and walked downstairs again, her hand gripping the rail so tightly she thought her fingernails might leave scratches in the paint.

Another search through the house uncovered no sign of a note, or anything that would indicate Lucy had meant to tell her where she had gone with George. For a minute, she stood in the kitchen doorway, her hand braced against the frame as she lowered her head and drew in as many deep breaths as she could manage.

"I-I need to return to Lady Rutledge's, please," she managed to say once outside again, the dampness of the evening air and the drizzling rain seeping into her bones and making her teeth chatter. "With as much haste as you can manage," she added, before stepping up into the carriage and swiping furiously at the tears that threatened to fall.

Chapter Nineteen

The rain ceased some time before midnight. Finnian looked up from his desk, surprised to find that the steady patter of drops against the window had stopped. The room had rapidly taken on a stagnant warmth, though the fire was in dire need of attention.

His chair scraped on the floor as he pushed it back and stood up. He undid the complicated knot of his neckcloth in a few swift tugs, the offending fabric ending up in a crumpled heap on a nearby bookshelf as he walked towards the window nearest his desk. A click, a soft whine from the wet hinges, and he looked out on the narrow strip of garden lit by the glow of various candles and lamps from behind him.

With both hands gripping the windowsill, he leaned forward, stretching the muscles of his back and upper shoulders while he breathed in the mingled scents of rain and lavender and greenery. Only a fortnight back in town and already he was tired of the smoke and stench of the place. For these few brief minutes, after the rain had washed the air clean, he could imagine that he was back at Denton Castle, with the windows of his bedroom flung open every night and the buzz of insects and the chirp of birds announcing the start of every day.

Two weeks, he thought. He ran a hand across his forehead, sweeping his hair back from his brow. An entire fortnight in London, attending to business and meetings and Parliament and more business should have been enough to sweep all thoughts of Sophia from his mind. Bess had said she would write to her, would make all the arrangements with Sophia about future visits, about the possibility of her and George eventually making Denton Castle their home. He had left the matter in his sister's very capable hands, and that should have been the end of it. At least until the time came to sort out such things as the child's education and the purchase of the boy's first horse.

Finnian tilted his head back and listened to the sounds of the house, a house already gone to bed for the night. Should he need anyone, he could ring and someone would rush to do his bidding at a moment's notice. But for now, he heard the ticking of various clocks, the scuttle of mice behind the moulding, and the soft creak of the building as it settled into its foundation.

What he needed...

He pushed himself away from the window and strode to the other side of the room. What he needed was to stop thinking about Sophia Brixton. There would be no happy ending there. She didn't care much for him as a person, that much was clear, though they had at least managed to arrive at a point in their acquaintance where every conversation didn't eventually dissolve into an argument. But she would never accept him as a suitor, and that was even if the notion of presenting himself as one would develop beyond the point of mere fantasy.

He picked up the brandy decanter, hesitated, and then set it down in favor of the whiskey instead. He pulled out the stopper and was about to pour himself a rather large portion when the distinct sound of a carriage pulling up to the front of the house—unusually loud against the silence around him—caught his attention. Only a few seconds later, a loud, insistent pounding began on the door, and he sent a brief curse towards the ceiling before he left his study and walked to the door. The pounding began again, louder than before, as he put his hand on the knob and started to unlock the door.

"Give me a minute!" His words came out on a tired growl. He wrenched open the door to find a slender, shadowed figure standing on his doorstep. A woman, most definitely, judging by the silhouette of bonnet and gown. Behind him, the sound of his Gleeson's steps shuffling through the foyer met his ears, and Finnian raised a hand to stay the man until he was certain whether or not he would be in need of a servant's assistance.

"Can I help you, ma'am?" Finnian glanced down at the carriage in the street. Not a hired vehicle, he could tell, even in the faint shreds of moonlight shining through the dissipating clouds.

The figure raised her head an inch, enough to allow the light from inside his foyer to illuminate her face. "Lord Haughton?"

"Dear God, Sophia!" His heart lurched at the sight of her, damp and disheveled as she was, her eyes red and strained from some obvious and recent upset. "What the devil...? Come in, already!" he amended, as soon as some semblance of his manners returned to him.

As Sophia stepped indoors, Finnian turned around and issued a series of orders to his butler. "We'll need something hot to drink, and food as well, I should think. Have you eaten?" He looked back over his shoulder at Sophia, but she made no reply, her mouth moving soundlessly as wide eyes blinked above the shadows on her cheeks. "Come along," he said, once he'd sent his butler to wake the rest of the servants. "In here. You look as if you need to sit before you fall off your feet."

He led her into his study, the nearest room that still boasted some light and warmth. He walked across the room, shut the window to keep out any chill, and turned around to find her still standing in the doorway, her gloved fingers tugging on one another with such fierceness he thought she might do an injury to her hands if he didn't do something to distract her.

"Mrs. Brix—" he began, but before he could utter another syllable, she interrupted him.

"It's George," she said, her voice an anguished croak. "He's gone."

Finnian shook his head. Did she mean...?

"Lucy's taken him," she said in reply to the look of question in his eyes. He noticed the quiver of her chin on the last word.

Lucy? It took a minute for his baffled mind to remember what role she had to play in the child's life. "His mother? But I thought she disappeared some time ago, that you hadn't heard from her."

"Well, she..." She spread her hands, her finger trembling violently.

"Right." He returned to her side, took her arm, and guided her into the chair nearest the fire. She was still in some sort of shock, and without saying another word, he returned to the drinks tray, filled a glass halfway with whiskey, and pushed it into her shaking hands.

Sophia looked at the beverage suspiciously and moved to give it back to him. "I don't want—"

"It will calm your nerves," he said, and nudged the rim of the glass back towards her.

She nodded once, then licked her lips. One small sip disappeared inside her mouth, and the reaction was instantaneous. "Dear heavens!" She coughed and spluttered, her eyes watering as she gripped the glass in one hand and smacked her chest with the other. "Oh, it's vile!" She coughed again and glared up at him from beneath the brim of her bonnet. "How do you drink something so awful?"

"One sip at a time," he told her, and tipped the glass up to her mouth again. "Simply pretend it's medicine. It will do you good, I promise."

Another sip followed, this one without the same spate of coughing, but not without a severe grimace distorting her features as she swallowed. When she'd imbibed nearly half of what he'd given her, he finally drew up a chair in front of her and sat down, his elbows balanced on his knees as he leaned forward. "Now, do you feel better?"

"Yes," she said, her voice hoarse. "Thank you."

"Then start from the beginning, if you please."

Sophia set the glass down on the table beside her and placed her hands in her lap. Her posture at that instant was such a study in anguish that Finnian wished for nothing more than to gather her up in his arms and hold her against him, to let her cry into his shoulder while he pushed her bonnet back from her head and kissed her hair, but he held himself still, waiting for her to speak when she felt ready and willing to do so.

"When I returned home from Derbyshire, Lucy was there. She'd arrived from Bath only a few hours before me." Her gaze darted over to the glass of whiskey beside her, but her lips tightened and she looked away again. "At first, she tried to dote on George, attempting to hold him, to play with him, to give him kisses and draw him into her embrace. But..." She looked up at him, the gold in her eyes catching the dying light of the fire. "He doesn't know her any longer, and I think he knew... I think anyone would have witnessed her behavior towards him and known it was insincere."

This time, she did reach for the glass. She took another sip, her eyes squeezing shut as the alcohol slid down her throat. "I know how cruel that sounds, and coming from her own sister, but..."

"No, no. I understand. You forget I have someone like David for a brother." Finnian's hand twitched, wanting to reach out and touch her, to offer her some form of comfort, but instead he leaned back, his arms crossing over his chest as he gave her time to continue.

"Well, three nights ago—or was it four? Oh, dear. What day is it today?"

"Friday," he supplied, and watched as her face fell.

"Four nights, then." She took a deep breath, and a quick flutter of her eyelashes betrayed the tears she fought to hold at bay. "Lady Rutledge invited George and I over for dinner, but Lucy—oh! I should have known better than to believe her! But fool that I was, I wished with all my heart to believe in the goodness of her intentions!"

She gave in to her tears then. Not a dainty cry like women of his experience had been trained to utilize, with only a slight sniff or a reluctant tear making a show of the emotions used to pull on the heartstrings of the men before them. No, this was an ugly display, raw with fear and anguish. Her heart was breaking, perhaps had already been rent to pieces, and Finnian tossed aside every reason he could invent against touching her, against offering her comfort in her pain. He slid forward in his chair until his knees knocked into hers, both of his hands held out to her, his palms upturned, his fingers unfurled.

"Sophia," he said, and her voice broke with another sob. But her hands found their way into his, her gloved fingers tightening around his bare ones.

"Lucy told me she wanted to keep an eye on him for the evening, so that he would begin to remember her again." She sniffed loudly, and without a handkerchief at hand, turned her head and indelicately wiped her cheek across the sleeve of her gown. "It was dark when I returned. I knew...I knew when I stepped into the house that something was amiss. I searched, but they were gone. Lucy had packed up all their things and disappeared, just as before. And this time, she took George with her."

Finnian released one of her hands long enough to reach for her glass and give it to her. She took a long sip, nearly choking again, before cradling it in her lap while her grip on his other hand only tightened.

"I told her you'd come to see me, about George," she added, and licked a drop of whiskey from the corner of her mouth. "I told her of your various offers, and how I was considering leaving Stantreath to make a home at Denton Castle with your sister, but she did not at all care for that plan. She wanted..." Another pause, another sip. "... something more significant from you."

Finnian lowered his head, his shoulders sagging as he exhaled. He wanted to be angry on her behalf, to siphon away some of her hurt and disappointment in her sister's behavior so that she could be free of the painful emotions. But he was not certain he had the power to do so. Instead, he ran his thumb across the back of her hand, while chiding himself for not remembering to relieve her of her bonnet and shawl when she'd first entered the house.

"Do you know where she is now?" he asked, but Sophia shook her head before he'd even finished putting the question into words.

"It's why I came here. Lady Rutledge again permitted me the use of her carriage and her servants so that I might discover if Lucy had attempted to contact you in any way, perhaps for money." Her face took on a sour expression at the mention of that last word, and her lips disappeared between her teeth as she seemed to pause long enough to once again gather her thoughts. "I fear she does not have any interest in George unless she has something to gain from him."

"And you're certain it is money she wants?"

Sophia's jaw tightened. "Along with a house, servants, a carriage, horses, a new wardrobe... Oh, and she did mention something about a private box at the theater."

"Good Lord." Finnian eyed the remains of Sophia's drink and wondered if it would be bad manners to take it and finish it himself. "I am sorry."

"She was not always like this," she hurried to say, her gaze seeking out his, pleading for him to believe her. "But when our parents died, she did not take it well. I think it hurt her more than I originally thought. And I didn't..." She sniffed. "I fear I missed it, her own difficulties, so wrapped up as I was in trying to make certain we would survive on our own."

"You are not to blame," Finnian assured her as he leaned forward, near enough to see the tracks of dried tears on her cheeks. Tracks that he wanted to sweep away with a brush of his hand.

Sophia smiled at that, though it was tinged with sadness. "Not fully, no. But a little bit, just as I'm sure you blame yourself for some of David's indiscretions, and as no doubt your father did before you." Her expression changed then, her eyes widening as she straightened in her seat. "Does this mean you've not heard from Lucy? She's not attempted to contact you in any way?"

"This is the first I've heard of it," Finnian said, sitting back again but without relinquishing his grip on her hand.

"So I take it you've not received any message from your brother, either?"

"David? Do you think...?"

Sophia raised one shoulder and let it fall on a sigh. "I've had several days in a carriage to think over a great deal, and I cannot help but find it to be more than a tremendous coincidence that my sister should take it upon herself to return to Stantreath within hours of my return from Denton Castle. I would not be at all surprised to discover that there is someone else guiding her hand."

"Neither would I," Finnian said, and let slip a curse from under his breath. "Forgive me." He released her hand, reluctantly, and left her to return to his desk.

"What are you doing?" she piped up from behind him, while he searched through the clutter for a clean sheet of paper and a quill that would not need to be trimmed.

"I'm sending for assistance," he told her without looking up. "I will admit to keeping a private investigator in my employ. He has been quite useful whenever my brother has decided to get himself mired in certain situations."

"And you think he can help us? To find George and my sister?"

He looked up from his uneven handwriting. "Without him, I wouldn't have found you." His words, he thought, held more import than he had intended, but whether or not she caught the deeper meaning behind them, he couldn't be certain. His message written and sanded down, he rang the bell and then returned to Sophia, where he held out his hand to her. "There's little more that can be done tonight. I suggest you eat and rest, and keep as clear a head as possible for whatever may lie ahead."

"But—"

"I doubt we'll find anyone tonight, and you'll be no use to George when we do discover him if you're dead on your feet with exhaustion."

She nodded and placed her hand on his arm. Despite her obvious tiredness from her journey and the stress of the last few days, he felt the strength that still radiated out from her touch, a fierceness that he had already well learned not to defy.

"I'll have a meal sent up to your room," he said as he walked her out of the study and across the foyer. "You can have Bess's suite while you're here. I doubt she'll mind," he added, making an attempt at lightheartedness that seemed to die in the air between them.

Sophia stopped at the bottom of the staircase, her grip tightened on his arm as she turned to face him. "Thank you," she said softly. "For all your help."

In the light of the foyer, her beauty was almost ethereal. The red of her hair shone like gold around her head, and her eyes... How he wished he could eliminate the sadness that darkened their normally shining depths. "I feel like I should be asking for your forgiveness rather than accepting your gratitude."

"I know. Which is why I'm making certain to offer it."

He could have kissed her then. If the circumstances were different, if she were not about to droop with tiredness, if he did not feel that he would be a disappointment to her...

"Here," he said instead, as the butler returned from the back of the house, with one of the maids—bearing a tray—at his heels. "Mary can show you to your room and see to your every need. And should I hear anything before morning..."

"Of course," she said, and took a step away from him, her hand sliding off his arm and falling to her side. "And again, thank you."

"Goodnight, Mrs. Brixton."

"Goodnight, my lord."

Chapter Twenty

Sophia opened her eyes, only to find herself gazing up at a shadowed ceiling she did not recognize.

London, she reminded herself, as her eyes fluttered closed again. Her fingers found their way to her forehead, kneading above her left eye where a headache throbbed with enough strength to make her feel as if she were still being bounced around in Lady Rutledge's carriage.

Her hands gripped the edge of the bed as she sat up, her breath hissing between her teeth as the pain in her head shifted and brought a surge of bile to the back of her throat. A deep breath, followed swiftly by another, and she dared to open her eyes again.

Someone had banked the fire during the night, though the candle she'd left burning in its holder on the nightstand had drowned in its own wax some hours before. The room was not cold, but as she swung her legs over the side of the bed, her bare feet sought out her knitted slippers and she took up her wrapper from the back of a chair where she'd abandoned it before falling asleep.

She shuffled towards one of the tall windows and pulled back the curtains. A faint green cast to the sky told her that dawn would soon be on its way, and also informed her that she must not have rested for more than a few hours since burrowing her head into the overstuffed pillows on Bess's bed.

The sill pressed into her hips as she leaned forward, until her forehead found the cool glass and the throbbing in her head subsided. She needed to eat, having only picked over the tray of cold meats and sandwiches sent up to her room after Lord Haughton had wished her a good night. She considered slipping down to the kitchen and searching for a snack, but then reminded herself that not only was it not her home, but with a new day on the verge of beginning, no doubt the lowest of the servants had already risen from their beds, cleaning out the previous day's ashes in preparation for another round of cooking for an entire household.

The maid had put her things away in the wardrobe, though her luggage had only amounted to a few gowns and accessories, everything that could be fit into one bag. She took down a plain gown, washed her face and neck and under her arms with the cold water and cake of soap beside the basin, and dressed before the sky had taken on a more pinkish hue. Her hairbrush was still in her hand when the bedroom door opened, and a maid—not the same girl as the previous evening—poked her head into the room.

Before a minute had passed, the maid had introduced herself—Maggie, her name was—and taken over the task of brushing and pinning up Sophia's hair. Maggie informed her that she could break her fast there in her bedroom, the morning room, or the dining room. That was, if she didn't mind sitting down to enjoy a repast in a large room without anyone to accompany her.

"Has Lord Haughton risen?" Sophia asked, as Maggie pushed a pin into the fashionable knot at the back of her head.

"Oh, I don't believe he went to bed, Miss," the young girl admitted, another half dozen pins clutched between her teeth. "If I'm not mistaken, he's kept to his study all night."

"Thank you," Sophia said, and once the girl had finished with her hair and fussing over the folds of her gown, she left the bedroom and attempted to retrace her steps to the study.

She knocked lightly when she reached the door, one hand already on the knob as she pressed her ear against the wood, listening for a reply. When a second knock elicited no response, she dared to open the door and step inside the dimly lit room. She found Lord Haughton immediately, though not in any stance or pose she had anticipated.

He sat at the desk. Or, more accurately, he sat slumped over the desk, his head resting on his right arm, while his left had at some point knocked over a bottle of ink, staining the cuff of his sleeve and several documents scattered about beneath him. She glanced up at the nearest window, which stood wide open, letting in a pale light along with a chill to the air that made her shiver slightly as the fire had been allowed to die down to dead coals and ash.

"My lord?" Sophia whispered, and placed her hand on his shoulder, giving him a gentle shake.

He responded with a sort of snuffling sound, and then a snore, and then he turned his head so that she could see his face.

Dark, untidy strands of hair fell across his forehead, while his beard had grown in even more since when she'd last seen him only a few hours before. But what caught her attention was the lack of lines and strain on the skin around his eyes and mouth, the smooth, almost boyish expression that graced his slumbering face, an expression she wondered if he was even capable of achieving during his waking hours.

But she felt sorry for him... No, not sorry. Strangely, it seemed to be more of a kinship that she felt with him, despite the differences in their sex and station. This man who strove to do what was right, even when he sometimes went about it in the most officious of ways.

Her hand still resting on his shoulder, she leaned forward until her mouth was quite close to his ear. "My lord," she said again, and did not back away until his eyelids flickered and he raised his head from his arm.

He blinked at her, his gaze bleary and unfocused. And then he passed his hand over his face, scratched his knuckles against his unshaven jaw, and looked up at her again.

"Sophia."

It was not the first time he had neglected his manners and failed to address her by her surname. Last night, she had heard her Christian name on his lips several times, though her own exhaustion and the urgency of the situation had deemed it one of the least of her concerns.

He looked at her this morning as he had the previous night. Gone was the disdain she remembered him exhibiting on their first meeting, several months ago in her cottage in Stantreath. It had been during her stay in Derbyshire, she realized, that the tension between them had begun to relent, and for the first time in their acquaintance, they had begun to work together towards making the best future for their nephew.

Another blink, and some of the shadows of tiredness returned to his face. The lines returned as well, and she thought he looked older than his years, though the state of his hair and his clothes were not helping him in that regard.

"It is morning," she pointed out, even though he was perfectly capable of looking over his shoulder at the light coming through the windows into the study. "I wondered if you had heard anything during the night..."

Lord Haughton rubbed his eyes and swept his hair back from his forehead, unwittingly setting it standing up in several directions at once. "If I had received any news, I would not have hesitated to wake you at once. I sent off a dozen messages, have garnered only a single reply as of yet, and did little more than twirl my thumbs until I... Well, until you found me here."

He sat up in his chair, only to notice the mess the spilled ink bottle had made of his shirt and the contents of his desk. "Damn it all," he muttered, and attempted to organize the mess while Sophia gathered up the papers he had knocked to the floor as he slept. "There's no need for you to..." he said, but stopped himself when she stood before him, a stack of crumpled papers in her hands. "Thank you," he amended, contrite, and took the stack from her.

"Did you get any rest?" he asked without looking over at her. She had given him her handkerchief to help sop up the ink, and she watched as he continued to fumble over the mess until she put a hand on his elbow to stop him.

"More than you, I gather." Her fingers tightened on his arm until he abandoned his cluttered desk and turned around to face her. He looked broken, she thought. Tired and disheveled and only half-dressed, and bearing the strain of a problem she had brought to his doorstep. "Is there anything that can be done right now? Anything we can accomplish beyond... twirling our thumbs over tea and buns?"

He shook his head. "Not unless you want to ride about London, scouring every inch of pavement and questioning every bystander to discover if they've recently seen a tow-headed infant in the vicinity."

"And that's if Lucy or George are even anywhere near London." Sophia shut her eyes and tried not to allow panic to overwhelm her. They could be anywhere in the country, she realized. And that was if they had even left Northumberland and hadn't simply sat back while she ran off to London in search of Lord Haughton's aid.

"The one reply I mentioned receiving?"

Sophia opened her eyes and found him gazing down at her, closer than she remembered him being only a moment before.

"It was from Mr. Winston, the man I keep on my payroll for incidents such as this. He said David is in London. He returned to town yesterday, from somewhere in the north," he said, placing a heavy accent on that final word.

Sophia drew in a breath. "Do you think...?"

"At this point, I won't allow myself to think anything without more facts. But if my brother is indeed involved with this..." He raised her chin with a crooked finger when she started to look away. "We will get him back. Do you understand?"

"Are we going about this the wrong way, do you think? I mean, we could be attempting to rescue George from his own parents."

"Can you honestly tell me that you haven't met people you thought should never be in the care of children? I wouldn't entrust David to the care of a flea-infested cat, let alone a healthy young boy."

"But Lucy..."

"I do not know your sister. Only you do, so I cannot make any decisions for you on that score."

They stood there, her fingers still clutching the loose fabric of his sleeve, her head still throbbing in time with the beating of her heart.

"If you'll excuse me for a few minutes," he said, and took her hand in order to remove it from his shirt. "I'll retire to my room in order to make myself more presentable." He raised his arm, the one with the ink-stained sleeve. "I'll have breakfast sent in to you, and I'll join you in here. That is, if you don't mind eating among the detritus of my work."

The tray arrived a few minutes after Lord Haughton left her. Sophia helped herself to a piece of toast and was spreading a thin layer of butter on the crusty bread as he returned to the study, his clothes changed, his hair combed, and his face cleanly shaven. He still looked tired however, and paler than usual as he took the seat across from her and helped himself to a cup of coffee from the pot.

"I doubt either of us is in possession of anything resembling an appetite this morning," he began, between swallows of coffee. "But we should do our best to eat our fill and fortify ourselves for whatever the day may bring."

Sophia did not argue with the wisdom of his words. She could not imagine where she may be by the time night fell, and after too many days of travelling and poor fare at poorer inns, she needed to do everything in her power to sustain herself.

After the toast, they each helped themselves to eggs and sausage and ham. They ate with perfunctory movements, neither of them seeming to take much enjoyment from the meal. But they both cleared their plates, and as Sophia wiped the last of the crumbs from her lips with the corner of her napkin, a knock sounded on the study door.

Sophia looked at Lord Haughton, and neither of them breathed. Then he pushed himself out of his seat and crossed quickly to the door. She had expected to see the butler or one of the maids come to retrieve the breakfast tray, but instead a small, undistinguished man with short brown hair and grey eyes stood in the doorway.

"Winston," Lord Haughton said, and Sophia watched as his shoulders rounded forward slightly before he stepped back and allowed the newcomer into the room.

The man called Winston walked towards the tight grouping of chairs where she and Lord Haughton had just finished their breakfast. He nodded his head towards Sophia, and offered his hand to her, as if she were a male business associate with which he was about to make his acquaintance.

"Mrs. Brixton, I take it?"

After a brief bout of hesitation, she placed her hand in his. He pumped it firmly and released her arm back to her care. "Mister...?"

"Winston. John Winston," Lord Haughton provided after he'd closed the door and joined them around the tray. "An old friend of mine, and a man possessed of the incredible talent of discovering things that other people would rather remain well and truly hidden."

Sophia studied the man, this John Winston. At first sight, she'd thought him to be of a middling build. But standing between beside Lord Haughton, she realized he was nearly of a height with him. Her gaze darted back and forth between the two men, Lord Haughton dressed in the finest clothing that London's tailors had to offer, while Mr. Winston appeared to favor nondescript colours and lines, somehow managing with the basic cut of his coat and trousers to render himself as unmemorable as possible.

"You have news?" Lord Haughton said, preempting any tedious conversation about the state of their health or the weather.

"I do." Mr. Winston reached into an inside pocket of his coat. Sophia couldn't help but wonder, considering the man's profession, how many secrets he concealed inside those pockets. "But it is news for which I am unable to take credit. I intercepted a messenger on your doorstep, come to deliver this." He held out a small letter, lacking a seal of any kind, and the paper bearing multiple creases and splotches of ink. "I asked the boy—because the creature didn't look to be more than nine years old if he was a day—who had hired him to deliver the note, but either he knew nothing, or was more skilled than anyone I've met at speaking falsehoods from behind an innocent face."

Lord Haughton took the letter, unfolded it, and tilted it towards Sophia, his way—she assumed—of inviting her to have a look as well. She stepped up to his side, her shoulder pressed against his upper arm, and read the spidery scrawl that slanted across the stained sheet of paper. Her eyes welled up with tears as she scanned the words, then swiftly transformed to anger as she read them again. The letter, signed by her sister, declared a wish to meet with Lord Haughton—and him alone—in order that they might discuss terms pertaining to George's upbringing.

"It is signed with your sister's name," Lord Haughton pointed out, though he had to have known she'd already seen the blotchy signature at the bottom of the missive.

"Yes," she admitted, her teeth clenched in an attempt to hold in the maelstrom of emotions threatening to tumble out of her at this turn in events. "But the letter itself is not written in her hand."

"I am aware of that," he said, and passed the letter over to Winston for his perusal. "Though he's attempted to disguise it, I have no doubt that letter was penned by none other than my dearest brother, David."

Chapter Twenty-One

Finnian sat in the carriage, while Winston occupied the seat across from him. He pulled at the shade that covered the window and glanced out at the city. They were well into the East End, judging by the quality of the streets beneath them and the sounds that reached them through the walls of the carriage. It was no surprise to him that David would choose such a disreputable neighbourhood for his supposed meeting with Lucy, Sophia's sister. Though Finnian was already wary of even finding the younger Miss Brixton there. He doubted his expression would register even a modicum of shock should he walk into the inn and find his brother waiting with a careless demand for several thousand pounds in return for the child.

"I believe we've nearly arrived," Winston announced, matching Finnian's glance beyond the shade of the opposite window.

As the carriage rumbled to a stop, Finnian gripped the edge of the seat while a round of curses sounded from somewhere outside the vehicle. He didn't wait for the door to opened for them but instead stepped down on his own before anyone had even jumped down to lower the step. He realized as the two of them departed the carriage that he'd made the right choice in opting for a more plain, conservative mode of dress for this particular errand. Together, they blended in neatly with the dull colours and ochreous layers of smoke and fog that seemed to cling to every corner and cobblestone.

"We shall meet back here in one hour," Winston said, glancing at the watch he'd tugged from the pocket of his waistcoat. "I'll proceed to the Calf's Head Inn on foot, while you meet with Miss Penrose at the Rose and Thorn."

Finnian tore his glance away from an altercation between a

crossing sweeper and a tradesman to look at Winston. "And you're certain that my brother and Miss Penrose were spotted together at the Calf's Head?"

Winston nodded, his right hand going to the outside of his coat, where no doubt his notebook was concealed inside. "Several witnesses report their comings and goings from there, and the innkeeper himself confessed to there being an infant on the premises. No doubt that's why they've arranged this meeting in another building entirely, to keep you off the scent. But if the child is indeed at the Calf's Head, I'll do my best to collect him while you're otherwise occupied with the sister. If all goes well, I'll return directly to the carriage and wait for you."

Finnian bristled. "All better go well," he muttered beneath his breath before checking his own watch. "Best be off now, rather than risk keeping anyone waiting."

They parted ways at the edge of the pavement, Finnian's destination only two blocks away while Winston set off with the silhouette of St. Matthew's behind him.

A ripple of guilt passed through him as he made his way towards the Rose and Thorn. Sophia had initially insisted on accompanying them, but he had asked her to remain in St. James's Street, to rest and help prepare the house for George's arrival, an arrival he did not doubt would be occurring before the day was over.

After a few words with the innkeeper, a tall, reedy man with yellow fingernails and yellower teeth—what he still had of them—Finnian was led into a private room in the back of the building. The place was small, furnished with scraps that looked to have been rescued from a previous century and propped up against papered walls that were stained and warped along every corner.

Lucy Brixton sat in a decrepit armchair, her dress and manner attempting to put forward the notion that she was of a higher quality than the room in which she resided. Her gown was some ghastly concoction of pale green silk and so many flounces and layers of fussiness that she resembled a petits four more than a young woman.

"Lord Haughton!" She extended her hand to him, fully expecting him no doubt to traipse across the cluttered room and plant a kiss to her fingers. Instead, Finnian remained at his post just inside the door and tugged at the cuffs of his gloves.

"I've little time for pleasantries and tedious bon mots, Miss Penrose. I've come to discuss your son, George, and the care and upbringing you wish for him." He took care not to reveal that he knew of Lucy taking George from Stantreath and absconding with him—and possibly David, as well—down to London. Neither did he have any wish to tell her that her sister had already arrived in London and was helping to prepare his household for the temporary addition of an infant guest.

"Well, of course," Lucy said, her face brightening with a sweet smile and a flutter of her eyelashes. "I would not wish to waste your precious time, my lord. I'm sure you've much more pressing matters to attend to, so I thank you for coming out of your way to see me this morning."

In colouring, Finnian realized, she did not resemble her sister at all. But their faces were remarkably similar, though Sophia's cheeks and nose bore a dusting of freckles to match the auburn in her hair. Lucy, on the other hand, possessed a clear complexion, though her cheeks bore enough rouge to make him doubt whether the paleness of her skin was a gift from nature or a bit of cleverly applied cosmetics.

"Will you sit?" Lucy gestured towards another armchair that nearly matched her own. It looked to have been created in the same decade, at least.

"I'd rather not," he replied, and watched as Lucy's mouth tightened. "What I would prefer is to move immediately and succinctly to the point of this little meeting you've arranged for us." When her response was nothing more than a raised eyebrow, he continued. "In plainer terms, what do you want?"

Though her smile lost some of its brilliancy, the light in her eyes failed to dim. She moved to the edge of her seat, the rustle of silk somehow loud despite the sounds of the noisy inn around them. "Three thousand pounds," she said, and paused long enough to purse her lips. "And a house. Not here in London, but neither do I want to be shoved off to some bucolic backwater like Stantreath. And do not attempt to offer me a room or two in a house you already own." She sniffed and raised her chin. "An offer such as that may be enough to tempt my sister, but I assure you that my tastes lean more towards the refined, and I will not be bought with little more than you would offer to the daughter of a country squire."

"And that is all you would request? Or should I fetch a piece of paper and some ink in order to make a list?"

"You may, if you wish. I'm sure you have an abundance of solicitors in your employ, all of them more than equipped to hammer out the details of our bargain. But there will be a carriage, and horses, and a fine array of servants. Male servants as well as female. I will not have anyone think I cannot afford to hire a footman or two."

"And we shouldn't forget pin money," Finnian added, not bothering to remove the disdain from his voice. "And perhaps a new wardrobe for you, fitted and sewn by the finest dressmakers in London, hmm?"

"Of course!" Lucy clapped her hands together in excitement as the sarcasm in his words dissipated into the air above her head. "I shall wish to entertain, and I certainly cannot do that in these..." She plucked at the skirt of her gown, her nose wrinkled in disgust. "...these rags."

"Of course not," Finnian agreed mockingly. "And after I've purchased these things for you and set you up in your own little house, perhaps you'll be able to spare a thought as to what should be done for your sister or even—dare I say—your son."

"Oh." Lucy sat back in her chair, her expression taking on a veneer of petulance that made her look more like the nineteen-year-old young woman hiding beneath the layers of poorly applied rouge and face paint. "I see. You have spent some time with my sister, haven't you? No doubt she's fooled you into thinking she's such a saint for all the supposed sacrifices she's made for me. Poor Sophia!" She rolled her eyes and blew out her breath in a huff. "Saint Sophia!"

He ignored her comments and took one of the proffered chairs near to the fire. He crossed one leg over the other, his ankle resting on top of his knee as he leaned back and drummed his thumbs against the shining buttons of his waistcoat. "I am prepared to agree to your request of three thousand pounds, and even increase it to five thousand. But on one condition: That single payment is all you will ever receive from me. Five thousand pounds, and you will leave your son to your sister to raise. You will relinquish all claims to him, and you will cease to use him as a bargaining chip in a pathetic scheme to extract more money from me at some future date."

When she opened her mouth to protest, he held up his right hand. Her mouth snapped shut again, and she narrowed her eyes at him but did not make another attempt to interrupt him.

"Or," he began, drawing out that single syllable with painstaking clarity. "You may continue to live with your sister, lend a measurable hand in the task of raising your son—my nephew—and agree to a modest income that will not leave any of you wanting for any of life's necessaries, including new gowns and a few extra servants. But you will not fly off to Bath, or Portsmouth, or London, or any other place contained on a map that is not also inhabited by your sister and your son. You will take on the responsibility of rearing your only child, and I will make certain that you and your sister are regarded as not only respectable, but marriageable, as I will also settle no less than a thousand pounds on you and Mrs. Brixton, in the event of your accepting a suitable offer, of course."

"How dare you!" Lucy straightened up in her chair, her hands gripping the armrests at her sides. She attempted to put on an appearance of being offended, but Finnian was not impressed. "Do you think you can put a price on my child's head? That I will be so easily bought by the promise of your modest income?"

He had already heard similar words from her sister upon their first meeting. But the difference between the two performances was that Sophia's reaction had not been a performance at all. With every part of her, she loved the infant left in her care. But Lucy, on the other hand...

"I presume you believe you have the upper hand," he continued. "That we'll continue on with this pathetic little farce of bargaining until you achieve what you desire and I'll finally be given the whereabouts of young George, correct?"

She shifted in her seat. "I don't know what you—"

"Or perhaps you'll attempt a different tactic. Perhaps you'll threaten to reveal that your sister is not really a widow, that she only pretended to lose a husband in order to lend your son a touch of legitimacy. I'm sure that consideration has already crossed your mind, has it not?"

She shifted again, her skirts rustling as the toes of her slippered feet poked out from beneath the hem of her gown. He watched as a half dozen different expressions slid across her face, until one that made him particularly uneasy settled into place on her brow.

"You like my sister, don't you?"

Finnian pulled in a breath. No, this was not a tactic he had expected.

"Oh, don't attempt to deny it!" She smiled sweetly, sickeningly sweet, with eyelashes fluttering over brilliant eyes. "You invited her to stay at your estate in Derbyshire, and from what your brother has told me, you became quite angered when he dared to suggest that there was anything... untoward between the two of you." Again, the eyelashes fluttered. "You might even love her, for all I know. I can't imagine why. All those freckles." Her nose wrinkled in disgust. "But marriage? Oh, that might be a tricky one, considering her own past and the potential scandal of less than savory familial connections." She gestured towards herself, the sickly smile never leaving her face. "Of course, you could always offer her a different sort of existence, though I'm not sure my sister is the type to accept carte blanche from anyone."

"Enough!" Finnian breathed again and reigned in as much of his anger as he could. "If your sister would have me, I would consider myself the most blessed of men to call her my wife. No amount of threats or blackmail or pitiful attempts to sully her character would change my mind, if indeed I ever choose to make an offer of marriage to her. Now," he said, and pulled his watch from his pocket. Nearly an hour had passed since he'd parted ways with Winston outside his carriage. "If you'll excuse me."

He rose from his chair and strode towards the door. Lucy leapt to her feet and made to follow him.

"Where are you going?" she cried, her voice a desperate screech behind him.

He turned to face her in the open doorway. Behind him, the cacophony of the busy inn sought to enter the quiet haven of their private room. "I need to return home, Miss Penrose. It might surprise you to learn that your sister arrived here from Stantreath last evening, and if all has gone well—" He gave his watch another glance. "—my associate should now have George in his care. It was the Calf's Head, if I'm not mistaken? Where you were hiding him? After spiriting him away from your sister's cottage without her knowledge, I might add."

Lucy's face crumpled. "B-But David said—"

"Ah, yes. My brother. I assure you he says quite a number of things, though not even half of them would I count as trustworthy."

"But…" Lucy repeated, her mouth opening and closing like that of a fish.

"Now, I will not simply take your child away from you," he interrupted while she continued to gape at him. "No matter that I doubt you would show the same consideration towards your own family. But the boy needs to be properly cared for, and using him to filch funds from my pocket will not be tolerated, do you understand?"

Chastened, she clasped her hands before her and nodded.

"I have already told you what I am willing to do for you and your family, Miss Penrose. You have a choice. Either I give you five thousand pounds, and you leave your son in your sister's care, or you can return with me to St. James's Street and we'll continue to discuss things in greater detail." He raised his eyebrows. "Which will it be?"

Her bottom lip disappeared into her mouth as she pondered the options he set before her. He had to admit, he hoped she would choose the latter. Though he would not agree to her absurd list of demands, he wanted to believe that love for her son would push her towards choosing a more modest existence with her family. But the renewed gleam in her eye as she leaned towards him erased any and all such hope. She smiled again, the powder on her face cracking around the lines that creased the corners of her mouth.

"I'll take the five thousand," she said, tilting her chin upwards in triumph.

Chapter Twenty-Two

There was nothing for it. Sophia had made an attempt at seeking out every possible distraction to fill up the minutes that slowly ticked away her morning, but it was to no avail. Books had been perused and tossed aside, newspapers and gossip sheets ignored, breakfast and luncheon both toyed with and finally pushed away in disgust.

Lord Haughton and Mr. Winston had left from St. James's street after taking their own breakfast in the study. At first, Sophia had considered demanding that they allow her to accompany them to their meeting with Lucy, but her sister was more likely to give in to hysterics and absurd demands if Sophia were present. Lord Haughton, she hoped, with his firm demeanor and stoic attitude would not allow a few tears on Lucy's part to sway him from his purpose: to find George and bring him—and hopefully Lucy—home.

Home.

Sophia looked around her, at the walls and furnishings of the drawing room in which she sat. This was certainly not her home. She thought of her cottage in Stantreath, a gift from Lady Rutledge. But that had never truly felt like home, either, only a place to stay, to lay her head and cook her meals until...

Well, Lord Haughton and his sister had already offered Denton Castle as a home to her and George, but would it ever be a place in which she could be comfortable? Would she merely feel like a guest for the entirety of her stay there, even if such a stay stretched into a span of years?

And Haughton—Lord Haughton, she reminded herself, though he was known as Finn to his sister and the enigmatic Mr. Winston. He had presented himself as such a formidable personage upon their first meeting, all stone and ice, an impenetrable wall without compassion or feeling. And now, months later, he had opened his home to her, had offered whatever she needed for the care and rearing of George. Even now, he was dealing with her sister's absurd demands and reckless, thoughtless behavior in wrenching her son from Stantreath only to use him as a means to acquiring what she wanted.

Sophia blew out a breath, tossed aside the piece of mending she'd borrowed from Lady Rutledge's maid in order to occupy her restless hands, and rose from her chair near the window. She began to pace, again, her footfalls quiet on the fine carpets that covered the floors. She had paced enough to have worn grooves in those fine carpets and holes in her slippers, but she could not bring herself to sit still for another minute.

Lord Haughton and Mr. Winston should have been back by now. She knew little of London geography, but she couldn't imagine their errand to see Lucy should take so many hours. Unless heavy traffic had waylaid them, or Lucy was being particularly truculent, or perhaps they were even having to wait as Lucy packed up her and George's things before returning to the townhouse. Or perhaps...

With a small huff of impatience, she left the drawing room behind her and made her way towards the study. She had seen some writing paper and quills in there, and she thought that writing a letter to Lady Rutledge, even a letter that might never be sent, might work towards settling her anxious mind.

She had her hand on the doorknob when something made her pause. A sound from inside the room caught her attention. Not the sound of a servant tidying or of even Lord Haughton himself moving about the room. It seemed to her ears that there was something... surreptitious about the noise. It was a shuffle, and then a brief clatter, and then silence. Someone, she thought, didn't wish to be heard.

Or perhaps that was only what her anxious mind imagined it to be. The last few days of travel and worry and little rest had no doubt left her wits in an addled state. Shaking her head, she grasped the doorknob with renewed strength, gave it a turn, and opened the door.

One step forward was all she took before her progress was arrested by the sight of David rifling through the papers stacked on the cluttered desk.

"Oh." The small sound slipped out of her mouth before she could stop it. David turned with a start, like a child caught in the act of committing a misdeed. Several expressions crossed his features in the span of a few seconds, from surprise, to embarrassment, and then settling on a furrowed brow that seemed to indicate frustration.

"What are you doing here?" The accusation lacked his usual charm. Gone was his grin, the rakish tilt to his eyebrows. There was no kindness in his tone, nor any of the overdone charm he had exhibited towards her at Denton Castle.

Sophia's mind worked at a rapid pace. David must be here without his brother's knowledge. She glanced at the desk behind him, as if she were looking around for the whereabouts of a tea tray or a missing glove, rather than at the small stack of papers and what appeared to be bank notes sticking out of a plain, brown satchel, one that David seemed to be taking pains to keep from her sight. "Lord Haughton is out this morning," she said, ignoring his question. Though of course he already knew his brother was absent. Why else would he be here now, searching through his brother's things?

"You're supposed to be in Stantreath." David took a step towards her. "Your sister said you were in Stantreath."

Sophia did not leave the doorway, neither did she close the door behind her. Lord Haughton may not be there, but at least there was a household full of servants stalking the floors above and below her. Should she need their assistance for any reason, all she would have to do is call out for one of them.

"So you have seen Lucy," she said. Her fingers were still on the doorknob, her knuckles swiftly turning from red to white as she gripped the cool metal. "And George, I assume? He is well? He has not been harmed in any way?"

"Geo—?" David regarded her strangely, before his eyes widened in recognition. "Oh, you mean the child? Yes, he's well, I suppose. Noisy, sticky thing, but he seems to be all right. For an infant, that is."

His callous remarks angered her, but she drew in a slow breath and tamped down any vitriol before it could spill out of her mouth and make the situation more precarious than it had already become. "So how did my sister so neatly effect her flight from Stantreath? With your help?"

"Of course." David shrugged, a return of his more familiar rakish attitude lending a tilt to his eyebrows. "We made good time, for the most part, though traveling with a woman and a child in tow does tend to slow one down what with all those damned stops for new horses or a wheel stuck in the mud."

She again glanced at the satchel. The bag appeared to be filled with a fair number of items, if its lumps and stretched seams were any indication. And was that a piece of silver she saw peeking out from one corner? "What now? You'll demand money from your brother in exchange for George's return? Or do you plan on keeping him? Tucking him into your pocket so you can bring him out again whenever you find yourself low on funds?"

David crossed the room towards her. Nothing in his movements appeared threatening. To be honest, he looked too tired and drawn to do more than push his hand through his hair and send out a string of curses from under his breath. "Your sister says you want the child. Well, you can have him. And Finn..." His expression soured at mention of his older brother. "He's taken with you, for whatever godforsaken reason I cannot fathom." He took another step forward, placing himself near enough to touch her should he only stretch out his arm. "But then, Finn always did have peculiar tastes. Red hair," he said, almost more to himself than for her benefit. His mouth curled in disgust as he eyed her hair, braided and pinned into a simple coronet around her head. "That would be just like him."

Sophia pulled herself up to her full height, taller than what was fashionable, she knew, and so she wondered if he would have any derogatory comments to make about that as well. Instead he seemed to deflate a little before he turned away and walked back to the desk. "No, you and my brother can have the brat, for all I care. Hell, the two of you can marry, raise him as your son, mold him into a miniature of my big brother. God help us if the next generation isn't complete with its own array of pompous asses throwing their unsolicited opinions at every poor sap to cross their path." He picked up the satchel and slung it over his shoulder. A tinkling sound from inside it confirmed her suspicion that it wasn't merely filled with bits of paper. "But if you want your nephew back in your arms, then Finn will find he has to agree to my terms. And if he doesn't..." David returned to the doorway, standing close enough to Sophia that she pressed her back against the door in order to put more space between them. "I'm sure you can convince my brother to see sense. If he truly is smitten with you, and you're already here beneath his roof... Well, what's a night or two in his bed in exchange for the return of your beloved nephew?"

She did not pause long enough to ponder whether or not she should strike him. The sound of her hand slapping the lower half of his face rang through the hall. She had never struck anyone before, and the pain that reverberated through her own fingers at the harsh contact drew a gasp from her own lips.

David winced and raised a hand to rub the part of his jaw she'd injured. "Yes, you and Finn do make a pair, don't you?" He stepped back, gave her a mocking bow and even clicked his heels together as he did so. As he straightened up again, Sophia saw the outline of her hand showing up as a vivid red splotch on his cheek. "Now, if you'll excuse me. I'd rather not be here when my brother returns from his little meeting with your sister. She may not be his type, but perhaps she's already managed to loosen the strings of his purse. I've found her to be rather persuasive when she puts her mind and, well, other parts to the task."

The leering grin on his face almost drew Sophia's hand to his cheek a second time, but before she could pull back her arm for another strike, a sound from behind David caught her attention. She leaned to one side and saw Lord Haughton standing in the hall, still wearing his coat and hat. But it was the small bundle in his arms that made her catch her breath. Her George, tucked half-inside his coat, his chubby, red cheek pressed to Haughton's breast as he napped against him.

"Oh, heavens." She raced across the hall, her encounter with David forgotten as she reached out to take the infant from him.

"He is unharmed," Lord Haughton assured her and passed the sleeping child into her arms. George let out a soft snore, smacked his drooling lips, and wiggled his bottom peacefully into Sophia's embrace. "And your sister... Well, we'll discuss everything at a more appropriate time."

Sophia pressed her cheek to the top of George's head and inhaled deeply. "Thank you," she said, her voice trembling with an entire catalog of emotions. She glanced up into Lord Haughton's face, at the tired blue eyes she had once thought to be so cold, so devoid of feeling. But there was something there now, something she was too exhausted, too overwhelmed with the events of the last few days to identify. "Thank you."

He nodded, nothing more. When he finally tore his gaze away from her face and glanced at the man still hovering behind them, he placed a hand on her shoulder and directed her towards the stairs. "Take him upstairs. Rest, eat, whatever you need. I have a few small matters to attend to, and then we can sort things out."

She glanced back over her shoulder at David, huddling in the doorway of the study, his shoulders hunched forward and his feet shuffling on the tile floor as if he were a recalcitrant schoolboy rather than a grown man. At the stairs, she met Mr. Winston, who gave her a nod and a "Good day, Mrs. Brixton," before she began the climb up to her room.

Once inside the bright, spacious bedroom, she sat on the edge of the bed, holding George to her chest. He was a sound enough sleeper that she could've put him down without disturbing him, but she had no desire to let him out of her arms until she could convince herself that he wouldn't be snatched away from her again. After a few minutes, she laid down on her side, tucking George against her as she drew her knees up and slid her feet beneath the edge of her skirt. She touched his cheek, the tip of his nose, traced the delicate shell of his ear with fingers that still trembled with the remnants of the morning's excitement.

"I do love you so," she whispered, before she closed her eyes, draped an arm over the sleeping infant, and followed him into slumber.

Chapter Twenty-Three

Sophia awoke when George did, his soft fussing drawing her from a deep, dreamless sleep. She glanced at the clock on the mantel. Only an hour had passed since she'd fallen asleep, and yet it seemed as if she'd slept the entire day away. Her head was foggy, and when George rubbed his eyes with his fists and crawled into her lap, she could summon no more thought or energy necessary than what it took to place her arms around him.

Oh, but he was filthy, she realized as she looked down at him, surveying him properly for the first time since Lord Haughton had placed him in her arms. Dried food clung to the ends of his fine hair, making it stand up in tangled tufts. His clothes, if she was not mistaken, were the same as the ones she had dressed him in the day Lucy had spirited him away from Stantreath. And his bottom...

There was a large damp spot on his clothes, one that had spread to the coverlet on the bed where he'd taken his nap. And on her skirt, she noticed as she picked him up and gave him a sniff.

"Pah!" she said. "When were you last changed?" She hoisted him onto her hip, regardless of the wetness he was continuing to spread to her own clothing, and gave the bell a hard pull. When the maid arrived, she ordered a bath, fresh clothing for George, and food for the both of them. Heaven only knew how well he'd been fed over the last few days, though if he was capable of soiling himself as well as he had, at least she was assured that he hadn't starved.

Another hour slipped away in caring for George, washing and combing the bits of food and miscellaneous debris from his hair, and changing her own gown for one not bearing damp patches all around it. After they ate, George devouring his bread soaked in milk with particular avariciousness, Sophia finally found the courage to inquire if Lord Haughton was still at home, or if anyone—she would not mention David's name—was still with him.

"He's in with Mr. Thompkins now," the maid informed her, as she changed the coverlet on the bed. "That's his solicitor, ma'am. They've been in there with their heads together for a good hour or more."

"And..." Sophia cleared her throat. "There is no one else... with him?"

"Not that I know of, ma'am. That Mr. Winston fellow departed only a few minutes after he arrived, him and his lordship's brother both in the same carriage."

"Oh." Sophia didn't know what to think of that. But it was a relief, to be sure, knowing that David was no longer beneath the same roof as them. "Well, thank you."

The maid finished her task, bobbed a curtsy as if Sophia were actually someone of importance, and left her and George alone again.

So David was sent on his way already, and in Mr. Winston's custody, for lack of a better term. And what of Lucy? Had Lord Haughton seen her? What had her sister said? And more importantly, what had he said that enabled him to return to the house with George sleeping so peacefully in his arms? Her sister would not have given up the boy without a fight, or a rather large sum of money.

She sat down in the middle of the bedroom floor with George, one of the maids having searched through the attics and found a few old, wooden toys that must have been leftover from when Lord Haughton and his siblings were children. The paint was worn off most of them, but George was delighted to have new blocks to stack and knock over, and an army of wooden soldiers to wave about until Sophia finally had to pry one from each of his hands before he poked himself in the eye with the dull end of a wooden musket.

Yet another hour slipped away, Sophia spending her time chasing George about the room as he attempted to toddle forward a few steps on wobbling legs before he dropped into a crawl that shot him from one end of the rug to the other faster than she could keep pace with him. She snatched him into her arms after following him around on all fours, growling like a bear, and had rolled onto her side with him, the both of them giggling as she tickled him beneath his arms, when she suddenly glanced up and saw Lord Haughton standing in the doorway.

"I did knock," he said, by way of apology, though his dark eyebrows were raised in amusement at the scene before him.

And what a scene it must be to him, Sophia realized, as a flush of colour warmed her cheeks. Rolling about on the floor, her hair falling out of its simple twist, and her skirt...

She yanked at the hem, which had worked its way up to her knees during her game with George. "I am sorry," she muttered, her gaze fixed firmly on anything that wasn't Lord Haughton's face as she attempted to surreptitiously fix one of her stockings that had worked itself free of its garter. "I didn't mean to...I didn't realize you had knocked. I didn't hear..." Her hands fluttered uselessly, her fingers glancing over her sleeves, her bodice, any and every other part of her gown that might have twisted itself around.

"Please, Sophia. Don't apologize." His voice was nearer, she realized. He was nearer. "Never before have I interrupted a more beautiful scene."

Her gaze flicked towards his face. The amusement was gone from his expression, replaced by...what, she could not tell. She swallowed, hard, and raised a hand to her hair. Too many strands had already fallen out of their pins, and there was nothing to be done unless she started over from scratch. "Your brother," she began. It was the first thing she could think of to say, and the best subject to divert him from his enigmatic expressions and the husky timbre to his voice. She was not sure she knew what to do with him if he wasn't going to be cold and distant with her.

"He is gone," Lord Haughton assured her, and held out a hand to help her to her feet when she began to stand up on her own. "I sent him away with Winston. I'll deal with him later, when I'm not so angry that violence seems like a sensible solution."

She hesitated, then slipped her hand into his. His fingers were warm, or hers were cool, she could not tell. There were callouses on the pads of his fingertips, on his palms, and she wondered what work or hobby it took to put them there. His thumb slid over the tops of her knuckles, then the back of her hand, before he touched the inside of her wrist. An accidental touch, she assumed. But there was that mysterious expression again. Thinking back, she recalled him looking at her in a similar manner once or twice during her stay at Denton Castle, but at the time she had been too wrapped up in her own dislike of him to consider what thoughts might lie behind that expression.

At their feet, George continued to tumble about, knocking over soldiers and blocks indiscriminately before setting them up again. He did not release her hand, but led her over to one of the chairs near the window.

"I've spoken with my solicitor," he began, and settled himself in the chair adjacent to her own. "Your sister has accepted the sum of five thousand pounds in exchange for giving full care of her son over to you. What she does with it, whether she buys her house and fills it with servants, or spends it all on befeathered hats is entirely up to her."

Sophia gazed at him in astonishment for several seconds. "Five thousand? How...? I can never repay so much. You should not have—"

He held up his hand. "He is my nephew as well, remember?"

She nodded, then swallowed over the rapidly forming lump in her throat. There would be tears soon, if she was not careful. "So she did not show any interest in raising George? In seeing him again?"

He hesitated. Unfortunately, that was all the reply she needed. "Perhaps she will settle down when she is older, when she has matured." She could hope, though Lord Haughton's younger brother was several years Lucy's senior and was not exactly proof that a few additional years were enough to bring wisdom. "Much older," she added, and cleared her throat of the tremble that might have been either the beginning of a laugh or a sob.

They sat together in silence as the mantel clock ticked away another five minutes. Before them, George alternated between attempts to walk and quick bouts of crawling accompanied by shrieking laughter as he pushed through rows of blocks and sent them scattering in all directions.

"And what of your brother?" Sophia ventured to ask when she was certain she could trust her voice again.

There was that hesitation again. "To tell the truth," he began, and rested his elbows on the arms of the chair before steepling his fingers in front of his chest. "I have yet to decide what course of action to take with him. I could force him into the army, though I fear his ability to wreak just as much havoc while wearing a uniform as he does without one. But he is my brother. Bess would wish me to be lenient, or at least not so harsh that we cut him out of our lives forever. It is fine line, I think, and it's difficult to see on which side lies the proper choice."

Sophia held out her arms to George as he crawled over to her and began to clamber up into her lap. Without delay, he started plucking at the buttons of her dress, grunting in frustration when they wouldn't immediately pop off into his chubby fingers. "I will see Lucy again," she said, and smoothed down a patch of George's hair that was determined to stick straight out from his head.

She had spoken the words without giving them a thought, but as soon as she heard them with her own ears, she trusted the truth of them. She would see her sister again, be it a matter of a few days or a few years, but she would see her again. Though the two of them were often at odds with one another, they did care about each other. They loved each other. And Sophia hoped that Lucy loved George. No, she knew that her sister loved her son. She simply wasn't ready to be a mother, or if that would ever be a role she was meant to fulfill.

"And what of you?" Lord Haughton's question broke through the fog of her thoughts. "Will you return to Stantreath now?"

"Yes," she replied, and looked up quickly enough to see a shadow of despondency darken his brow. "But," she continued, her gaze still on his face. "If the offer still stands, I think I would like to return to Denton Castle. If not permanently, at least for an extended stay."

His shoulders visibly relaxed. "Of course, I will write to my sister at once, let her know of your plans."

"Thank you." She kissed George's head before he squirmed out of her lap and took three steps away from her before dropping again to all fours. "I will, of course, need time to pack up my things, to give my farewell to Lady Rutledge, but I cannot imagine that should take up more than a few days. The cottage is small and there is not a lot in it, as I'm sure you remember."

She tried to smile, but failed miserably in the attempt. Now that George had been returned to her, now that Lucy had been given what she wanted, now that David was under the watchful eye of Mr. Winston, and the decision finally voiced aloud that she would be returning to Denton Castle, it seemed all the former impediments of their acquaintance had been cleared away. He was no longer the cold, haughty member of the peerage come to impose his rule on her. She was welcome in his home—homes, she amended to herself—and even sat with her now, quietly, companionably, as if their first meeting had not been heated enough that she had been sorely tempted to strike him.

"I will leave you now, as I'm sure you're still exhausted. You'll need your rest if your intention is to leave tomorrow." He rose from his chair as she did and bowed towards her. "Sleep well, and I will see you in the morning, if not before."

She stood there as he left the room, only a step forward from her chair while George continued to scatter toys and crawl in and out from beneath the hem of her skirt. Lord Haughton had only been courteous in coming to speak to her, only wanting her to feel welcome and wanted after all the difficulties of the last few days. But she couldn't help feeling that something had shifted in their acquaintance. That enigmatic expression on his face, the light in his eyes that she had so much difficulty trying to identify...

He's taken with you...

David's words flickered through her mind. She tried to assure herself that he had said such things solely to unnerve her. There couldn't be any truth to it, surely not. But still she played those words over and over in her mind, even as she knelt down onto the rug and began lining up the wooden soldiers for George.

He's taken with you...

She thought of Lord Haughton's eyes, how cold they had always seemed to be, so many weeks ago. She realized she hadn't seen that same chill in them for quite some time. And when she'd slipped her hand into his only a few moments ago, she'd had the distinct feeling that he hadn't wanted to let go.

"No," Sophia said aloud, and tried to shake such thoughts out of her head. Her exhaustion was getting to her. That must be it, nothing more. Once the preparations for her return to Stantreath were made, and she was once again on the road with George tucked in beside her, well... everything would be so much clearer, she was sure. No more muddled thoughts or idle fancies that Lord Haughton—Haughton, of all people!—was falling in love with her.

"No, certainly not," she said, and bit at the soft flesh inside her bottom lip. And she definitely wouldn't pause to wonder why that repeated assurance should bring out such a dismal feeling from within her.

Chapter Twenty-Four

Finnian peered out the window of his coach. They had already made the turn through the gates, the wide, even lane that led up to the main house curving smoothly into the trees and out of sight.

The first leg of his journey from London to Derbyshire had been a trial, the rain becoming a ceaseless impediment, rendering the roads nearly impassable until the worst of the deluge had passed. At one point, several miles outside of Luton, he had considered ordering the driver to turn them around and begin the journey back towards London, but he demolished that thought before he could give it a voice.

He'd already written to Bess and informed her of his impending arrival. Should he fail to show himself at the end of the designated frame of time allotted for his journey, no doubt his sister would send out a search party in order to ensure he hadn't tumbled headlong into ditch somewhere along the way.

Bess had written to him to inform him of Sophia and George's arrival at Denton Castle, and then proceeded to write every other day for the following three weeks. From Sophia herself, he'd received not a word. In fact, the last he'd seen her had been when he'd helped her into a carriage in front of his townhouse in St. James's street. A word to the footman, and the step was put up, the door closed, and she began her journey back to Stantreath.

The farewell had been remarkably short, a perfunctory demonstration of all things they'd both been trained to say in such a situation. A wish for a safe and pleasant journey. A few words of gratitude from her for his help. A slight squeeze of her gloved hand and a brief tousle of George's hair, and nothing more.

He'd done nothing to delay her. Her intentions to leave London as soon as possible could not have been clearer. That she'd hoped to receive some word from her sister, he did not doubt. But though several notes were sent out to Lucy's place of lodging, no reply had been forthcoming. Her sister, having achieved her promise of five thousand pounds, seemed to no longer crave further communication with the rest of her family.

Finnian glanced out the window again, the brilliance of the afternoon sun dappling the graveled lane with rays of light that shone through the branches of the trees. At the edge of his view, a large stream wound its way through the woods, its swollen surface catching the light as it snaked towards a stone arch bridge over which the carriage rumbled only a few minutes later.

The house would be the next thing to come into view. Rolling lawns and stately elms forming a frame to his childhood home. But he let the shade fall back into place. He leaned back in his seat, his eyes closed as he pressed his head against the quilted upholstery behind him. He would arrive at the door, and a flutter of activity would commence. And there would be Bess in the midst of it all, ready to chastise him for not arriving sooner. As if he had not had more than enough business with which to occupy his time before he could deem it prudent to depart from London.

The carriage rolled to a halt. The usual shouts began, along with a tilting of the vehicle as driver and footmen climbed down and changed positions and immediately began to remove his luggage. The door opened, the steps were lowered, and he emerged into near blinding sunlight. He raised his hand to the brim of his hat as he squinted against the glow, made even brighter by the jewels of moisture that still stubbornly clung to every stone and blade of grass.

He glanced towards the front doors of the house, fully expecting his sister to rush out to meet him. But there was no sign that Bess had even been alerted of his arrival. And so he went indoors, passing his hat and coat to the butler while he inwardly bristled at such a silent welcome. Without realizing it, he'd become accustomed to the flurry of conversation and tea things being foisted on him within minutes of his arrival in Derbyshire.

"Is my sister at home?" Finnian asked as his gloves were also taken from him.

"Yes, my lord." The butler handed off the various accoutrements of Finnian's outerwear to a nearby footman. "She is..." The elderly retainers brow furrowed slightly. "Outside, I believe. With Mrs. Brixton. They are taking the air before dinner."

"And do you happen to know where their search for air has taken them?"

"They began in the rose garden, my lord. But where they may have gone from there, I could not say."

Finnian nodded and instead of heading towards his study or upstairs to his suite of rooms as the butler seemed to assume, he passed through the main part of the house and let himself out onto the terrace that provided a fine view of several of the gardens and a portion of the lawn that led down towards the lake.

The grass was still wet from the rain, though a breeze had picked up that would no doubt dry everything before night fell and a damp chill could set in. He strode in the direction of the rose garden, but changed his mind at the last minute, instead veering towards the edge of the lake, not far from where they'd had their picnic some weeks before.

He found no sign of them there, and neither could he discern them on the path that led down through the trees and towards what had been one of his father's favorite fishing spots. Looping around, he worked his way up the low hill that backed the house, his destination a folly commissioned by his mother, a structure that would afford him a view of half the park.

His boots were soaked when he arrived at the top of the hill, and coated with bits of leaves and grass he'd accumulated during the walk. His valet would not be pleased with the state of his dress when he returned to the house to prepare for dinner, but any consideration for his servant's sensibilities were banished from his thoughts as the folly came into view, inside of which were seated his sister and Sophia.

The edifice was a crumbling thing, though its age could be traced back to within his own lifetime. The ruin of the piece was all a pretense, an act of architectural artifice, and Finnian would have had the small building, with its cracked columns and tumbledown roof, demolished and taken away once his father had passed away, but for the fact that Bess had taken a liking to the folly and visited it regularly during her daily walks out of doors.

Bess, he saw, immediately spied his approach. A broad smile stretched across her face, and she waved him over with her hand. Sophia, who was turned partially away from him and so had not detected his climb up the side of the hill, looked back over her shoulder and saw him.

Her lips parted a little. He noticed that first. But she closed her mouth again quickly enough, her back straightening and her chin lifting as she shifted in her seat. She did not smile as his sister had, but neither did his arrival appear to cause her any sort of consternation. For that, at least, he told himself to be grateful.

He stepped up to the edge of the folly, the sun at his back as he bowed to both ladies. Bess nearly leaped up from her seat in her eagerness to embrace him, while Sophia nodded politely in return, her gaze never leaving his face.

"How intolerable of you to make us wait for such a time!" Bess stepped back from him enough to give his arm a pinch, before she rose onto the balls of her feet and kissed his cheek. "I'm sure you'll regale us with all of your tales of bad roads and worse inns and bridges torn from their foundations by floods of most biblical proportions, but you're here now, and I refuse to allow you to leave again until you've spent enough time away from London to erase those dark smudges from beneath your eyes. Sophia!" She turned towards her companion while keeping one arm tucked against her brother's side. "Doesn't he look in need of a rest? All the time he spends in town has aged him beyond his years, and I think we should do everything within our power to keep him here until he's regained a bit of health and colour in his cheeks."

Sophia wasn't given a chance to reply, Bess having commandeered both the conversation and where she believed he should sit, which just happened to be in the place his sister had abandoned only a moment ago, directly beside Sophia.

Finnian looked up at Bess, though he could detect nothing in her expression that gave away her intentions to make a match of the two of them. But he knew his sister, and despite every effort she'd made in her numerous letters to avoid the subject, he'd caught the subtle hints scattered across her lines referring to her desire for him to settle down and find himself a wife, a wish that was always closely followed by a long list of Sophia's charms.

But he didn't need his sister to tell him of what he was already well aware, though he wasn't sure Bess knew how often Sophia had invaded his thoughts over the last several weeks. Bess, he assumed, had taken it upon herself to ignite a spark, but he doubted his sister perceived that a fire had already been kindled long before.

"And where is George?" He managed to slip the question into a brief lull in Bess's commentary. He looked towards Sophia, who lowered her eyes and fidgeted with her hands in her lap before she began to speak.

"Sleeping, perhaps. Though he might be awake by now. I had just put him down for his afternoon nap when your sister suggested a walk, since the rain kept us confined to the house for the last several days."

He watched her as she spoke. She looked better than when he had last seen her, after the stress of finding George and dealing with David and her sister. Now she looked rested, vibrant, and lovely enough to make him wish his sister far away.

Sophia looked at him again, her eyes catching the light of the afternoon sun as it dipped low enough to shine beneath the roof of the folly. Her chest rose and she opened her mouth as if to speak again, but a glance at Bess made her hesitate.

"I received a letter," she began, and paused long enough to unclasp and clasp her hands again. "I received a letter from my sister earlier this week. It was the first she had written to me since—" She cleared her throat and pressed on, though Finnian wondered how much of the situation Bess knew aside from what he'd told her himself. "Well, she's returned to Bath, and set herself up very well. She has undertaken the role of a companion to an elderly spinster, the sister of a marquess, if I am not mistaken. From what I gather, the role affords her access to all of the fine parties and entertainments Bath has to offer."

A line appeared between her eyes, the only sign that her sister's current life caused her some distress.

"And she is happy there, you believe?" he asked, the question making another line appear across Sophia's brow.

"I do," she said, and met his gaze, her face again clear of the shadow that had passed over it before. "And I find that I want nothing but for her to find some happiness. I would not have wished her to remain in Stantreath, to force herself into a role for which she was not suited if it would only bring her misery. In turn, all of us would have been made miserable, and there could have been no good in that."

Whether she believed in the truth of her words or only spoke them out loud in order to make herself believe them, he could not be sure. But a small smile teased the corners of her mouth, and in reply he sent up a silent request towards Heaven that Miss Lucy Penrose would indeed find some happiness, if only for her sister's sake.

"Oh, goodness!" Bess chimed in, and clapped her hands together beneath her chin. "I nearly forgot! I was to meet with Mrs. Ketchum this afternoon and go over the menus for next week, now that Finn will be with us." She stood, muslin and lace and embroidered rosettes twirling as she gathered her shawl about her shoulders and gestured for Finnian to remain seated. "No, no. You stay here and give Sophia some company. I would not wish to cut her walk short simply because I lost track of the time."

Bess was gone before either of them could protest, though he knew any sort of argument against his sister's behavior would be as effective as shouting at a mountain in the hopes that it would lift its roots from the ground and step aside. He would not be in the least surprised to discover that Bess had no planned meeting with the housekeeper at all, and was simply contriving to toss the two of them together.

He watched Bess walk down the hill, towards the house. Once he was certain she was far enough away to not overhear them, he returned his attention to Sophia. Her gaze had found someplace beyond the artfully deteriorating walls of the folly to fix upon, the breeze stirring the fiery curls of her hair that touched her neck and the high, ruffled collar of her gown.

"Are you well?" he asked, and waited for her reply.

He watched as her chest rose, her nostrils flaring slightly as she drew in a deep breath. "I am, yes," she said, without turning to look at him. "Your sister has been most kind, doing everything in her power to make George and I feel at home here."

"And does it feel like home to you?"

She turned the full force of her gaze on him then. "Not yet. George, of course, behaves as if he has never been anywhere else. But he is so young. He won't remember any of what happened before we arrived here." Her brow furrowed. "And I think I envy him that."

There was more, he thought. He could see the troubles etched in every line of her face. He had a sudden wish to wipe those cares away, or more specifically, to possess the power to achieve such an end. "I've heard from David, or I should say that Winston has apprised me of my brother's arrival in Toulouse, though where he'll wander from there, I cannot say."

"Do you expect him to stay on the Continent for any considerable length of time?"

Finnian shrugged. "Things have settled there over the last year, and as long as he continues to receive his allowance in a timely manner, I cannot see any reason why he would wish to return to England and what he perceives as my tyrannical rule."

Her mouth moved as if she would speak, before it transformed into a grimace. "I've no doubt Lucy viewed my behavior in a similar light. I think she resented my taking charge of everything after our parents died, but I had little choice."

"But were there no relatives, no aunts or cousins to step in and fill the breach left by your parents' demise? I cannot imagine two young ladies, left without someone to protect them."

Sophia pulled in another breath and let it drift away from her on a sigh. "The few relatives of which we knew could not afford to take us in. I considered seeking employment, as a governess or nurse, but I could not leave Lucy. And then when she discovered she was with child... Well, what penniless cousin would have anything to do with us then?"

I'm sorry. He nearly said the words out loud, but he had no wish for her to think he was uttering nothing more than the standard niceties expected of him. Instead, he reached out and took her hand. She wore no gloves, and her fingers were cool even though she'd had them tucked in her lap for the last few minutes. When she did not immediately pull her hand away, he turned her hand upwards in order to trace the lines in her palm with his thumb.

He dared not raise his eyes to look at her face. As bold as he had been when he'd first met her, barging into her home like a bull, and now the slightest change in her expression held the potential to destroy him.

He gave no thought to his actions, but only continued to sit there, her hand in his, his fingers gliding over the rough patches on her skin that gave away the difficulties of the life she'd led before arriving in Derbyshire a few weeks before. Eventually, he thought, those callouses on the pads of her fingers, on her palms, would fade. Her knuckles would be smooth again, her brittle nails no longer bearing the evidence of having done her own washing for the last several years.

His thumb slid over the heel of her hand and up to her wrist, where the freckled skin of her forearm disappeared beneath the printed cotton of her sleeve. "I should walk you back to the house." Still, he did not glance up at her face. Her skin mesmerized him, and he feared that should he release her hand, he would lose something that might never be returned to him.

"My lord," she began, but he shook his head.

"Please don't call me that." He lifted his gaze to meet hers, the afternoon light glinting off the red and gold in her eyelashes. He wondered if she knew how beautiful she was, or at least how beautiful she was to him. He had been given the impression that Sophia thought her sister to be the great beauty in their family. But Lucy, with her soft curves and pouting lips, stirred nothing inside of him. It was Sophia he could not banish from his thoughts. Sophia, with the fire in her hair and the liberal sprinkling of freckles across her cheeks.

"Your sister has been very kind to me," she said, and withdrew her hand from his grasp. The abrupt change in subject was as unexpected as a glass of water splashed into his face. "I could not have imagined feeling more welcome, more...a part of a place, of another person's life. Outside the realm of my own family, that is."

"As opposed to myself, do you mean?" The words slipped out, a reaction to her movement away from him. And though he had added a touch of lightness to his voice, there was a seriousness to his question that drained some of the illumination from Sophia's face. "No, no. Do not attempt to deny it," he went on before she could interrupt. "I am well aware of the sort of behavior I subjected you to earlier in our acquaintance."

"Well." She cleared her throat. "I wouldn't say—"

"I was a boor. And I gave not a thought to the ideas or wants of anyone but myself."

"Yes." She said finally, and again folded her hands in her lap. "You were, and you did not." Her gaze lifted from her lap and met his. "But despite the way you went about it, your motives, I believe, were in defense of your family. And since then, you have done so much to prove that you are not the villain I at first perceived you to be. If not for you—"

"If not for me," he interrupted again, feeling wholly disgruntled with the direction the conversation had taken. "You would still be in Stantreath with George. I would never have caused even the slightest ripple to disturb the life you'd made for yourself there. Your sister—"

"My sister acted of her own free will. It had nothing to do with you."

But Finnian shook his head as she spoke. "I spoke with my brother. This entire... scheme they concocted came about because of David finding out about his son, finding out about *you.* Which would not have happened if you had not been in Derbyshire when you were, a journey that ultimately came about because I blundered into your life several months ago, in order to throw a bit of money at you so that I might never have to deal with you again." At that last comment, he inwardly recoiled. What if she had accepted his offer when he'd first met her in Northumberland? What if that had been the beginning and end of their acquaintance, aside from the most emotionless of notes and instructions passed from solicitor to solicitor?

But she hadn't accepted his offer. If she had, she would have proven herself to be a different person than the one sitting across from him now, a person with whom he would never have fallen in love.

"I am thoroughly ashamed of the behavior I exhibited to you earlier this year," he said, still holding out his hand, as if her own still resided within in. "And I find I must ask for your forgiveness, even if you have no inclination to provide it."

She sighed, and when she looked at him again, he noticed the flecks of green and gold twining together in her eyes. He wanted to tell her that she was beautiful, that at some point during their unusual, tumultuous acquaintance, he had fallen in love with her. But the words necessary to make such a proclamation would not rise to his lips. Was it her rejection he feared? Or that any advances on his part would frighten her off her plan of remaining at Denton Castle?

"It was not your sudden appearance on my doorstep that threw our existence into chaos." She tapped her thumbs against each other, and when he glanced down, he noticed the toe of her right foot bouncing out a similar rhythm. "You forget that Stantreath is not even our original home, but a place we retreated to in order to escape the scandal George's birth brought down on our heads. You forget that I lied, putting myself forward as a widow and claiming George as my own son, to free my sister from the stigma of bearing a child outside of marriage." A soft sound escaped from her throat. Finnian almost took it for a chuckle. "We both of us did all we could to sweep our siblings' transgressions beneath the rug instead of tackling them directly, no matter what our neighbours might have whispered about us behind their hands. And look at where it's brought us! My sister and your brother, driven to stealing their own child in order to ransom him for a small fortune."

He raised one eyebrow. "Do you mean to say you blame yourself for your sister's behavior?"

"No," she confessed. "At least, not entirely. But can you tell me with all honesty that you have never once gone back over the course of your brother's life and thought about what you or your family might have done differently in order to bring everyone to a different outcome?"

He leaned back in his seat, as far as the stiff, unyielding stone of the seat would allow. "I cannot."

She swallowed, then cleared her throat before speaking. "It may surprise you to hear me say it, but I've begun to entertain the notion that you and I... Well, that we share some common traits, at least as far as our characters are concerned."

Was she mocking him in some way? He watched her, but there was no sign in her manner or expression that she was about to lash out at him with her tongue.

"We are both the firstborn children in our families," she explained, apparently impervious to the look of incredulity creasing his brow. "And we each bear the brunt of responsibility that comes with such a position."

When he said nothing in response, if indeed she expected him to provide one, she took up her shawl and her bonnet from the seat beside her and stood up. "It is getting late, and I'm sure that George has already been awake for some time."

As she wrapped the shawl around her shoulders and pulled the bonnet down onto her head, Finnian rose and tugged at his coat, only realizing then that he still wore the same clothes he'd arrived in. Once they both had set themselves to rights, he stepped forward and held out his arm to her, but she made no move towards him.

"A little while ago, you asked for my forgiveness." She held her arms crossed over her chest, the ends of her shawl held tight in her hands. "I believe I'd already pardoned you, for my own benefit, some time ago. But if it is the words themselves you need to hear, then..." She held out her right hand to him, as if she were offering it for nothing more than a simple handshake. "I forgive you," she said. "After all you've done for us, for me and George, while we were in London, and even—"

He grasped her hand fiercely, drawing it upwards before he kissed the tops of her fingers. Another kiss was pressed to the sensitive skin of her palm, before a third one found its way to the inside of her wrist. It was the same path he'd traced earlier with his thumb, and he brought himself to a halt when his cheek brushed against the edge of her sleeve. "Sophia," he said, his breath reflecting off her skin and sweeping across his jaw.

It was the first he'd spoken her name out loud in weeks. Propriety, he knew, would dictate that he refer to her as Mrs. Brixton or Miss Penrose or whichever name she chose to take on for herself. But propriety and its strictures had ruled too much of his life for far too long.

"Sophia," he said again, his gaze never leaving her face. She watched him, her eyes wide, her lips slightly parted as her breathing quickened.

"My lord," she began, but he held up a hand to interrupt her.

"Finn," he corrected her. "If you will."

She licked her lips. How such a small movement possessed the power to affect him so strongly, he could not tell. "Finn," she whispered. "Before you speak... Please..." She shook her head and placed her free hand flat against the center of his chest. "I do not know enough of your life before I entered into it, but allow me to assure you that things will not be easy from here forwards. There will always be George, and you and I would be setting ourselves up as fools if we thought our dealings with my sister and your brother were over and done with. And there are so many other things," she pressed on. "George's illegitimacy, and my lack of status and fortune, and then there is—"

"No."

She blinked.

"No," he repeated. "Think of what you know of me, and ask yourself if any of those things will make me reconsider what I am about to say to you."

Her mouth closed into a firm line. Her gaze dropped to the vicinity of his chin, but when she looked up at him again, he thought he saw something like amusement brightening her features.

"I love you." He put the words out there, tasting them for the first time. "I wish to marry you, though I've no doubt you'll continue to voice every reason why we should not. And yet I cannot comprehend there existing a single one that would matter to me."

Her hand, he realized, still rested against his chest. Slowly, her fingers pulled inward, until she'd formed a loose fist that tapped out a restless rhythm on the front of his waistcoat. "And to think I wanted nothing more than to toss you into a mud puddle the first time you set foot in my home."

Finnian allowed himself to sigh. That she had not grabbed him by his collar and threatened to pitch him into the lake after his declaration had to be taken as a sign in his favor. "Sophia?"

Her mouth quirked, and her gaze again dropped to the level of his neckcloth, battered and flattened by the day's journey as it was. "You're waiting for an answer from me, I know. And it is poor behavior on my part to have given myself so much time to think it over, and yet still not have a ready reply when the topic is finally broached."

"What do you mean...?" he began to say, but she waved his words away with a flick of her fingers.

"You may flatter yourself with the knowledge that I have already allowed my mind to wonder what it would be like to have you as a husband." She laughed, a soft sound that escaped her throat and made him want to kiss her. "But I must admit it is still quite jarring to hear the words spoken out loud."

He ducked his chin until he could see her eyes and the brilliant light that glowed from within them. "And to what conclusion have all your silent ponderings brought you?"

"That your sister would no doubt be the happiest woman in all of Christendom to discover you'd decided to settle down once and for all."

He tossed back his head and laughed. When his mirth subsided, he looked down to find Sophia watching him, her expression more serious than it had been before. He noticed, too, that subtle alteration in the feeling between them. Behind her, the sun dipped lower, the edge of it disappearing beneath the hills that formed a backdrop for the house. Finnian leaned forward, though he did not have far to go. Sophia's hand was trapped between them, her fingers sliding up and plucking idly at the already rumpled folds of his neckcloth before he pressed his lips to her cheek. Her breath warmed his chin as he shifted his mouth to pay equal attention to her other cheek, and then he kissed her lips, parted as they were, her teeth still tugging at the inside of her bottom lip until she tilted her head up to better meet his.

She was not a slight thing, certainly not a wisp of a female to wilt in his arms the minute his hand found its way to her waist, and yet his first inclination was to hold her as if she were the most ethereal of creatures, ready to dissipate when his fingers sought out greater purchase. But instead of fading away, Sophia stepped into him, the hand that had been making a further mess of his neckcloth sliding over his collar to brush the edges of his hair.

This woman, he realized, and no other.

By the time he pulled away from her, the sun had disappeared below the horizon. The glow of an early summer twilight still lit the sky above, but a definite chill had seeped into the air along with the loss of daylight.

"Your sister will send out a search party for us if we tarry much longer," Sophia said, her voice strangely quiet against the cacophony of crickets and other insects that had sprung to life once the first few stars lit up in the eastern half of the sky.

"Then you don't know Bess," he mused, and tucked an errant curl of hair behind her ear. "No doubt she's already settled herself before the fire, and is dandling George on her knee while she crows to herself about her abilities at making a match between the two of us." Finnian lowered his head and kissed her again, this time a light brush of his lips on her brow.

"I still haven't given you an answer," she reminded him as he slipped out of his coat and draped it over her shoulders.

He said nothing as he offered his arm to her. She took it without hesitation, her fingers warm on his sleeve. Leave it to her to draw out his suffering for as long as possible. If she did agree to be his wife, she would always keep him from becoming too complacent. Which was undoubtedly one of the reasons he found her so attractive.

"George will most likely be in my care until he is grown." She turned to face him, her shoulders rising and falling inside the folds of his coat. "I have always looked upon him as I assume I would my own children. But he is your brother's son. Will you be able to raise him as a father should, without any of your difficulties with David marring your opinion of him?"

He sought out her hands, raising both of them to his lips in order to kiss the tips of her fingers. "I will do my best. That is all I can promise."

"And that is all I will ever ask of you." She shifted forward onto the balls of her feet and kissed him, her hands slipping out of his grasp in order to frame his face with them. "It is all either of us can promise to each other," she whispered against his lips, and kissed him again.

She took his arm when he offered it, and they began the walk back down the hill and across the lawn towards the house. The windows were already lit with the glow from the candles and fires in the various rooms, the preparations for dinner well underway. They halted on the terrace, the doors only a few paces ahead of them.

He kissed her once more, away from the light that spilled out through the windows. "So, shall you be the one to tell my sister, or should I?"

"Together," Sophia said, and shrugged out of his coat in order to return it to him before they went inside. "And not until after at the least the first course. Should she discover it before then, I doubt we'll be permitted to sit down to a proper meal for the remainder of the evening."

"Very good," he remarked, while attempting to bite down on his smile. "I'll meet you in the drawing room?"

"Agreed." A dip of her head, a smile of her own, and she slipped inside, pausing only long enough to glance at him over her shoulder, the previous lines of stress replaced by a slight crinkling at the corners of her eyes. Lines of happiness, he realized. And he—cold, boorish fellow she'd once accused him of being—had been the one to put them there.

Acknowledgments

I'm sure everyone says this, but there are really are too many people to thank. But I'll go ahead and try, because I like to prove folks wrong.

To Kay, Ash, and Mandy. Not only my editors, cover designer, and proofreaders, but the ones who listen to me meeble when the self-doubt attacks and who are ready and waiting to attack it right back.

To everyone else from World Tree and that-place-formerly-known-as-Breaking-Quills, for all of your friendship, your support, your late night chats, your amazing advice and support as I fledged my way into becoming a full-time author.

And finally to my family, for putting up with me when a fresh, shiny plot sinks its claws into my brain and supporting me through all of this. The house is a mess and you don't care. You have no idea how much that means to me.

Also from World Tree Publishing and Quenby Olson:

Knotted

When seventeen-year-old Olivia Davies receives a phone call from her estranged father in the middle of the night, she's in for a huge shock. Her father is getting married - again - and he wants her to be at the wedding. So over summer break, Olivia packs her bags and makes the trip back to England to meet her future stepmother. But instead of the middle-aged woman she expected, Olivia finds herself introduced to Emmy Balfour, a stunning blonde young enough to be her sister. And if that wasn't enough, she also finds herself dealing with the disapproval of Emmy's older brother, Ian, a man for whom "polite" and "respect" seem to be four-letter words.

With only three weeks until the wedding, Olivia struggles to stay afloat while navigating the treacherous waters of wedding planners, aristocracy, and bridesmaid's dresses - not to mention the bridesmaids in the dresses. But just when she thinks everything is finally settling down, a few well-timed lies threaten to destroy her father's chance at happiness. As a last resort, Olivia must work with Ian in an attempt to set things right, a partnership that forces her to decide if keeping him at a distance or disregarding her first impressions of him will cause her to step up and make a few changes in her own life.

The Half Killed

Dorothea Hawes has no wish to renew contact with what lies beyond the veil. After an attempt to take her own life, she has retired into seclusion, but as the wounds on her body heal, she is drawn back into a world she wants nothing more than to avoid.

She is sought out by Julian Chissick, a former man of God who wants her help in discovering who is behind the gruesome murder of a young woman. But the manner of death is all too familiar to Dorothea, and she begins to fear that something even more terrible is about to unleash itself on London.

And so Dorothea risks her life and her sanity in order to save people who are oblivious to the threat that hovers over them. It is a task that forces her into a confrontation with her own lurid past, and tests her ability to shape events frighteningly beyond her control.

The Crimson Gown

Lydia Hunt is familiar with the concept of sin. Reared beneath the strictures of religious zealotry and abuse, she has heard again and again that her nature is wicked and her soul bound for eternal damnation. But when she is sent to work at Mowbray Hall, ancestral home of the enigmatic Lord Cailvairt, Lydia begins to fear just how wicked she might be.

For although Cailvairt makes no effort to hide his pursuit of her, his insistence on challenging the ideals imposed upon her as a child—even while speaking to her as an equal—leaves it difficult for Lydia to resist his attentions. As her inhibitions crumble away and the foundation of her beliefs threatens to falter, she must determine if giving into temptation will destroy her... or be the act that saves her.

Coming from World Tree Publishing, August 2017

The Bride Price

Chapter One

Lord Edmund Winthrop, Viscount Marbley.

Emily Collicott whispered the name under her breath, her own voice added to the susurration of sound that rippled from one end of the ballroom to the other. From where she stood, she could not see him. There were too many other heads in the way, heads bedecked in various arrangements of ribbons and pearls and feathers. The feathers were the most dreadful of them all, flopping and tickling and occasionally smacking her across the face when she failed to keep a wary eye.

Miss Fauntley had called on them this morning for the sole purpose of relating the news that Marbley had returned to town, after a nearly year-long sojourn in Paris. But he was back in London, the obnoxious Miss Fauntley had tittered between bites of marzipan and candied fruit. He was back, and his reappearance had succeeded in setting every drawing room abuzz.

To tell the truth, Emily had found herself a bit underwhelmed by the news. This was her first season in London, and what was this Lord Marbley fellow to her but a tedious portion of gossip bandied about like a borrowed novel? But she was soon swept along by the bubbling, frothing tide of London society, and now that he'd arrived in Lady Halloran's ballroom, she craned her neck as much as every other young woman in order to gain a glimpse of his reputed beauty.

He was tall, the women around her had whispered. He was broad-shouldered, another group had said. His hair was black as ebony, his eyes like amber pools, his nose a perfectly formed proboscis that would have sent the Romans into fits of envy. His smile was reputed to have caused no less than eight—eight!—young ladies to faint, leaving them as unresponsive heaps of silk and lace in his wake. He was witty. He was graceful. He was all that was kindness and benevolence.

And he was here, Emily thought. Not more than half a ballroom's length away from her.

She stood on the balls of her feet, her balance wavering as she was pushed and shoved from all sides—the result of several dozen women surging forward as the news of Marbley's arrival spread through their ranks. Emily struggled to catch her breath before another bundle of feathers walloped her in the face and she was suddenly extricated from the press of bodies.

"Did you see him?" Josephine's lilting voice tumbled out in a rush.

Emily looked down and only then noticed the other young woman's hand on her arm, the same hand that had rescued her from the crush that was still shifting and moving in time with Marbley's circuitous path along the outskirts of the room.

"Thank you," Emily said. "And no, I did not." She looked up at her friend with an expectant air.

"Oh, I've seen him before," Josephine crowed, and opened her fan with a practiced snap. "I even danced with him, once. It was my first season, and I was silly enough to believe that a scant few minutes of attention from the likes of him would be enough to secure my prospects."

Emily blinked rapidly and lowered her gaze to the floor. It was an easy matter to forget that Miss Barrowe was seven years her senior and currently celebrating her ninth season in town, a season the redoubtable Miss Josephine Barrowe claimed would be her last.

"You'll do better than I." Josephine's mouth crooked in a smile while her eyes gleamed. "You've a look about you that sets you apart. They can say what they like about this complexion being in fashion or that particular shade of hair, but toss out the fripperies and men want nothing more than a pretty, healthy girl who can smile at a party and produce a viable heir or two."

Emily tugged nervously at her gloves as the crowd continued to buzz with excitement around her. "You're forgetting a fortune. A few thousand pounds tacked onto that smile and most men could forgive a woman having a wooden leg and a moustache."

"Would that all of us arrived in town with a fortune in tow," Josephine sighed. "I'd have been a married woman these last nine years if I had more than three shillings to call my own."

"But if you were married, then you might not be in a position to aid me during the trials and travails of my first season," Emily countered as she linked arms with her friend. "You would no doubt be off at your country estate, lobbing a few chastisements at one of your strapping young sons for leaving a trail of muddy footprints through the house."

"Your fantasies are too kind," Josephine said, barely controlling her laughter. "I would have daughters instead of sons, and I would spend all of my time tearing out my rapidly graying hair as I struggled to find tolerable husbands for the lot of them."

As the two women laughed, the crowd shifted again, the bulk of it moving backwards until they found themselves pressed against the doors that opened onto the lamplit terrace.

"Chin up!" Josephine warned, a moment before she nudged Emily in the ribcage with the point of her elbow. "Here comes Mamma!"

Emily glanced up long enough to see Lady Barrowe emerge from the line of assembled guests, her dark eyebrows raised and her thin mouth set in a disapproving line. Emily would have felt a greater inclination towards fear if this hadn't been the only expression she had ever seen on Lady Barrowe's face.

"Of all the things!" Lady Barrowe chided as she approached. The heavy silk of her gown swished and rustled as if it, too, shared in the older woman's obvious irritation. "The Viscount Marbley finally deigns to make an appearance, and here I find the two of you giggling in the back of the room like a couple of misbehaving schoolgirls!"

Emily's spine straightened under Lady Barrowe's narrowed gaze. The woman shared a nearly identical build with her daughter, the both of them tall and lean, their matching dark heads each shot with a liberal amount of auburn highlights. But while Josephine's eyes were often creased with laughter, her color heightened from the amusement of a shared joke, her mother preferred to look down on everything with a cool, criticizing eye.

"Shoulders back," Lady Barrowe said to her daughter. "Just because you're tall does not give you leave to slouch. And you," she turned her sharp gaze to Emily. "You've gone white as a sheet! Should any man look at you, he'd think you wouldn't survive the winter."

"Ow!" Emily bit back a shriek as Lady Barrowe proceeded to pinch both her cheeks.

"There!" Lady Barrowe declared triumphantly. "That's put some life back into your face. Now, eyes up, and don't let me see you sniggering behind your fans when the Viscount comes this way."

With a forceful prodding from behind, they were pushed back into the crush. Emily nearly stumbled as someone stepped on the hem of her gown, and then a hand touched her arm, holding her up as she regained some measure of her equilibrium.

"Thank you." She expected to look up and see that Josephine had once again come to her aid. But it wasn't a woman's hand that gripped her forearm with a mingling of strength and delicacy. "Oh," she managed to say, when she found herself looking up into no other face than that of Lord Edmund Winthrop, Viscount Marbley himself.

Of course, she hadn't been introduced to him yet. This was the first she had laid eyes on him, but there was no mistaking that this was the man who had single-handedly set London society on its ear.

Not one of the descriptions had done him a whit of justice. He was tall, yes. And dark-haired, and broad-shouldered, and impeccably dressed, and his eyes...

They were more gold than she had originally imagined. Not that she had spent a great deal of her day musing over the particular shade of hazel that his eyes would prove to be, but their brilliance startled her, and she found that she could not look away.

"Are you all right, Miss...?"

She blinked. His hand was still on her arm. He should have released her some moments before, but his fingers were wrapped around her, his thumb stroking a portion of skin an inch above her elbow. It was scandalous, that touch. At least, it felt as if it was. And Emily couldn't believe that every other person in the room hadn't sent up a cry in outrage at the liberties he was daring to take in front of so many.

"Yes, I..." She swallowed, an action that sounded so loud to her own ears that she imagined it could be heard all the way down to the kitchens below.

And then there was a flurry of movement at her side as Lady Barrowe pushed forward, the maelstrom of silks and feathers and turbans beginning again as everyone adjusted to make room at the front of the line.

Emily heard the perfunctory introductions, the words seeming to fly over her head. Here was Miss Emily Collicott, lately arrived from Cornwall; eldest daughter of Sir Richard Collicott...

... sent to London in hope of making a good marriage, her own thoughts continued. With two more sisters at home, the both of them relying on her success in society to raise their own fortunes. And her mother gone for two years, leaving her in the hands of Lady Barrowe, who treated the search for a marriageable man with all of the finesse and romance of a military campaign.

Her gaze slid to the floor, to the tips of her own slippers peeking out from beneath the hem of her ballgown. A wave of inferiority washed over her, that one of these finely dressed ladies or gentlemen would suddenly notice the small stain on her gloves, or how her figure was bare of the usual jewels that so many of the other women wore. Her pale hair was simply styled, her gown bore none of the more fashionable decorations that would have cost more money than her father had entrusted to Lady Barrowe's keeping. She was small, and plain, and unadorned. And her entire family was dependant on her not making a single mistake during her stay in town.

"Say yes, child!" Lady Barrowe hissed in Emily's ear.

Emily raised her eyes, her breath stuttering through parted lips as she found herself once again staring into Marbley's beautiful face. "I'm sorry?"

There was a glimmer of amusement in his eyes, and the corner of his mouth twitched with the promise of a smile.

A beautiful mouth, Emily thought, and forced herself to exhale.

"A dance, Miss Collicott," Marbley said, his voice carried by the impossibility that a single person around him was not dangling on his every word. "That is, if you are not otherwise engaged for the remainder of the evening."

Engaged? She had not been approached by a single gentleman since her arrival two hours before, for all that Miss Barrowe insisted her appearance would set her apart. "N-no," she stammered, as the warmth of a blush flooded her cheeks. "That is... I mean, yes. I would be honored."

His hand was still on her arm, she realized, as his fingers slid down to her wrist, the heat of his touch soaking through her glove like water. Behind her, the sounds of the musicians preparing to play filled the air, as if they had been waiting for Marbley's permission to continue. He led her out onto the floor, the other couples following suit as the renewed murmur of conversation rose to a heated pitch behind them.

The music began, a sprightly melody that sent a thrill of fear through Emily's frame. Despite her diminutive size, she had never believed herself to be particularly light on her feet, and she wondered what her marital prospects would be if she accidentally trod on Marbley's toes before the end of the evening.

As they moved through the patterns of the dance, Emily strove to look everywhere but at her partner's face. It would be too much, she thought, to have to struggle with the awkwardness of her steps while gazing into his shining eyes.

"Miss Collicott," he whispered as their hands joined for a moment and they moved towards their next positions in the line. "I do believe you're trembling."

She looked up at him, startled at the sound of his voice so close to her ear.

"Are you afraid of me?" he asked. She was horrified that he would pose such a question, until she recognized the same twitch at the corner of his mouth, the spark of laughter in his golden eyes.

"No, I'm only a little nervous, my lord."

He smiled at that, a small smile, revealing a brief glance of even, white teeth. "I take it this is your first season?"

"Yes," she said, and returned his grin with one of her own. "In fact, this is my very first ball."

"Really?" Dark eyebrows lifted a half an inch. "And what is your impression of our fine city?"

"It is overwhelming," she admitted. "I have seen only small portions of it so far, and always from a carriage window or the same wide pathways in the park. But I feel that should I spend a lifetime here, and able to travel onto any of the streets of my choosing, I could not succeed in viewing everything it has to offer."

"Very well said." He nodded, before they were parted again by the figures of the dance.

Emily reminded herself to breathe while there was some distance between herself and Marbley. She had spoken about being overwhelmed by London, but she might as well have been describing her reaction to his presence.

There was something about him, something that went beyond his handsome face and well-tailored coat. Emily attempted to find the proper word, but the only thing she came up with before the pattern of the dance returned him to her side was simply... *more*.

"A pity," he whispered as his fingers once again claimed her small, gloved hand. "A pity that we are being so closely watched by the vultures of London's drawing rooms, that they would seek to prevent me from stealing your companionship for the remainder of the evening. I believe my heart will sink back into the doldrums when it comes time to return you to the care of your chaperone."

She glanced up at him and saw a glint of his smile, and though she told herself his remarks were purely facetious, she thrilled that perhaps...

It was too soon that the music dwindled towards its conclusion. A small bow marking the end of the dance, a polite bit of applause, and Marbley offered his arm before they began the brief walk that would take them back to the outskirts of the room.

"It was an honor, Miss Collicott." Marbley bowed once more, this time over her hand. Emily's mouth opened, ready to reply, but when he turned and walked away, he seemed to take her breath along with him.

"Well," Lady Barrowe began, and Emily heard the elation in her voice. "Wasn't that a fine thing? A fine thing, indeed! You'll have no shortage of suitors now, I'm sure. And maybe even Lord Marbley himself..."

Emily turned around and saw Lady Barrowe tugging at the lace on her sleeve, her brow creased in thought.

"I'm sure Lady Prescott will know of several invitations he's accepted," she continued. "And if we can continue to throw you into his path..."

"Refreshments!" Josephine announced suddenly. She snagged Emily's elbow and pulled her towards the punch bowl before the elder Barrowe had an opportunity to protest.

"Keep a wary eye of my mother's efforts to see you wed,"

Josephine warned between sips of punch. "She can be a bit overzealous if left unchecked, and I would not wish to see you hauled out before every eligible gentlemen as if you were nothing more than a prime piece of horseflesh up for sale."

Emily held her own cup between her hands, waiting for the trembling in her fingers to abate before she dared attempt to take a sip. "But is that not why we're here? To secure a husband?" It was a fact she had reminded herself of on countless occasions, to the point that she now wondered if the words were permanently etched across every corner of her mind.

"Yes," Josephine admitted, with obvious reluctance. "But I think my mother will never forgive me for turning down my one and only offer of marriage. She will believe herself to have failed some time-honored quest of motherhood if she doesn't see at least one young lady assigned to her care sent down the aisle." She took another sip, her mouth quirking above the rim of the cup. "And since she produced no results with me..."

"Someone made an offer to you?" Emily pounced on this tidbit of information. "Who was he?"

"Oh, I hardly remember," Miss Barrowe waved away Emily's questions as if they were nothing more than insects. "But he was old, and rheumy, and I would've been his fifth wife, if I'm not mistaken. Poor Mamma, I don't believe she's ever recovered."

All of this was said with such a mischievous gleam in Miss Barrowe's eye that Emily had to bite down on her lip to keep from snorting with laughter.

"Now," Josephine said as she set down her empty cup. "Are you ready for another dance?"

Emily followed her friend's line of sight. Two young men were making their way through the crowd toward their place near the punch bowl, their expressions leaving no doubt as to what had brought them across the entire length of the ballroom.

"I don't believe they're coming all the way over here for a mere glass of punch," Josephine remarked.

Emily pushed her shoulders back and nodded slowly. "Neither do I," she said, and put on her brightest smile for the approaching gentlemen.

Printed in Great Britain
by Amazon